THE HARD TARGET

MEN OF DELTA SERIES

BOOK ONE

M.M. ROSE

Table of Contents

CHAPTER ONE DORA 5

CHAPTER TWO RICHTER 15

CHAPTER THREE DORA 22

CHAPTER 4 DORA 26

CHAPTER 5 RICHTER 31

CHAPTER 6 RICHTER 40

CHAPTER 7 DORA 49

CHAPTER 8 DORA 54

CHAPTER 9 RICHTER 60

CHAPTER 10 RICHTER 67

CHAPTER 11 DORA 73

CHAPTER 12 DORA 78

CHAPTER 13 DORA 84

CHAPTER 14 RICHTER 93

CHAPTER 15 RICHTER 101

CHAPTER 16 DORA 109

CHAPTER 17 DORA 116

CHAPTER 18 RICHTER 127

CHAPTER 19 DORA 132

- CHAPTER 20 DORA 139
- CHAPTER 21 RICHTER 146
- CHAPTER 22 DORA 154
- CHAPTER 23 DORA 160
- CHAPTER 24 RICHTER 168
- CHAPTER 25 DORA 176
- CHAPTER 26 DORA 182
- CHAPTER 27 DORA 190
- CHAPTER 28 RICHTER 195
- CHAPTER 29 DORA 201
- CHAPTER 30 RICHTER 208
- CHAPTER 31 DORA 215
- CHAPTER 32 RICHTER 222
- CHAPTER 33 DORA 229
- CHAPTER 34 RICHTER 238
- CHAPTER 35 DORA 245
- CHAPTER 36 RICHTER 248
- CHAPTER 37 DORA 257
- CHAPTER 38 RICHTER 263
- CHAPTER 39 DORA 268
- CHAPTER 40 DORA 273

CHAPTER 41 DORA	278
CHAPTER 42 DORA	289
CHAPTER 43 RICHTER	294
CHAPTER 44 DORA	302
CHAPTER 45 DORA	308
CHAPTER 46 DORA	316
CHAPTER 47 RICHTER	322
CHAPTER 48 DORA	331
CHAPTER 49 DORA	340
CHAPTER 50 RICHTER	348
CHAPTER 51 DORA	355
CHAPTER 52 RICHTER	360
CHAPTER 53 RICHTER	367
CHAPTER 54 DORA	372
CHAPTER 55 DORA	381
ABOUT THE AUTHOR	386

CHAPTER ONE
DORA

There are moments that define a life. What came before or what happens after fades into insignificance. It's like standing at the edge of a precipice and seeing the world open up below.

Or, in my case, the corner of East 275 and 276, Dale City, VA.

I've never been here before. From what I've seen so far, there's no reason to come back either. There are no lights on in the three-story building opposite. There are no lights on in the whole block, period. Two blocks away, traffic lights at an intersection blink on and off. Distant headlight beams point my way and swerve away. For some reason, I press myself into the shadows.

What I do tonight will make or break me.

Hell, I'm scared. I don't even know if I should be here. I got a handwritten note, left by a nameless person with door security at the office of the newspaper I work for. It told me to come here after ten p.m. if I wanted secret information about Senator McGlashan. Eternally curious journalist that I am, I found the offer hard to ignore. The magazine I work for is a small start-up, and we focus on political gossip. There's a big market for it in DC, as you can imagine. I've been following McGlashan ever since the Ethics Committee raised questions about his campaign funding sources. Multiple shell companies in the Bahamas. I have no idea who left the note for me, or how they knew I was looking for a story. It's not like I've published anything yet.

Security mentioned the person who dropped the note was a short, slim man. He had his head covered with a hoodie and wore dark glasses. We don't have CCTV at our office, so no images of him exist. The envelope he left the note in contained a key. I'm guessing the key is for the front door of the building opposite me.

I digress. Goosebumps prickle my skin. I remember the words of my fellow reporter and best friend, Julia: *A scoop will make your career.*

Yeah, right, I said. *What if this guy turns out to be some psycho who targets female reporters?*

So I left the address with Julia, and right now, on my iPhone, I'm sharing my location with her. This is something the man who delivered the note told me not to do. But as desperate as I am to get a scoop, I'm not stupid. I've got my mace spray with me. The digital recorder on my phone will switch on the second I enter so Julia can hear every word and sound.

The cordless earbuds are in my ears. "Julia?" I whisper.

"Hey, you. All set?" she whispers back.

"I'm not sure this is a good idea."

"I know, but just think. In our business, you never turn down a source, right? Especially if he has some info that can make your career."

Julia got a scoop like this by meeting a man in some seedy hotel in New York. She actually went up to Times Square to meet him. He turned out to be the husband of a politician who was taking kickbacks from a Mexican cartel. When the story broke, Julia went from unknown reporter to star journalist.

"Remember what we discussed?" Julia asks softly.

I pause for a second before replying. "Don't go inside. Open the door and wait for him to show himself. He just wants to be sure I am who I say I am. Then ask him to come out for a coffee or something."

"Correct. You got this!" Her tone is meant to be encouraging, but all I get is a sinking feeling of dread.

And yet I know I need this. The rent in DC is expensive; that alone takes up two-thirds of my salary. I got used to certain comforts growing up, and I can't live without those. Add in bills, and I'm virtually broke. Wearing the same dress every day of the week or shopping in thrift stores is normal for me. But it would be nice to spread my wings once in a while.

"Yeah, I got this," I say, more to myself than to Julia.

"Atta girl," she whispers. "Break a leg."

Unfortunate choice of words, Julia.

I say nothing and hang up. I take a deep breath, eyes fixed on the foreboding building in front of me. No way am I going inside. Lights come on in a house at the end of the block, gaining my attention. More of them do, and a couple opens the door and steps inside. It helps to relieve the darkness surrounding me, and I breathe a little more easily.

I look to either side. No car comes down the street. I grab my phone and spray and cross the street quickly. The front door looks huge and intimidating. The brass key in my pocket digs into my fingers. I take it out and, taking a deep breath, fit it into the keyhole.

The latch is well oiled, and the key opens the door without a sound. I push it gently, and it falls open. The streetlights illuminate a wide hallway. It's dim, but I can make out a switch on the wall. I reach in to flip it. A bulb in the ceiling springs to life, washing the place with sudden light. It's an old place, and it's seen better days.

The carpets are threadbare, and paint peels forlornly from the walls. A musty smell prevails in the air, thick like fog.

The front room is to my left, light slanting across its opening in a triangle. The hallway stretches into a landing, with more rooms leading off it and a staircase going up. Darkness swallows the stairs as my eyes follow them up.

I wasn't aware I was holding my breath. I let it go, exhaling slowly. The place looks deserted, but anyone could be hiding in here.

"Hello?" I say tentatively. "Is anyone here?"

Silence greets me. I wait then repeat my question. Silence again.

Right, this is silly. I can't do this. I need to turn around and head back. Part of me wants to call Julia again, but this is not her gig. She might have advised me, but the decision was my own. Whatever I do is up to me.

Trouble is, I'm not good at stepping away or letting it go. A voice is whispering inside me, saying this could be the start of something big. The person who wrote the note was specific.

This will change everything—their exact words. Sure, they could be a psycho or a lunatic. But should I not at least try to find out now that I'm here?

I'm wearing my running shoes, yoga pants, and a light jacket. I can take off fast if I sense trouble. Leaving the front door open, I peek inside the front room. What harm can it do? I have a Maglite I can use as a weapon if need be. Heart thudding against my ribs so loud I swear someone standing next to me could hear it, I step inside.

I glance back to the relative safety of the street. The parked cars are all empty, with no sign of life. I click the latch of the front door out, ensuring it can't slam shut. My mouth is drier than the Mojave at full noon in August.

Another five, six paces, and I'll reach the door of the front room. Its windows face the street, and I've already checked that the curtains are drawn. If there's anyone in here, they're waiting in the dark. The thought chills my spine, and I come to a halt.

This is madness. What the hell am I doing?

My mind goes back to the informant. What could be so important he has to meet me like this? For no reason, thoughts of my father also come to mind. My media tycoon father, who has always disapproved of every path I've taken. I didn't want to work for one of his TV channels. He didn't want me to work for what he called "a shitty nest of liars."

If my dad was here, he'd be shaking his head and clicking his tongue. I can suddenly hear his voice in my head, like a distant echo against the fading, parched walls of this age-worn hallway.

Dora, Dora, Dora. What are you doing with your life?

My father is used to making people do what he wants. When I didn't follow the neat plan he had for my life, he shut me out. Strange as it sounds, that's okay with me. There is no scope for variety in my father's life, only drab routine. His life is cold and impersonal, and his manner toward me has always been distant, aloof. I've never understood why.

Resolve strengthens in the pit of my stomach like an iron fist. I can do this. I can get the scoop of a lifetime. I can show my father what I'm capable of. The news anchors at one of his TV stations will be dying to interview *me* one day.

A sudden creaking sound splinters into my consciousness. Like air collapsing from a burst tire, my daydream vanishes. The hair stands on the back of my neck, and my spine straightens. What was that? I'm pretty sure it came from the direction of the front room.

The ka-boom of my cardiac muscles almost drowns out rational thought. I swallow hard and find my voice. It's a croak, and I clear my throat. "Hello? Somebody there?"

Silence again. Damn it. Whoever is in there won't give himself up. I remember what Julia said. *This guy's just as scared as you are, Dora.*

I raise my voice a notch. "Listen, it's just me. Dora Simpson. I came alone, like you asked."

Great, well done. If he's a psycho, he now knows you have no backup.

Still no sound. Why doesn't he show his face?

"Look, I'm coming in, okay? Don't be scared. I won't hurt you."

I know how ridiculous that sounds, but I need to make sure this guy doesn't do something silly. The front door behind me is still open. I can still make a fast getaway if I need to. I don't have to step inside. I creep forward, shining my Maglite.

The door to the front room is open. I shine the flash beam inside. It tracks up the wall and around the sides. I see a light switch again, and after thinking for a few heart-stopping seconds, I reach out and flick the switch.

Light floods the room, and I yelp when I spot the man standing before me. He's tall and broad shouldered, with a well-trimmed beard on his cheeks. I flinch back against the wall, but my eyes are on him.

He's drop-dead gorgeous. His brown hair is cut short. The cheekbones are high and handsome, the nose sharp, and the pink lips full and sensuous. Delicious light-gray eyes complete the look. But those eyes are like thunder, and he's staring at me with rage.

"Who are you?" he bites out from between clenched teeth. His voice is a low rumble from his spacious chest, and anger spikes in his words.

I cannot speak, as I'm still staring at him. My eyes move to the large hands hanging loosely by his sides.

I swallow hard. "I...uh...are you the informant?" Deep down, I know it can't be him. The informant was small and wiry. This guy is tall, dark, handsome, his looks a cross between Keanu Reeves and George Clooney.

His brows meet in the middle of his forehead. "What? Did you say informant?"

His hypnotic eyes hold me captive, but part of me wrestles free from their hold. Just because he's good looking doesn't mean he's not a freak. I start to inch toward the hallway.

"Stop," his voice rings out. My feet stop moving, but my mind is screaming *RUN*. I glance at him, and he has not budged. I tear my eyes off him and step toward the door.

Now he moves. I sense more than see him come toward me. But he stops at a comfortable distance as if he knows I'm scared.

"I'm not going to hurt you." His voice is not a growl this time. It's still deep, and for some reason it sends shivers down my spine.

"Who are you?" he asks.

I find my voice at last. "I could be asking you the same question."

The frown returns to his face. "You came in here after me. Where did you get the keys?"

There is a hardness in the lines of his face, and his eyes are flint. But he stands still, watching me closely. I feel his eyes move up and down my body.

My mind is whirring away. Could this guy know something about the informant? I guess I don't have anything to lose by asking him. If he lunges for me, I can run out the doorway. I tense myself, ready for flight in case he moves.

The frown is back on his face. "You need to start talking. How did you know about this place?"

"Someone left a note at my workplace, asking to meet me here. Do you know him?"

That might have been the wrong question. His eyebrows lower farther, and the thunderous look returns. Still, he remains stationary. I see a muscle twitch in his strong jaw.

"I have no idea what you're talking about. Look, lady, this is important. We don't have much time. Who told you to come here?"

"If I knew about that, I wouldn't be asking you, would I?"

His eyes move to my ears then back to me. "You're wearing earbuds. Are you in contact with someone right now?" The growl is back in his throat.

Damn it. My white iPhone AirPods. I forgot to take them off.

I don't remove them. If this guy is dangerous, I need to stay in contact with Julia.

I meet the fire in his eyes with a lift of my chin. "I might be. None of your business. Who told *you* to come here?" My reporter's gut instinct is telling me this guy is hiding something. Something important. What's going down here tonight?

Good going, Dora. Well done, really. He could be a serial killer for all you know, and here you are baiting him.

Frank bewilderment spreads across his face, and he shakes his head slowly. He squeezes his eyes shut then opens them as if he's staring not at me but at an apparition. He begins to say something, stops, and drags a hand across his face. His huge chest rises and falls as he takes in a deep breath and then lets it go, not taking his eyes off me.

CHAPTER TWO
RICHTER

I keep staring at her as if I've never seen a woman before. Her large eyes are wide with surprise and concern. Light-brown irises deepen to darker pupils into mystic depths. Her nose is small, but her mouth is full, with generous lips. She's beautiful, even in those yoga pants, light mascara around her eyes, and a ponytail. A need stirs inside me, an ache that sends blood flowing to my cock. I've not seen a woman like her for a long, long time.

And I'm on the fucking operation of a lifetime.

Shit.

Get a grip, dickhead.

A lifetime's training kicks in. I check out the now-lit hallway and the street outside then move my eyes back to her. She's a civilian, I can tell that much. She could be carrying a piece in her jacket, but if she is, it's well hidden and a small weapon, like a 9mm Beretta. The fear in her face makes me relax, in fact. This woman is not an operative. First off, she doesn't have an accent. She's American, East Coast. Again, she could be hiding a foreign accent, but that would make her one hell of an actress. I've seen female agents before though—Russian KGB. She's not one of them. Confusion clouds my mind then clears as the urgency of the situation hits me again.

I need to take action. There's no time to lose. Waleed and his men could be on their way, could arrive any minute. With the hall light on and the front door wide open, there's no way on earth they'll step inside. I won't be able to get my hands on him. This carefully laid-out plan will fail.

"I need to turn the lights off," I say and feel stupid immediately.

Her face turns ashen, and her mouth opens. "Why?" she squeaks.

"Because... look, you need to leave now. Just go." *And I'll forget I ever saw you*, I think to myself. Somehow, I don't think I will. That sexy gym wear hugging her sleek hips and those wide eyes are imprinted on my gray matter.

"You're planning something clandestine. A secret meeting. Who do you work for?"

Not just a pretty face, obviously. She's figured out stuff most government agencies would take weeks to work out.

"I can't tell you anything. Just leave. Please." I take a step toward her, and this time, despite the flicker of fear in her eyes, she holds her ground. Her chin comes up in defiance.

"This is what the informant left the note about, right? What's happening here tonight?"

She's got backbone, I'll give her that. "I have no idea what you're talking about." I move closer to her.

Her right hand dives inside a pocket, and she brings out a spray. Her eyes are flashing, and her voice trembles. "I'll spray this into your face. Don't come near me."

I check the floor behind her. If I were to disarm her gently, she's still going to fall against the doorjamb and probably hit her head.

The microphone in my earbud comes to life. It's my brother, Cal. "Who the hell is she?"

I don't reply. His voice rasps. "Get rid of her. Now."

"What does it look like I'm doing?" I hiss back.

The woman is staring at me before she narrows her eyes, which flick to my ear. "Who are you speaking to?"

"It doesn't matter." I turn my head to look at the window, hoping she'll follow. She does, and I reach out a long arm and pluck the spray from her hand. She gasps and staggers backward. Her head hits the door, and she winces, rubbing the back of her skull. "Ow."

Before I know what I'm doing, I'm at her side. She smells faintly of lavender and a musky odor that is strangely appealing, comforting. I lower my head toward her, taking care not to touch her.

"Are you all right?"

She doesn't say anything, just lifts her head. Her eyes are melting like chocolate. Despite every instinct that is screaming at me to get rid of her, those twin lakes of light hold me captive.

What the hell am I doing?

She stumbles backward fast. Her hand stays frozen on her head, eyes holding mine. Her back hits the wall of the hallway.

"Will you get a move on? You can play *When Harry Met Sally* later!" Cal's voice contains a hint of humor but is scathing nonetheless.

I move past her, and she shrinks away. I shut the front door and turn off the lights, and the building sinks into darkness again. I pick up the Maglite she dropped and hand it to her. Then I switch my own flashlight on, cupping a hand over the beam.

Parting the curtains, I have a quick look outside. I count the seven cars I saw parked out there before I entered by picking the lock on the back entrance. No new vehicles.

When I turn around, I see she has the Maglite on, hand covering the beam. Without moving, I speak to her softly.

"Please go. Now."

She surprises me by coming closer. "Tell me what's going on. I took a big risk coming here tonight. I deserve to know."

I don't know who the hell this woman is or how she's suddenly got the *cojones* to demand information from me. All I know is that the seconds are ticking down, and this situation is getting more dangerous. She's a civilian. Last thing I want is for her to get caught in a crossfire.

"You're in danger." I sharpen my voice. "You need to leave."

She asks, "Does this involve Senator McGlashan?" I can barely see her face in the gloom.

"Who?" The name means nothing to me. Cal will know, though, and he chirps in my ears.

"Head of the Senate Intelligence Committee." Cal says the words slowly, and I know what he's thinking. This is getting weird. I push the thoughts to the back of my head.

"No, it doesn't. Like I said, I have no idea what you're talking about. Now leave if you don't want to get…" I check myself at the last minute.

"Get what? Go on, talk."

I groan audibly. So does Cal.

I say, "I'm meeting a friend who's in trouble. His wife has kicked him out because he's having an affair."

Jeez, that's lame. She doesn't swallow it, as expected.

"You'll have to do better than that," she snaps.

"Yeah. That was garbage." Cal, my helpful brother, snickers.

"Are you an undercover cop?" The sharpness of her tone betrays her intelligence. How the hell is this woman starting to figure me out?

"No, I'm not a cop."

"FBI? DEA? You're not alone, right? A team is watching you and recording everything." She actually folds her arms across her chest. I can make out her shape vaguely in the dimness. I turn off my Maglite, but hers is still on. Sensibly, she keeps it tucked into the crook of her arm.

"Well, guess what? Your secret's safe with me. I want to see what happens. All you have to do is tell me the name of who you're waiting to meet."

I'm glad it's dark so she can't see my jaw hit the floor. Man, I've been in conflict zones all around the world, seen shit so twisted it still gives me nightmares. But this woman trumps everything. And I'm not in some godforsaken corner of Afghanistan; this is freaking Arlington. My own country. Who knew a five-foot-seven, hot bundle of feminine contradiction would throw such a monkey wrench into the works?

"Sweet Jesus," Cal whispers in my ear.

I can't even speak. How did she figure it out?

"I'm not wearing a wire. Don't worry about me," she tries to reassure me. "If you must know, I'm a reporter."

Oh no. That's the last thing I need.

"I don't care about who you are," she says as if she can read my mind. "Or who you work for. But whoever it is you're waiting for, he has to be someone big, right? Worth a large operation?"

A rocket-propelled grenade hurled by the Taliban has nothing on this woman. She's showing her true colors. Spellbinding as they are, I need to get a grip. I shake my head, clear my throat.

"That's enough. You need to—"

"GMC Yukon approaching from the south, followed by a Lincoln Escalade. ETA two minutes." The voice of Randy, my Delta teammate and close friend, sounds in my ear.

"Happy now?" Cal says.

"Shut up," I growl at Cal.

"Get the fuck out of there. Move it!" he growls back.

CHAPTER THREE
DORA

He moves so quickly he takes my breath away. Just like when he plucked the spray out of my hand, he's standing next to me in the twinkling of an eye. I move backward, but my heel catches the carpet, and suddenly I'm falling, hands pinwheeling for balance.

An iron arm hooks around my waist like a life support. Fingers grip my arm gently, and I find my feet again. I jerk upright and slam into his chest. Totally not intentional. Warmth blossoms in my face, and we separate instantly. But not before I smell him like I did before. It's a deep, humid, and raw masculine essence. No aftershave here. Warmth floods between my thighs. During the brief moment we touch, I can feel the unmistakable slabs of his hard pec muscles. Breath catches in my chest as I move back.

I see him as a dark, tall shadow rising up before me. He's still a mystery, but he doesn't scare me anymore. If he wanted to hurt me, surely he's had enough chances.

"So, who is it?" I mumble. "Just one name, please."

His voice is harsh. "Listen, lady, this isn't a movie. There's no story here. You need to get the hell out, now." He strides forward, propelling me by the elbow. His hand slips inside my jacket pocket and picks out my phone. He drops it on the floor and smashes it beneath his boot.

"No!" The shout escapes my throat before I can stop myself. "What the hell are you doing?"

His hand holds my arm in a viselike grip as he grinds my phone again. Then he bends down and separates the battery pack and takes out the SIM card.

"Now no one can trace you," he pants.

I'm furious and about to shout at him when twin headlight beams cut into the room. There's a sound of cars being parked in front of the house. Doors slam.

"Hurry," he whispers urgently. His right hand curls around my wrist, exerting gentle pressure. This time, I need no encouragement. Whoever those guys are outside, if he doesn't want to meet them, then neither do I.

"What's your name?" I ask as we hurry down the hallway.

After a split second, he says, "John."

"Try again," I whisper back.

Behind us, a key turns in the front door, and it swings open. He moves faster, and I follow. Voices float over to us from behind. "John" seems to know where to go. He opens a door and steps into complete darkness. All I can smell is the musty smell of old carpets and furniture. Through another door and a hallway, we come to a back passage that seems to lead to a garden. John, or whatever his name is, stops in front of another door. Hand on the handle, he turns to me.

"Run to the end of the garden. There are stones you can climb over to the fence. Jump over the fence, and you're on West 360. Don't look back. Just walk."

"And what will you do?" I ask.

An edge of moonlight cuts across the long windows next to us. The silver shine catches his dark beard and the glint in his eyes.

"Don't worry about me. Get the hell out of here. Go." He opens the door. The warmth of the summer night floats across the garden. John puts a hand on the small of my back and pushes gently. "Now."

"But—"

"These are bad people." His whisper is fierce in my ear. "They'll kill you without a second thought. Do you want that?"

I gulp, fear suddenly spreading like icicles along my limbs. Before I can say anything, John pushes me out into the garden and shuts the door firmly behind me. I hear the key turn in the lock.

Great. I'm alone. The moon-washed garden lies to my right and a high brick fence to my left. I try the door handle once again then duck as a beam of light cuts through the open window.

I feel bad about leaving. Fear and sweat congeal into a morass of indecision, weighing me down. What should I do? Call 9-1-1, of course. But if the cops are involved, will I ever find out what really happened here? I know what cops are like. I'll be chasing police officers at the precinct, while they'll keep stonewalling me.

If I stay, I might get killed. John said as much. I don't believe that's his real name, but he was speaking the truth about this place being dangerous. Maybe I should heed his advice.

I creep out into the overgrown lawn. I keep taking cover as flashlights shine outside the windows on the first floor. I notice a Japanese rock garden toward the back of the yard. A couple of the rocks are big enough for me to climb so I can grab hold of the top of the brick wall. I hear muffled shouts behind me. I turn around, but there's not much to see.

John's face comes to mind again: those sharp gray eyes, the strength in his jawline. Oh, damn it. Why did this stranger have to be so good-looking?

I need to do the right thing. My hands grip the wall, palms resting on the wet moss over the bricks. I'm ready to haul myself out of this hell.

Something circles around my ankles and pulls. I scream and hold onto the brick wall, but I don't find much purchase. Whoever is pulling me is stronger. I'm dragged down, and a hand clamps over my mouth. I'm fighting, kicking, but go still when a cold metallic object presses against the side of my forehead.

"Make another move," a menacing voice says, "and I'll splatter your brains. Got it?"

CHAPTER 4

DORA

Nausea is making me gag. His hand smells horrible, like old, rotten meat. I nod quickly. The muzzle of the gun leaves my forehead and presses against my back. Hard. He shoves me forward, keeping a hand on my jacket collar.

Another man meets us inside the door I've just come out. He shines a light in my eyes, and I flinch.

"Found her trying to escape."

The other guy beckons us forward, and I stumble inside with them. My heart is practically beating out of my chest. Sweat pools at the nape of my neck. What the hell did I get myself into?

We go into one of the back rooms that face the garden. They're as spacious as the front room, and they're in a similar state of dereliction.

The light is on. A group of men surrounds John, who is kneeling on the floor. A gun is pressed to his head, and all the men have their weapons drawn. Tension crackles in the air.

A man in a light summer suit, clearly the leader, steps out to meet me. He's slim and tall, and his beady eyes run all over me. I look away.

"So, who is this then?" He turns to look at John.

John's eyes are on me. There is a silent message in them, but I'm not getting it. He nods gently, still staring at me. I gulp and nod back.

He turns his attention to the man in the suit. "How the hell should I know?" John seethes.

The man in the suit laughs. "I just saw your little interaction."

John says nothing. I feel the cold steel muzzle press against my forehead again.

"If you don't know who she is, then maybe I should put a bullet in her head?" Mr. Suit asks. "She means nothing to you, right?"

John looks up, and I see pure, unadulterated rage in his eyes. "Viktor. Just let her go."

Mr. Suit—Viktor—gestures, and the pressure of the weapon on my forehead grows, forcing my head to one side. I whimper and shut my eyes. Is this how it's going to end?

"Viktor." John is speaking through clenched teeth, and his voice has steel in it. "Stop this."

I sense a presence and open my eyes to see Viktor peering closely at me. "Why?" he asks without turning, a lecherous grin on his face.

"She's our analyst," John says. "She knows where Jozdani is."

Viktor's pupils dilate, then he peers at me with renewed interest. He steps back.

"Search her," Viktor says.

A man steps forward while the one holding my arms stiffens his grip.

"No," John says. "You don't have to."

Viktor tells me, "Take your jacket and shirt off."

For me to do that, the man holding me has to let go of my arms. He does so, and I stare at John on the floor. His eyes are blazing, teeth bared in a snarl. He shifts, trying to move, but there are three men holding him down, one with a gun to his head.

Silently, I take off my jacket. I have a T-shirt on underneath. The man in front of me steps forward and lifts it without ceremony. I feel his sticky hands touching me, and I close my eyes.

"She's not wearing a wire, goddamn you!" John shouts from behind us.

"Lower your pants," Viktor tells me calmly.

There's a commotion behind him, and my eyes open to find John struggling to rise. There's a flash of metal as the butt of a gun rises and strikes his head. The dull thwack is a sickening sound. John grunts but doesn't fall. He fights the two men on either side of him, even with his hands cuffed behind his back. His face is mottled with rage.

Viktor seems the essence of cool. He tells the man holding the gun to my head, "Shoot her."

"No," John says.

He's breathing heavily, and I see a trickle of blood pouring down the side of his forehead. The two men holding him are leaning back, and he's straining forward. I can see they can't hold him back for much longer. I have a feeling if I wasn't here, John would have finished these guys off. I can't help feeling I've messed this up badly for him.

"Then get back down," Viktor says to John. He turns back to me. "Pants off."

"You're gonna die for this, Viktor." John grinds out the words.

My eyes are closed, palms clammy. I lower my pants all the way without stepping out of them.

"Shoes off," Viktor says. I have no choice but to do as he says.

My panties and sports bra stay on, but I have to remove my socks and shoes. I have to turn around, and Viktor walks around me as if it's a show he's enjoying. My cheeks are burning, and I look up to the ceiling, avoiding all eyes.

"Get dressed," Viktor says eventually.

When I'm done he takes photos of me, as well as of John. Then he looks at me, angling his head. "So, where is Jozdani?"

I don't have a clue what he's talking about, but I know one thing: John is trying to save my life. I need to come up with something fast. What's the farthest place inside the United States I can think of? Or should it be abroad? Viktor is watching me closely, blocking John. I think as quickly as I can. I need to pick a place far from here that will take time to get to.

Jozdani sounds like a Middle Eastern name. It seems reasonable to guess Viktor is looking for this Jozdani character.

Whoever this Viktor is—from his accent, I think he is either Russian or Eastern European—he's here, right? He must be following a trail. Safer to stick inside the United States.

"In a town outside Seattle," I say.

John's voice is loud. "She knows half the address. I know the other half. Kill us and you get nothing."

Viktor's eyes are searching my face, and I can see a glimmer of excitement in them. Did I say the right thing? I hope so.

He gestures to his men. "Put them in the car. Take them to the safe house."

He moves, and John's eyes connect with mine again. There are four men around him now, two with weapons pointed at him. All of them look worried, as if he's a raging beast who can tear them apart any second. The look on his face is scary, too. His eyes are flecks of hard gray, and his jaw is set tight. But his eyes relax when they see me. He mouths a silent "sorry." I nod, and he shakes his head. His eyes dart to the left, then back again. He does this twice, and I realize he's trying to tell me something. What exactly I have no idea.

CHAPTER 5
RICHTER

I keep my face impassive, but I'm boiling inside. Viktor had no right to do that to her. There will be payback, I promise myself. My heart drops to my shoes when I see the look on her face. I'm ashamed I couldn't protect her. Thankfully, the body search is over quickly. As I look at her being herded out of the room, my thoughts and feelings are all swirling colors on the canvas of my mind.

I don't even know her name.

I can't forget those come-hither eyes and the delicacy of her curves. She's hot, and wildly inappropriate thoughts play havoc with my imagination at this, the worst of times. I need to keep my shit together.

What she did just now probably saved both of our lives. How did she know to come up with a location in the United States? Pure guesswork, I'm sure, which means she's really smart. I met this woman only a few minutes ago, and she's already in sync with my thoughts.

I'm pushed out into the hallway and toward the front door. The lights are all off, and only flashlights guide our way. That and the barrel of a gun pressed hard against my spine. I can make out the woman in front of me. I walk faster to get closer to her. The men around me speed up, too.

I know for a fact that the rest of my team is outside. Many of the buildings on this block are deserted, and Cal and I did a recon yesterday. Randy, our sniper, is keeping watch from one of the buildings opposite. Ken and Brandon will be around the corner. My own car is parked two blocks down.

The earbud has been ripped from my ear. My hands are in plastic cuffs behind my back. The woman in front of me is similarly bound.

All my senses are on fire. Every sight and sound is amplified ten times. As we go through the doorway, I stiffen myself. There's another three-story building opposite us, and I know Randy will be up there with his rifle, night scope trained on us. *With any luck.*

I need to prepare for what's going to happen.

The doors of the Lincoln Escalade are open. I can't see Viktor anymore. He must be inside the car. Any second now, we will be put inside the car. If that happens, my boys will be chasing us. I know how they function. If there's going to be a firefight, best to do it when the enemy's exposed. I look up at the dark building in front. My heart leaps in my chest when I spot the faintest movement in a second-story window. It's open, and—only to the trained eye—the almost-black shape of a weapon is visible.

Randy's in position.

"Wait," I call out loudly enough for all to hear.

Everyone stops. Heads turn toward me. I take a swift step forward till I'm right behind the woman. I can sense her go rigid, like she knows something's going to happen.

It happens so quickly it's a blur. I fall forward, hooking one leg around the woman's. With a sharp cry, she falls, and I fall with her, covering her body with my own.

Bop! Bop! Bop!

Suppressed gunfire suddenly flashes all around us. Viktor's men open up as well, but they're firing at an invisible enemy.

"Stay down," I shout at the woman. Her body is soft, and it molds to mine like a glove to a hand. I don't want to crush her, but at the same time, I need to cover all of her.

With a screech of tires, the Lincoln takes off. The guns fire twice more, then there is an abrupt, eerie silence.

A man groans a few yards from my face.

"Are you okay?" I ask the woman, shifting my weight off of her.

"Yes, I think so," she says, her voice breaking.

I'm still not leaving her, and my head swivels from side to side. From one corner of the block opposite, a black shape detaches itself and scurries over to take cover behind a car. Was that Brandon? Sure looks like him.

"Richter?" a voice calls out.

Relief floods through me. It is Brandon.

"Over here," I call out. I see the now-familiar shape, weapon on shoulder, rush toward me. I stay down to protect the woman and also to ensure my own safety. Only a fool stands up in a firefight without a weapon or adequate cover.

Another shape rushes from the left, and it's Ken. Brandon gets to me first and snips away the plastic cuffs with his knife. I know Ken is keeping watch, ready to fire at the first hint of trouble.

But it's all gone very quiet.

It's all gone wrong.

We have dead men lying around us. We are an ultra-secret team that operates outside U.S. soil. To say we have no jurisdiction inside the United States is putting it mildly. Not even the Department of Defense knows of our existence. Cal will have to explain this to the DoD, and I feel sorry for him.

I'm just grateful the woman is alive.

But it's still a clusterfuck of epic proportions. I help the woman to her feet. Her cheeks are wet with tears.

"I'm sorry," I say, meaning it. "What's your name?"

"Dora. And don't apologize." Her voice quivers, and she sniffs, wipes her face with her sleeve. "It's me who crashed your party."

I shake my head. "You had a reason to be here, right?"

She nods. "An informant left a note for me."

Brandon steps up to face me. He's ex-Delta Forces like me, our bond forged in fire and blood. I quickly explain to him what happened. Ken hands me an earpiece and hooks me up to the comms channel.

"What the hell happened?" Cal asks.

When we've finished talking, Brandon leaves us to get his car.

"What are we doing with the woman?" Cal asks. "What's her name again?"

"Dora," I say. "She needs protection. Viktor has seen her face and thinks she knows where Jozdani is. He also took photos of us, and he could've sent them to the rest of his group."

Cal swears under his breath. "So what the hell do we do?"

Ken and I have moved to one side, leaving Dora standing against a car. She can't hear our conversation.

I've bluffed Viktor to save our lives. I don't know where Jozdani is. He's an Iranian nuclear scientist who's gone missing. Viktor, an undercover agent for the KGB, is looking for him just like we are. Jozdani has the latest knowledge of Iran's nuclear program. Finding him is critical. If the enemy have him, then the U.S. and its allies are in deep trouble.

Cal says, "You need to disappear, bro. If the Russians think you know where Jozdani is, they'll come looking. Viktor's still alive, right?"

"Affirmative," Ken says. "He's spread the news by now."

Cal nods. "I can get you a new identity. You need to lie low while we do our research, find out what's happening."

There's a pause, then Ken voices the thought in all our minds. "What about the woman?"

I bunch my fists and exhale. "Guess she stays with me. We have a duty to protect her until we find Jozdani and this shitstorm blows over."

Cal says nothing. I can read the thoughts in his mind.

I say, "Viktor and his men will be onto her like a flash. She's not safe and won't be for a while."

Cal says, "Her being here is a serious threat to OPSEC." That's CIA speak for operational security. He continues. "She can't have any contact with the outside world. No phone calls, no social media."

It's my turn to pause, letting it all sink in. We have a lot more than we bargained for, and then some.

Cal says, "You need a new name. And the woman, well, she can be your fiancée."

I do a double take. "Fiancée?"

"Not in real life," Cal says, and I can hear the smirk in his voice. "In case anyone wonders who she is, that's your story. You're starting a new life in the country. Left the city life behind. All that jazz."

"You've got to be kidding me," I say, shaking my head.

"You got a better idea?"

I'm silent. I glance over at Dora. She's watching me in silence. A car turns the corner, and all of us look up quickly. It's Brandon in his SUV. He flashes the headlights once to let us know it's him.

"Right," Cal says to me. "Head over to our place in Montrose."

Montrose is a small town near the Appalachian Mountains, straight down the I-95. Nice place and safe. It's a touristy place in the summer as well, so a new couple moving in won't be seen as an anomaly. Our parents owned a farm there. The farmhouse is well looked after, and we use it occasionally to relax in.

I'm of two minds about this. I walk away from the team to speak to Cal in private.

"We've never used our place as a safe house," I whisper at him. "Why don't we use one of the other properties around DC?"

Cyborg Securities, the firm Cal and I formed, has grown to have several safe houses around the country and a few abroad.

"We can," Cal says. "But I'm not sure if it's safe, given we just had a security breach. Best to check them out first and wait a few days to make sure they're not under surveillance."

I think for a while. Cal's thinking makes sense. We don't know who Dora's informant was. And the angle with Senator McGlashan...the more I think of it, the more uneasy I get.

"Alright," I breathe out. "But we move from Montrose in less than a week. That should be enough time to ensure the safe houses are clean."

"Gotcha."

We get into the car. Another member of our team, Oliver, is on his way to take the bodies to the morgue. Brandon will drop us off at my car, which is a new hire, paid in cash.

Ken hands me a backpack. "This has cash, extra ammo, two handguns, and a change of clothes."

"What about Dora?" I say.

When Ken doesn't reply, I make it clear to them. "Get Samantha to do some shopping for her and send it over." Samantha is the sixth, final, and only female member of our team. She's also our baby sister. Well, that's how I think about her, anyway. I'm the oldest in the family, then Cal, and finally Sam. She used to be an FBI agent, but it didn't take much coaxing for her to leave her job and join us. We're Delta guys, so we don't have much experience in domestic law enforcement. Sam is a huge help in that field.

I glance at Dora. "Any special requests?"

Her voice is clear. "Is makeup too much to ask for?"

I shrug. "Nope."

"Can I speak to Samantha?" she asks.

Not just me but the rest of the guys stop and gawk at her. She said Samantha's name as if they were old friends.

"There's things I need that only she will understand," Dora says, her eyes flicking from me to the others. Her eyes constrict, and I see her jaws clench. She looks back at me.

"That's all," she says.

I step toward her. She's been through enough already. I dial the office, ask for Samantha, and hand the phone to her.

"Go ahead," I say softly. "It's okay. She knows you're here."

Dora turns her back to us and speaks to Sam briefly, then hands the phone back to me.

Sam's voice is brisk and businesslike as usual. "I'll send Brandon a list of the items she wants. He can drop it off. You get straight to the safe house now."

I'm the boss of this outfit, but Samantha is well versed in giving us men orders. She's extremely good at her job, and I respect that. More than once, she's saved our lives by doing background checks and making sure our asses didn't end up in jail by breaking the law. It pays to listen to my kid sister.

"Roger that," I say.

Brandon drives slowly to where my car is parked. I climb out alone and check over the car quickly. It's a large four-by-four with bulletproof, tinted windows. There's no sign of tampering. I start the engine then get out and open the passenger-side door for Dora. She's said virtually nothing all this time, and her eyes are downcast. Without looking at me, she gets into the car then looks straight out the windscreen. I don't know why, but seeing the tension on her face and her pale, drawn cheeks, a pain twists inside me. I want to reach out, grip her shoulder, tell her it's going to be okay.

But I don't know that for sure. I shut the door gently, anger flaring inside me again. Damn Viktor for treating her like that. I'll tear him apart when I see him again. Resolve strengthens inside me like molten metal hardening in a blacksmith's forge.

I don't know this woman, but I'll protect her with the last drop of blood in my veins.

I get inside, and my hands tighten over the steering wheel. Not in my wildest dreams did I think this could be happening.

Ken walks over to my window. There's a big smile plastered on his face. I feel like punching him.

"Shall I stick a 'Just Married' sticker to your back window?"

"Fuck you," I growl and pull out.

CHAPTER 6
RICHTER

TWO YEARS AGO

MOSCOW

RUSSIA

The snow is falling so hard it's almost blinding. The night is inky black, and across Tverskaya Prospekt, the dark waters of the Moskva River rustle restlessly. Snow has the ability to absorb sound, and the noise of traffic is subdued. But not the currents of the broad river from which this magnificent city gets its name. I've been to Moscow several times on clandestine operations, mainly security jobs like protecting important politicians. Since I left the Delta Force, this is what I do.

But this time I'm on a personal mission: a hunt for my father's killer.

I'm sitting inside a café, one of those little rooms that sells everything from vodka to coffee. The wizened old babushka who's served me also helped to confirm the address: 1379 Tverskaya Prospekt. Viktor Megdinov would be there tonight, I was told.

His name and photo arrived at my old Army letterbox last week. The letter from the KGB headquarters was dated 14th December 1992. It authorized Viktor to assassinate the CIA agent who had taken photos of the nuclear submarine yard in northern Russia, close to the Finnish border.

I didn't question the intelligence. Over the years, I'd sent out enough feelers into the intelligence community. So had my brother Caleb, an Army Ranger. Nothing had come of it. Till last week.

So here I was.

I don't have to wait for long. A Lada saloon car arrives, tires churning snow. The windows are black tinted. It stops in front of the address. I drain my coffee and step outside the shop.

A man steps out of the Lada. His size and shape are similar to the photos I have of Viktor. Then he looks up and sideways. The car moves away slowly. He turns to the left, and our eyes meet. He goes completely still, watching me. Like most Russian men, he's wearing a furry hat, called a *shapka*, and a long black cotton overcoat.

There's no one on this snow-swept street but us. Under the streetlights, I can see his face clearly. It is Viktor, there's no doubt. He's older than what the photos show, but he was young then, much younger than my father, Julian Blane.

I don't know why, but Viktor is holding my gaze. I step toward him, and he knows something's wrong. He moves toward the door of the building, and I break into a sprint. If he gets inside, my hopes of catching him are slim.

I crash into him just as he climbs the first step. We smack against the wall then tumble into the snow. We're roughly the same size, and he fights back. But years of Special Forces training and combat have made me into a killing machine. Viktor is no match for me. Two hard punches to the face make him go dizzy. I hold him up against the wall and search him quickly. He has a belt holster, and I throw his weapon away.

"Look at me," I growl. I have to hold his head up. "I'm the son of Julian Blane. The CIA agent you killed in 1992. Remember?"

Something flickers in his eyes, then they widen.

I bare my teeth. "This is payback, asshole. You're coming with me to the U.S. embassy. You're going to confess to your crime."

He smiles then. It's a nauseating, shit-eating grin, and it makes me sick to the core.

His English is faultless. "Really? If I confess, what do you think will happen? A diplomatic war between Russia and the U.S., that's what. Maybe even a real war. Is that what you want?"

"I want the truth," I snarl. "Did you kill my dad?"

He goes quiet. The smile vanishes. There's almost a sad look in his eyes, but then it clears, replaced by a calculating glint. "Who told you?"

"It doesn't matter. Answer me!"

He smiles at me again.

I take out my knife and press it against his neck. Fear dilates his pupils.

"OK." His voice is shaky. "I did it. All right? Put the knife down."

I don't put the knife down, but I lessen the pressure. I have no intention of killing him. I'm not a cold-blooded murderer. I want him to face justice, even if every fiber in my body is screaming at me to beat him until he ceases to exist.

But that makes me as bad as him. No, this evil bastard is going down for what he did. To make things worse, I know he works for the Russian mafia, or Bratva, now. He's used his old KGB contacts to supply information to the mafia network, which makes him valuable to them. The Bratva have chapters all over the world, including the United States.

I rest my elbow against his neck, crushing him. "Talk," I growl.

"Okay." He swallows. "But you need to know something first."

I know delaying tactics when I hear them. As Delta, I did field interrogation on terrorists in Ramallah and Fallujah.

Something's wrong here. Keeping up the pressure on his neck, I glance sideways. The river is to my left. But to my right, I detect movement. A black shadow separates itself from the corner of a building about fifty yards away.

"You got a big problem," Viktor says. The sick grin is back on his face.

I don't hesitate. I pull him toward me as two men start running toward us. One of them is about to fire, but he stops when he sees me using Viktor as a shield.

43

"Let me go," Viktor shouts.

"Negative, asshole," I growl. "You're coming with me."

I punch him in the guts, twice, hard. He bends over. I lift him onto my back and run for the river. I know the men won't shoot. There's too much risk of them hitting their boss.

Viktor is screaming something in Russian. Some of them are swear words, but the rest I don't get. They're probably instructions to his men. Which means I need to haul ass.

I have an escape route prepared. There's an RIB—a rigid inflatable boat—bobbing on the water, moored to a small jetty. It's right across the building, and I run to it. I'm slow due to the snow. Luckily, the heavy snow means there are fewer cars on the road. My boots sink in the white mush as I cross the road and onto the broad pavement. There's a gate then stairs that lead down to the dark waters of the Moskva, where my rental RIB is moored.

I can hear shouts behind me. I ignore them.

I jump down the last two stairs and land on the wooden jetty. Viktor is still on my back. I lose balance and fall to my knees. It hurts like hell, but there's no time to waste. I can still stand on my two feet. Viktor is shouting in my ears. I ignore him and stand up, ready to run the last few yards to my boat.

I come to an abrupt halt. A figure materializes out of the darkness. He's as tall and wide as me. I'm in combat mode now. If I had a gun, I would shoot him. Especially since he's pointing one at me.

"Put him down," the man shouts in English. The gun is pointed at my legs. He won't hit Viktor if he shoots me there. And he's close enough to take my knees out.

"Do it now!" he shouts.

I hear men scrambling down the stone steps behind me.

Shit. I'm cornered.

I need to survive this. Come back for this asshole later. At least I got a confession out of him.

"I'll be back, Viktor," I whisper in his ear. "Remember that as long as you live."

I grab him around the waist, lift him in the air with both hands, then throw Viktor as hard as I can toward the man pointing the gun at me. I bellow with the effort, feeling my chest and shoulder muscles contract powerfully.

Viktor flies into the man like a missile. They crash together then fall into the river.

I dive into the water myself. Gunshots ring around the jetty. Bullets hit the woodwork then splash into the water. I take a deep breath and dive under the freezing waters as bullets streak past me.

There's a loud humming sound. It gets louder. I can't see anything in the murk. My lungs are bursting, so I kick up to the surface. I lift my mouth and take a grateful suck of the cold night air. I hear the sound again, and I look to see a boat heading toward me.

I duck back down, but the people on deck have clocked me already. I swim underwater, but I'm on my last breath. I have to breathe again. It's that or pass out underwater.

I swim for as long as I can then lift my face. This time, a strong light shines on me. With it comes a voice I recognize. I can't believe it.

"Richter! Richter! It's me, Cal!"

I must be dreaming, but I know this ain't no dream. A rope is thrown down to me, and I grab it gratefully, pulling myself into the boat.

*****

A thermal blanket is wrapped around me, and someone hands me a steaming mug. I sip from it, grimacing.

The boat is chugging downriver, headed for safety. A bulb hangs overhead, casting a yellow light over fishing nets and an old anchor. And my brother, Caleb Blane, sits opposite me.

Caleb's my height but slimmer and clean shaven. He's looking at me with calm, steady eyes.

"How did you get here?" I ask, incredulous. I wipe a hand over my beard, squeezing water out of it.

"Who do you think sent you the intel?" he counters.

I blink in surprise. "You did? Why the hell didn't you tell me?"

In response, my younger brother takes out something from his pocket and chucks it at me. It's an ID card bearing his picture and job title fixed to a lanyard.

I gape at it. "CIA? Since when?"

"I joined two years ago. They wanted more special ops men. I fit the bill, plus you know I speak Arabic."

I frown at him. "And you never told me? Why?"

"Because they wanted to form a group of operatives who were not employed by the CIA, Army, or any government institution. I was under a strict NDA." He passes a hand over his face. "Until I found this shit. Someone sent me the intel about Viktor. I couldn't act on it, given my current role. But I knew you would."

I'm trying to process all of this, but my brain still feels numb. "Who sent you this?"

Cal shakes his head. "Darned if I know. But I got authority to follow this up. It's a big deal. Dad's death was always ruled an accident, right?"

We hold each other's eyes. All our lives, we never believed the official version. Neither did our mother, God bless her departed soul.

Our father drowned in a boat carrying five other men—Russian and American. His body was never found. Before his death, he had sent the photos he took of the naval shipyard.

He was a careful man and an experienced agent. The CIA swallowed what the Russians told them, and the matter was never investigated.

But Cal and I never forgot.

"There's got to be a reason someone's sending me the intel now. It came to my personal email. No one in the CIA knows anything about it," Cal says.

"Weird," I say, frowning. "Files on Dad would be top secret, right? CIA property."

Cal nods in silence. "To be honest, it's one of the reasons I took the job when the CIA asked me."

I feel a rush of warmth toward him. "You did the right thing. Plus," I say drily, "you just saved my ass."

His lips quirk. "I didn't join the CIA to save your ass. But you're welcome." He becomes serious. "We need to get to Viktor."

My jaws twitch. I feel the fire returning to my veins. "Don't worry. I will."

CHAPTER 7

DORA

I sneak a look at his face, illuminated by the dashboard lights. His eyes are fixed on the road. We are still inside Dale City, going past blocks of one- and two-story townhouses. When he talks, he doesn't look at me.

"Do you need to speak to anyone?"

"Yes, I do," I say, struggling to keep my voice even. "But you destroyed my phone, remember?"

He sighs. "That was for your own good. Did you want those people to get hold of your phone?"

"I didn't *want* any of this," I snap. "All I want is to go home." Anger simmers inside me. This whole... mess I've landed in is ridiculous. Why did I have to come to this godforsaken place? I don't even know who I'm angry with—myself or this person sitting next to me.

"Don't you want my address?" I ask. "I live in Alexandria."

He doesn't say anything. I frown. "Did you hear what I said?"

In reply, he sighs deeply. That admittedly large chest rises and falls like an ocean wave.

His next words throw me completely. "I'm not taking you home."

"Excuse me?"

When he tells me, I stare at him, thunderstruck. After the shock of what I've been through, this is just too low a blow.

"What?!" I'm not aware I'm shouting. "You want me to live in this small town with you? Are you kidding me?"

"There are people looking to kill us." His voice is unruffled, and he still hasn't as much as turned to look at me. "They can easily find out where you live. When they find you, they'll kill you."

I sink back into my seat, hands pressed over my face. "Okay, that's enough. Stop the car."

"I can't do that."

"I said stop the damn car!"

He doesn't reply. I can see his jaw tense. His large hands grip the steering wheel tightly.

I wind the window down and unbuckle my seat belt. I try to open the door, but he's locked it.

"What are you doing?"

"If you're not going to pull over, I'm going to jump out the window."

"You're in shock right now." His voice is low, as if he's speaking to a child. "Believe me, I'm doing this for you."

"Don't patronize me." This guy might be good-looking—okay, smokin' hot—but he's also infuriating. I want answers, and he's not giving me any.

"Who are you?" I say.

"I told you. My name is—"

"John, I know. If that's your real name, then I'm the Queen of England."

He stays silent. I fold my legs and put my feet on the seat. I grip the window edge and lift myself. If I hoped to get a reaction out of him, I'm disappointed. He barely moves a muscle.

Instead, in a resigned voice, he asks, "What are you doing?"

"Jumping out the window. What does it look like?"

Another sigh, then he signals and pulls over. He keeps the engine on, but the car is stationary.

I glare at him. "Right, *John*. Start talking."

He actually lowers his head and grips his forehead as if he's tired. That doesn't work with me. If he's going to take over my life, I need to know what the hell I'm getting myself into.

"I can't tell you anything," he says in a tired voice. "These are very bad people. They won't hesitate to kill you."

Staring at his face, I remember the moment when he looked at me with a gun pointed at his head and said the name—Jozdani. He'd pronounced it slowly, staring at me, as if he wanted me to memorize it. A shiver had passed through me. There had been a signal in his eyes, a silent communication, and we'd had a connection.

"Who is Jozdani?" I ask.

His shoulders slump, and he groans loudly. He raps his knuckles on the windowsill.

"You don't need to know that."

"I don't even know your real name!"

That makes him pause. He lifts his head, and gray eyes stare at me. Then he nods. "My name is Richter."

For some reason, the name fits his rugged, muscular build.

Before I can say anything more, Richter glances at his watch. He starts the engine. "I shouldn't have stopped here." He pulls out as he tells me, "We can talk while I drive. But there's one thing I need you to remember."

I'm in no mood to take orders from him. "Just the one thing?"

"Dora." He says my name for the first time, and he utters it slowly, as if it settles on his tongue, snug and comfortable. "There can be no negotiation on this. Do you understand?"

"Okay," I say.

"You have to follow my lead. If I say take cover, you do it without asking questions. Otherwise, I cannot protect you. Got that?"

"Crystal."

I remember what just happened. How he bumped into me from behind then covered my body with his. He just saved my life. I close my eyes and huff in silence. I'm just angry I can't go back home. I don't know what sort of a mess I've landed in, but I sure as hell need his help to get out of it.

"When can I go back home?"

He ponders the question in silence. The ramp for the I-95 comes up, and he takes the southbound route.

"A few days. My colleagues should let me know soon."

I cradle my head in my hands. I have a headache. I'm shattered, exhausted. I've had a sheltered life. Rich dad, prep school, good college, overbearing brother. No one's ever shot at me except with words. And that's mostly been my dad. But even his often cruel words come nowhere close to the real bullets flying around me today.

"You know, I have a life," I mumble. "I need to get back to it."

"I know. So do I. Trust me, I don't want this any more than you do."

"Well, that makes two of us."

"Right."

There doesn't seem to be much to say after that. We drive on, delving deeper into the darkness of the highway. My head rests back in the seat. I can hear Dad's voice in my head, scolding me as if I'm a little girl. *What have you done this time?*

His face morphs into Julia's, sitting by the phone, a red-nailed finger twirling her strawberry blonde highlights. I need to call her and tell her what happened. Thoughts bump and slide into one another then fade into the darkness, where the beams of the headlights don't reach.

CHAPTER 8

DORA

There's a burning in my eyes. It doesn't hurt, it's just bright. So bright my eyes blink open. Daylight. I'm on a bed. It's big and comfortable, with fluffy blankets. I sit up straight, heart pounding, confused. Where am I? In a flash, memories of last night come back like a thunderbolt. I must be at Richter's place. We drove here, and I must've fallen asleep in the car.

Thank God, I'm still fully dressed. And alone in the bed. I put my feet on the solid wood floor. There's a rug on it. I walk to the windows and part the curtains slightly. There's an open field in front running for miles before reaching the mountains. The hills look close by, so massive they take me by surprise. Sunlight catches the rock formations as rays of light peek through the cracks, early-morning shadows playing hide-and-seek. Together with the mist rising like a curtain from the fields, melting in the sun, it's a beautiful sight, and I can't help but stare at it.

The knock on the door almost makes me yelp. After a gentle nudge, the door is pushed open.

It's Richter. He's wearing a white T-shirt that clings to his body and blue jeans that hug his hips. The T-shirt leaves little to the imagination. The corded muscles of his biceps strain the sleeves. There's a tattoo on his right biceps and ink on his upper chest visible through the thin fabric. His forearms have thick veins traversing their length and coarse, chocolate-brown hair on top of the knotted muscles. The shirt molds to the slab of his pecs and the flat abs. His face is stunningly handsome, and his presence fills the room, head nearly touching the top of the doorframe. Last night, in the darkness, I didn't get a proper look at him. He looks older than me by a few years at least. If I had to guess, I'd put him somewhere in his late thirties or early forties.

My gaze sweeps down to his legs, trying not to linger on his powerful hips, on that mildly arrogant, cocky posture he has as he stands with his arms hanging by his sides. The stance is open, direct, and begs my eyes to look at him again. I slap my brain and drag my eyes away. For no apparent reason, I suddenly envision him naked, the line of hair moving down from his belly button...*Fuck! Stop it, Dora!*

I'm looking out the window again, eyes fixed on the mist. I swallow, aware my lips are parted.

"Did you sleep well?" His voice is deep but gentle.

"Um, yes. Did you?" Okay, head smack, stupid question.

He says nothing, observing me silently. His strange, quiet gaze settles on my face as if he's trying to memorize my features. It's so unnerving I have to look away. The mist again. Swirling and diffuse, opaque. Like my brain right now.

Another question arrives silently in my mind. I decide to ask him. "How did you know I was awake?"

There's a quirk to his lips, an almost smile. It vanishes quickly. "It's very quiet around here. I heard the wood creak."

So he was waiting for me to wake up.

"There's coffee downstairs," he says. "And a bathroom in here." He jerks his head toward the end of the room. I've seen it already.

He stares at me silently for a little while longer, and an inscrutable look, like a shadow on the hills, passes across his face. Then he turns and goes down the stairs.

I gulp and breathe. His absence leaves a sudden vacuum in the room, and the space seems to expand back to its normal size. Richter is the type of man who can make a room look smaller just by being in it. He has to be six three or four and two hundred pounds plus. Hell, I felt that weight when he threw himself on top of me last night. Warmth touches my cheeks as I hurry into the bathroom.

I don't need makeup really, but a touch of mascara would help. My eyes look pale. I leave my shoulder-length dark hair as it is. There's nothing to change into, a problem that has to be rectified soon.

The smell of coffee invigorates me as I come downstairs. The place is surprisingly well decorated. Artwork hangs in small frames on the wall. Fluffy cushions are placed on the deep sofa set. The wooden fireplace, with logs burning, is a nice feature to one side.

Stacks of logs are placed on either side of the fireplace, which takes up almost one side of the floor. There's a massive flat-screen TV on the wall and a pool table to one side.

It's large and cozy. The kitchen is next to this living area. I step inside to find Richter with his hands on the sink, staring out the window. He turns as I come in.

"Coffee?" he asks.

I nod, tuck a loose strand behind my ear, and sit at the table. He reaches for a cup from the shelf, and the hem of his shirt rides up. I catch a glimpse of toned abs and the enticing curve of a hip bone. The tattoo on his biceps catches my eyes again. It's a black knife imprinted on what looks like a red clover leaf.

He pours the coffee from the machine and puts it in front of me. Then he picks up his own cup and leans against the counter. I sip, aware of his eyes on me.

The coffee's good, but the silence is unnerving, for me anyway. I'm a city girl used to the background hum of invisible cars, millions of human beings shuffling, stepping around—the rhythm of urban life. Here, I can't hear a thing. Only emptiness.

"So, you come here often?" I ask.

"Actually, it's my home."

Right. I'm totally out of my depth here. I don't like it. I put the cup down and stare at him. The smoky gray eyes return my gaze.

"Look, Richter, I know what happened last night was a mess. And you saved my life. Thank you for that. But I got no answers last night, and I'm sure as hell not going to stay here if you don't give me something right now."

He stares at me with that impenetrable, rock-hard gaze for a few seconds then looks away. His eyes are softer when he speaks. "I'm sorry. I can't tell you much." He shifts, standing taller, and changes the subject. "You need to speak to your family, right?"

"Yes. And my friend."

He scratches the stubble on his jaw and ponders. "We can divert the signal so it looks like it's coming from New York. Just so anyone eavesdropping can't get a trace on it. But it's best not to call your friend. Only family, and that too if they have a burner phone."

Burner phone?

Jesus. What sort of trouble am I in?

Richter rolls his shoulder and puts the cup down on the table. He really is a man mountain, his muscles popping like they're hewn from the rocks around us.

"Who do you need to contact?"

"My father, for one. Or maybe my brother."

The thought actually nauseates me. I can hear their snorts of derision from here. I get on better with Robert, my older brother. But he's too much like Dad, although he tries not to be, for my sake. From the time my mother died, Dad made it his life's obsession to mollycoddle me with teachers and helpers. I was the rich kid who got dropped off at high school in a fancy car every day. My friends were vetted by my dad. Only those deemed rich enough and from stable enough families were allowed into our home, which is ironic considering Dad is on his fourth marriage.

Michael Simpson, the media tycoon. My dad can buy and sell companies like he's shopping for groceries. He spends his whole life working, and I barely remember seeing him until I turned into a teen. From then on, he wore a stern-faced mask, never to be questioned, always to be agreed with. Fun? I never had a good time with my father. Sure, he cares about me, loves me too, in his own way. But he loves me because I do as he says.

His choice of college. His approval of my friends and boyfriends. Even his choice of profession. But I demurred when he wanted to groom me to become a TV anchor. The latest edition of my stepmother is one, and she's a Stepford clone, a country club–visiting, silicone-boobed, Botoxed blond bimbo. Looks great on my father's arm. Fucking nightmare to have a conversation with.

It might sound harsh, but I'm tired of having to get on with Dad's parade of wives. He has this weird fixation on showing the world how close he is to his children and family. I have no time for it.

"Who is your father?" Richter rumbles.

"Who is Jozdani?" I counter.

His wide shoulders slump, and he bends his neck, chin falling on his chest.

His voice is barely a whisper. "You need to forget that name."

"Why?"

"Because it's dangerous." His nostrils flare, and light glints from the smoky grays. There's a beeping sound, and I look down to see his hand reaching into his pants pocket.

CHAPTER 9

RICHTER

Cal's number flashes on the screen. I take the call, walking out of the kitchen through the back door into the garden porch.

Before Cal and I set up our security firm, he used to be a CIA agent. He's our main intel guy, but lately we've also got our very own smart-ass sister Samantha. Between the soft-spoken but intense Cal and my wisecracking sister, I don't get a moment's rest from work-related updates and general ball busting about being the boss but not pulling my weight.

"Done some digging on Dora Simpson," Cal said. "Her father owns several TV stations all around the country. Mainly news oriented but also lifestyle. You know the America Live station that operates out of DC? That's one of her dad's." Cal reels off a few other familiar and not-so-familiar names I see on TV.

"He's loaded. Top connections as well. Does a charity ball every year on Capitol Hill. Knows everyone worth knowing."

I'm leaning against the logs, a summer breeze cool on my chest. "He's gonna have a coronary when he finds out what's happened to his daughter. This could get out of hand."

"Just sit tight and wait for my signal." Cal pauses. "Are you sure you're going to be okay?"

"What the hell's that supposed to mean?"

"Mission safety is critical. She can't know anything about us."

"I know that, Cal." I'm getting pissed off now. "What are you trying to say?"

"Nothing. It's just that...after Charlotte, you haven't been with a woman—"

I cut him short. "You really think I'm going to let that get in the way? You don't think I know how important this is?"

My voice is hard, and we're both quiet for a while. Cal is the first to speak. "I'm worried about you, big bro. You keep it all under wraps. Act like it's all cool. But you don't fool me."

I move the phone away from my ear. I don't need to hear this. A change of topic right now sounds good.

"Any news of Viktor?" I ask. "Or Jozdani's whereabouts?" *Focus on the mission.* It's what I've done for the last three years—hell, for most of my life. I need that focus now more than anything else.

"Jozdani has a son from his first marriage. Studies in Vermont. The son doesn't have his father's last name, which is why we didn't track him down sooner."

"Are you sure J is in the U.S.?"

"He traveled on a fake passport. Facial recognition picked him up at JFK."

"You think he's here to see his son?"

Cal hesitates before replying. "I'm not sure. He doesn't stay in touch with his son. The boy has an American mother, one of Jozdani's friends when he was at Stanford doing his PhD."

Both of us are silent, thinking. I say, "Whatever. We need to find him, right? That's the whole mission."

"Unless Viktor finds you first. He thinks you know where Jozdani is. Well, you and Dora."

"I'll keep an eye on her. Don't worry. Find out as much as you can about her family and her father."

I hang up. Holding the phone in my hand, I stare to the end of the garden and the mountains looming in the distance. Morning light is painting them in pastel shades of dark brown and ochre. It gives me a sense of peace. One of the reasons I call Montrose my home is the isolation and the distance from the real world.

"I can tell you about my father."

Her voice makes me jump. I stand and whirl around. Did this woman just get the drop on me? I curse in silence. How in hell's name did that happen?

She's leaning against the porch door, arms folded across her chest. She has a tank top on beneath the loose-fitting dressing gown, and her breasts rise up in a soft, inviting bulge. The cleavage is barely visible above, and blood rushes to my cock like a river breaking its banks. I step back, rubbing a hand over my face, praying she can't see my hardening manhood. I look away. It's been a while since I've been so close to a woman. Not since Charlotte, in fact. Three years. The memory dims the sunlight, darkens my day.

"His name is Michael Simpson."

Her voice is the sound of wind rushing through the trees. She carries on, telling me about his business empire.

I turn to her. She's younger than I imagined. No more than mid-twenties. She's slender but filled out at the right places. Those dark-brown eyes are luscious, and whenever I can wrench my eyes off them, they fall on the smooth swell of her hips. I remember how pliable her body felt when I covered her last night. My cock comes alive again.

This isn't working. You'd think I'm some sex-starved man, and, well, you'd be right, but I have discipline, damn it. I didn't live through Army Ranger school, get deployed, then become a Delta operative for nothing. Being tough is ingrained in me.

Then why am I falling apart every time I look at her? It's not because I haven't been close to a woman since Charlotte. I have. But none like this one right in front of me. She's a curious mix of innocence and confidence, her eyes at once demure and sparkling, her words demanding then downcast.

I don't know what to make of her. All I know is my body goes into overdrive when she's near me. Just like she is now. I try not to show my surprise as she comes forward and sits down on the step, looking at the overgrown garden as if it's her own house.

Did she just do that? And what the hell am I supposed to do? I could go back inside, leave her here, but that would be rude. And besides,

I have a duty to look after her. If Viktor's men find her... I can't even finish that thought. All I know is I cannot let that happen.

"Nice place you have here." Her voice has that rustling, soft quality. The words lie on my heart like a soothing balm, and I have no idea why. I find myself sitting down on the porch, keeping a good distance from her.

I get the phone from my pocket. "Do you know your dad's number? You can call him. This number's untraceable."

She presses her lips together and looks down. "I'd like to get dressed first."

She sure as hell doesn't seem keen to call her own folks, which makes me wonder. But I don't push it. "Okay. I can take you into town. There are some clothes shops. You won't find Neiman Marcus here though."

She smiles at that. "I'm more of a Macy's girl. But any store will do right now."

I shrug and head back inside. At the porch door, I say, "Remember, we're a couple, right? Just in case anyone asks."

She turns to look at me, her eyes bright. "Yeah, sure."

In the kitchen, I've started to unload the dishwasher when I sense her behind me. She's not moving, so I straighten, a stack of plates in my hand.

Her eyes move from my hand to my face. She's chewing her lower lip, and her brows are furrowed. "Those men would have killed me last night, right?"

I put the plates on the table. I nod without speaking.

"How many of them died last night?" Her voice quivers then breaks at the end. She seems small all of a sudden and very lonely. Her earlier confidence has gone like a winter branch with shed leaves.

Deep inside, so far I barely feel it, something snaps in two. I shut the dishwasher door, and the soft click resonates in the rusty chambers of my heart, spreading to the hard corners of my soul like ripples in a pond.

Dora has her back to the counter, facing me. Her chin sinks to her chest, hands rising to cover her face. In a flash, I'm at her side. I'm so close I can feel her trembling. Without thinking, I lift my arms to engulf her. She's crying now. I can hear the tears, which sound like the whisper of rain down my window on a stormy night, sniffing, sobbing. Those whispers of pain and loneliness coat my insides like dried lava in a volcano. I hear them in her lost, woeful voice as I hold her close to me as if I can do something about it, even though I know I can't.

Her arms circle my torso, and the first contact with her body, even through the layers of cloth, is like a benediction, a calming salvation that closes my eyes and opens my mouth. I feel the wind rushing through a distant galaxy, a space opening up inside me as big as that invisible sky way up there, full of twinkling stars that send us their light even though they died millennia ago.

Her tears drench my T-shirt, and I hold her tighter, whispering words I'm barely aware of. She shudders, and I rub her back. It seems so natural, holding her like this, even if we are strangers. My hand slips down farther, and suddenly I feel the swell of her hips, so smooth and round. My splayed fingers are long enough to stretch from one side to the other.

Blood stirs up in me again, making my cock twitch. *Damn*. I bend my fingers, or I'll end up stroking her hips. And if I do, with her face and coral-pink lips being so close to mine…

I clear my throat and separate myself from her gently. Dora sniffs once then looks up at me through red-rimmed eyes.

"I'm sorry," she says.

"Don't be," I say, hoping my voice is firm. "What you went through last night would test the hardest of men. Not only did you survive, you acted like a real pro."

"You think so?"

"I know so."

I step away, giving her some space. "Now, let's get ready. We need to buy food and clothes for you."

CHAPTER 10
RICHTER

Before we get into the car, I give her a ball cap and dark sunglasses. I'm wearing both myself. I think she will get annoyed at the frayed old ball cap and the definitely unstylish glasses, but she puts them on without a word.

I've got my Glock 22 in the underarm holster and a knife strapped to my left ankle. My jacket's undone for easy reach, just in case. I lock the house and turn on the alarm.

She's looking out the window at the residential blocks giving way to flat grassland, rising up to the somber stacks of malachite. I struggle with what I want to say. I always have. Words don't come easily to me, and feelings I bottle up. Something changed when I held her in the kitchen—that felt...different. But now, when I want to speak, I can't find the words.

She turns to me, and I sneak a look at her. She watches me for a while, but it doesn't make me feel uncomfortable. I don't understand why. She's a stranger—if she stares at me, I should feel weird. But it feels the opposite.

"Don't talk much, do you?" she asks.

I shrug and raise my eyebrows. I feel more than see her smile. That puzzles me as well. By all accounts, she should be scared, nervous, worried. Instead, she seems to be taking this in stride. There is a strength in her, radiating out from her vulnerable, gentle core, and I can feel it hitting me like invisible radiation from a power source.

"So, you can't tell me what this situation is about. But I figured you out last night, remember? You work for the government, right?"

"Hell no." It slips out of me before I know it.

"Okay," she says slowly. "You're undercover. More than a cop though. You're FBI. If we were abroad, I'd say you're CIA or even Special Forces."

She's smart. Damn smart. I knew this last night, but now I know I'm in trouble. She's nothing if not persistent.

"You must be missing your family," I say.

She leans forward until her face is closer to mine, forcing me to look at her. "You're gonna have to do better than that to throw me off. I'm a reporter, don't forget."

Holy fuck, of course she is. Damn. Double damn.

"That tattoo on your arm, it means something."

When I say nothing, she continues, "I worked on a story about the SEAL team and their counterpart in the Army, Delta, once. It's not mandatory, but many of the Tier 1 operatives have ink done, don't they? Sort of like an initiation rite."

My hands tighten on the steering wheel, so I relax them quickly. I shrug again, not saying anything. She's still leaning close, and I'm glad my jacket's sleeves are hiding the tat. My nostrils are aflame with her scent, the faint lilac still wafting from her hair and a light flowery perfume that I can't help but inhale deeply. It settles inside me, the memory of that scent.

She sighs and falls back against the seat.

I ask, "Which newspaper do you work for?"

I can tell she's examining me for another change of topic. Luckily, this time she goes with the flow.

"It's not a newspaper. More of a current-affairs magazine with some lifestyle thrown in."

"Daddy's brand?" I ask.

"Why would you think that?" Her tone is sharp and angry.

I sneak a look at her. Her brows are boxed in the middle, nose crinkled.

I think of the flat tone in which she spoke of what her father does. There was no warmth in it like one would expect. I'm starting to wonder about the Simpson family dynamics.

"Wanted to strike out on your own, huh? Make your own way?"

She looks out the window, avoiding my eyes. "Something like that."

I know there's more to it, but I leave it for now. None of my business, to be honest. In a couple of days, Cal and Samantha will know where Jozdani and Viktor are, and we can get back to the mission: pick Jozdani up and get rid of Viktor.

And Dora Simpson will head back to her own life.

The thought shouldn't leave me feeling empty inside, but it does.

I don't want it to.

But it does.

I of all people should know what it's like for someone like me to...make connections. I'm trained to kill and maim. Violence has been the mainstay of my life. First for my country then for our private security company. The job is all I have, and there's no point having relationships when I don't know if I'll be alive the next day. If I do fall for someone, it makes me the asshole who doesn't learn from his mistakes.

Well, one mistake. One whose scars will remain on my heart for as long as I live.

As we approach the mall, I pull the GMC Yukon into a parking lot and pay for a couple of hours. I check my appearance in the mirror and then look at Dora. Her ball cap is pulled low, and the dark glasses cover her eyes effectively. It's a sunny day, so we should get away with it.

The parking lot is busy. We walk down with families around us. I come to Montrose twice, maybe three times a year. Apart from my neighbors, who don't know my real identity, I don't know anyone here. I like it that way. But I stay on high alert, noticing every shape around me.

When she slips her hand into mine, it catches me by surprise. She leans closer and whispers, "If we're meant to be a couple, we should act like one. Right?"

Of course she's right. I feel like an idiot but also relieved she thought of it. A couple sticks out far less than singletons. Her hand fits snugly into mine, and a shiver passes up my arm, making the hairs on my forearm stand up. It's been a long time since a woman put her hand in mine. Trust? Wouldn't go that far.

We're walking around the clothes aisle in a shop when a voice stops me.

"Richter?"

I turn. Dora is walking a few paces ahead, but she hears it too. I have no choice but to answer, even though I don't recognize the voice.

An old woman peers at me from behind thick glasses. I'm still confused, but then my memory jolts: old Mrs. Carruthers from the end of our block. I saw her a couple of times when I went out running the paths in the hills and once I brought her stray cat back home. She made me a carrot cake to say thank you, and I found out she had a son who died in the second Gulf war. I felt bad I couldn't tell her what I did, but lying about my profession comes naturally to me and my brethren. It's actually the worst aspect of our jobs, having to keep people we care about in the dark about what we do.

"Hello, Mrs. Carruthers," I say, glancing around. There's a family and another couple down the aisle, but they can't hear our conversation. My glasses are off, and so is the ball cap. Dora still has hers on.

"Thought it was you. My eyes are still sharp, you know."

I smile back at her and notice she's checking out Dora. The old lady's sharp as a tack, and I have to watch myself around her. I gave her a story about being a retired military policeman. Not sure if she believed me.

"Who's the young lady?" Mrs. Carruthers asks with a knowing smile.

I introduce Dora as my fiancée. They shake hands.

"So how long are you here for, my dear?" the old lady asks.

"Less than a week. Isn't that right?" Dora looks at me.

"That's right. We have to head back to see her parents soon," I say.

A few more polite questions later, it's time to move on.

"Do come and see me sometime," Mrs. Carruthers says. "It's Tom's death anniversary next week, and I've been feeling lonely."

I feel like an asshole. "Sure thing. I'll drop by."

Just as we're moving off, Mrs. Carruthers asks, "Where's the engagement ring?"

I go rigid. Hell, I hadn't even thought of that. I wouldn't even know where to look for one here in Montrose. The old lady is looking at me with a quizzical expression on her face. I need to give an answer, but I'm tongue tied.

It's Dora who answers without missing a beat. "It was the wrong size. So we had to send it back to the supplier for a refit. He surprised me, so there was no time to get the right size."

Mrs. Carruthers looks mollified. I sigh in relief.

CHAPTER 11

DORA

Richter acts as if he's made of bricks, not flesh and blood, but I'm starting to see the real him—which sounds strange, because I've only just met him.

There are people who show their real selves not with words but with deeds. This man mountain is one of them. He must have carried me upstairs from the car last night and tucked me into bed. I woke up with the covers over me this morning. Fully clothed.

He probably kept an eye on me overnight, and he knew when I was awake. That might sound creepy, but now I know he sees it as his duty. And it makes me feel safe.

He was there when I lost it and couldn't help the tears. When I put my arms around him, his wide, colossal presence was like holding onto an immovable rock in a fast-moving river. He was my support.

And the way he interacted with that little old lady, it's not hard to see she dotes on him like a son. The fact that she's lost hers in a war speaks volumes about who Richter is. A former soldier, no doubt. Probably an elite one. But Richter is made of flesh and bone, not bricks or steel.

Yes, I see him. There's something deeper to him as well. Something I haven't figured out yet. Again, there are people with whom I can tell. Maybe it's something sad. Misery and bereavement can cast a cloak around a person's shoulders. That cloak never really lifts, no matter how much they get on with life and act normal. It's in the fractured, hollow look in their eyes, the sudden drop of their lips. I don't know what he's been through, but I'm willing to bet it's something that took a heavy toll on him. It's not something I can ask him either.

We get all the stuff we need and are in the car when he excuses himself and runs back. He emerges a few minutes later with a bag. He gets in the car and puts it in my hand. It's a brand-new iPhone, the exact model I had.

I look up at him, smiling. "You didn't have to do that."

He shrugs as he backs the Yukon out. "I did break it. It's only fair."

I don't want to say I'll pay him for it. iPhones aren't cheap, and I don't know how much money he makes. But I don't want to say something he won't like. Mentally, though, I make a note. He's paying for everything right now, and I have my dad's Platinum credit card. The day I leave, all debts will be squared.

When we're on the road, he says, "I also have to thank you for saving me from the ring explanation."

"That old lady is observant."

"Most old ladies are," Richter says drily. "But thank you anyway. You've got great presence of mind. You know what to say in tough situations. It's a good skill to have."

The compliment lights up my heart. My dad and brother never compliment me for anything. There was never any need to, since I never showed any initiative—apparently. Which is why Richter's words leave me with a warm, fuzzy glow.

"Thank you," I say, trying not to smile.

"Pleasure is all mine," he drawls in a low voice.

*****

Richter helps me carry my stuff into my room. I'm happy with what I got. I'm going to spend some time arranging the double dresser now.

He stops on his way out. "I'm going for a shower."

I nod at him, desperately hoping he can't see the warmth creeping into my cheeks. Richter naked in a shower is an image I suddenly can't erase from my mind. I look down at the iPhone in my hands quickly and start to fumble with the battery.

"Don't open the door for anyone. The windows are all locked. Please don't open any."

Soap suds moving down his water-slicked pectorals, pooling at the deep groove in the center of his chest, then sliding down his six-pack. Muscular thighs—

"Did you hear me?" he asks. My head shoots up, and he's looking at me with a puzzled expression.

This time I can't help the heat fanning up my neck. "Uh-huh," I say, turning my back to him quickly.

He leaves the door open and walks into his own room before he steps out again. I realize there's only one room in the house with an en suite bathroom, and he's given it to me.

I hear the shower turn on and Richter moving around. I get up and work fast, moving my clothes into the dresser. Then I head downstairs. I need to do something to keep my mind off the shower upstairs. Food seems to be a good option.

I must admit, I suck at cooking. Ready meals nuked in a microwave are how I spend my evenings alone. When Julia comes around, we get takeout. That's pretty much my social life these days. Men and I don't mix very well. Mostly, I meet the men my father approves of at social functions and such gatherings. I still haven't found any of them remotely interesting, yet another fact that rankles my father. I've even been told I might be left on the shelf at this rate. I'm twenty-four, and the only real relationship I had was in college, where my dad and brother couldn't pry into every aspect of my life…until they did and pissed off my ex-boyfriend so much he dumped me. There's no escaping my family.

Guilt rips into me. I need to call Julia. And my dad. Despite everything, he is my father. I have to let him know. But it's Julia I feel bad for. I know she'll be worried sick about me. As soon as Richter's out, I need to ask him to let me call Julia.

I open the cupboards and look for frying pans. I can't cook, but I know how to fry. I'll heat some oil in a skillet and the chorizo that Richter bought. I take out a chopping board and slice the chorizo while the skillet heats up. I reach for the oil, and my side brushes the pan. Instantly searing pain runs down my side as the ultra-hot metal touches my skin.

I can't help the scream. It comes out louder than expected because oh god, my skin burns like hell. I bend over, clutching my side, grimacing. The fire is still on, and the pan gets hotter.

There's a crashing sound above, then the whole house seems to shake as thunderous steps charge down the stairs.

CHAPTER 12

DORA

Richter suddenly appears at the kitchen door, wearing nothing but a towel wrapped around his waist.

Momentarily, I forget my pain.

This man is seriously ripped. I don't know what he does to keep himself in shape, but the steely stack of pecs and the ridiculously well-defined six-pack are straight out of a male bodybuilder's magazine. His hair is still wet, and a drop of water courses down the V of his chest. His eyes are wild, checking me out along with the kitchen in general.

There's ink all over his chest, dark green and blue, and it lends depth to his muscles, as if any was needed.

"What happened?" he asks, striding into the kitchen.

I can't look away from him. It's as if my hormones have a viselike grip on my head. A single trail of dark hair trails down from his navel, disappearing beneath the towel.

Desire pools between my legs, untangling a knot deep inside my belly. I clutch the back of the chair in front of me.

"I... uh..."

He comes close enough to touch. Then he reaches around me and switches off the stove. He lifts the pan and places it in the sink. It sizzles like I imagine my fingers will if I place them on his chest. His brows are lowered, and I can see droplets of water sticking to his beard.

Now that he's close, I'm hypnotized by his lips. In fact, I realize with a jolt it's his lips and mouth I find the sexiest, that gut-clenching combination of hard lines on his jaw and chin and the ruby redness of his lips.

"Talk to me, Dora. What happened?" His voice is almost a growl.

I come to my senses. "It's the frying pan. It was heated up, and I rubbed against it. Just an accident. I'm fine. Really." *Okay, stop babbling. That's enough.*

He gives me a close look then looks at the window. The door is still locked, and he leans over the sink to check the window before he looks back at me. His eyes are softer, his nostrils not flaring anymore.

"Where did you hurt yourself?" he asks.

I'm still trying to catch my breath. He's close enough to touch, feel, sink my teeth into. Without a word, I point at my waist. The muscles on his forearm ripple as he reaches for the hem of my T-shirt. He stops before he touches it. The smoky-gray eyes flecked with green look up at me.

"May I?"

I'm unable to speak. I only nod. He bends down on one knee, the towel straining and dipping lower. He lifts my T-shirt and peers closely at my burn. Then he moves his face closer, so close his beard touches my skin, and he blows.

That's right.

He blows air onto the burn, and it's the most mind-blowing experience I've ever had.

His cool breath brushes over my skin, making the hair on my arms stand up.

I have to sit down; I can't stand any longer. He senses that and pulls over the chair to help me sit.

He stands, and I'm inches away from his rock-hard abs. That dusting of fine hair that snakes its way down beneath his navel is close enough to touch.

I'm hypnotized, unable to look away.

"Hold it up. You need some ice."

My eyes must be dazed as I crane my neck upwards to look at him. He seems even taller, looking down at me. I can smell every aspect of him. The musky aroma of his masculine essence, the light steam still rising off his body.

He bends at the waist to get closer. He frowns. "Dora. Are you okay?"

I gulp. "Yes."

"Then hold up the shirt."

I do as I'm told. He turns around to open the fridge door, and I get a view of his back. It looks like a marble sculpture, every muscle carved and grooved by nature's perfect hands. He has ink on his back as well, just on the top, near the shoulder blades. Blue and black swirls of barbed wire blend with the taut symmetry.

He takes out an ice tray and crushes some with an ice pick then wraps it in a small towel. He bends down to where I am again and looks up at me, the smoky grays asking permission. I nod, and he presses the towel to the burn. I gasp at the cold touch. Then he does something I didn't expect. He holds my hand and lowers it to the towel pressed against my side. I know we held hands before, but this is unexpected, for me at least. And he glances up at me as our hands touch. The warm sensation sends tingles up my arm and down my spine.

The green flecks in his gray eyes seem to condense and converge as the pupils dilate ever so slightly. Then he clears his throat and looks down. He presses my hand to the towel. His touch is so comforting, the warmth of his hand and the coldness of the ice such a contrast, that a moment stops and settles between us, heavy with meaning. My heart is spinning like a washing machine on high. I can feel it crash and rebound against my ribs, the sound a hollow echo in my ears. I can't hear anything else.

Richter lets go of my hand and stands up. He moves away, leans against the sink, and brushes a hand through his hair.

"Should be all right in a few. Keep it tight. If a blister forms, just let it pop. Better to let the fluid drain out."

I clear my throat. "How do you know about burns?"

"Basic wound management."

"Are you a medic?"

He doesn't reply. I point to the tattoo on his right biceps.

"What's that?"

He gives me a slight shake of the head. "Persistent, aren't you?"

"It's my job," I say.

"You're not at work right now," he says, lifting his eyebrows. His eyes narrow. "What were you trying to do with the pan?"

"Fry the chorizo." I point to the diced meat on the board.

"Chef, huh?"

I roll my eyes. "Hell no. Can't cook to save my life."

He begins to say something then stops.

I'm still pressing the ice to my side, and my fingers are going numb. "But I figured that if I'm staying here, I should pull my weight."

His lips quirk, then go still. "Without burning the place down."

"The only thing I burned was myself." My tone is stronger than intended. I look down. "I know I'm useless at cooking."

I'm used to being told I'm useless at most things. That I can't get by without help, namely the help of my dad and brother. The litany of discouragement that has littered my life has also made me the person I am. I feel I won't ever be worth anything. Even when I succeed at something, I put myself down. I applied to Ivy League colleges and didn't get in. My dad was a donor to Vermont College, and he never tires of telling me I only got a college education because of him. When I chose to join the magazine start-up, he saw it as a betrayal. He never tires of telling me that either.

"Have you tried to cook much?" Richter asks. His eyes are contemplative, gazing at me as if he's trying to figure out my thoughts.

I shrug. "Sometimes. Not really. Always had someone to cook for me."

When I lived in Dad's ten-bedroom mansion, there was always a cook. And a driver, a butler, a gardener.

I don't know what to expect from Richter. He doesn't show the condescension to a spoiled rich girl that I've felt in the past. I don't know anything about him, but I'm guessing he wasn't brought up like me. We're polar opposites in every way.

"Well, if you haven't tried to cook," he drawls, "then how do you know you're no good at it?"

I stare at him. He stands straight and stretches his arms. The biceps flex and bulge, and the ropelike cords of sinews in the forearm tighten. There is a raw power to his physique, tightly coiled, waiting to be unleashed. I've never seen anything like it this close. I *hate* the patch of warmth in my cheeks, but I can't stop it.

"Let me get dressed," he says. "Then maybe I can show you how to make a chorizo pasta with red wine?"

"You can cook?"

He shrugs without replying. Then he's gone.

CHAPTER 13

DORA

When Richter comes back down, he's wearing a T-shirt again, brown this time, with the same dark-blue jeans. I don't know what size he buys, but this shirt hugs his body as well, the sleeves tight around his biceps. He digs into his pocket and pulls out a cell phone. It's not an iPhone or any make I've seen before. There's no brand name on it.

"You can call who you want from this phone. It will seem the calls are coming from New York." I take the phone from his hand while he continues, "You can't use your phone yet because it doesn't have the bouncing software loaded on it. My brother sorts that out normally."

He checks himself suddenly, snapping his jaws shut.

I raise my eyebrows. "So your brother's in this as well? Family business, huh?"

"Like I said, the less you know the better." He pauses to move the chopping board. "Do you want to make the call? By the way, a few rules about phone calls. Don't tell anyone my name or where we are. And only call people you really need to. Understood?"

"Yes." What else can I say?

"I'll get the ingredients ready." He looks up at me. "Only if you want to cook, of course."

I nod, trying to hide my eagerness. No one's ever shown me how to cook. That might sound strange, but it's true. I go outside, and the first memorized number I call is Julia.

Her squeal of surprise is followed by a hushed whisper. "Shit, sorry. I'm at work. Hold on."

I hear her moving out of the office and into the hallway then onto the stairs. Her voice echoes.

"Dora? What the fuck is going on? I called the cops, but no one can find you."

"Have you called my dad?" Silently, I'm praying she hasn't. Julia is the only one who knows about my conflicts with him. She comes from a very happy family, but somehow she gets it.

"You know, I was about to call him today. I wanted to give you a day at least before I did anything. But I had to call the cops. Now tell me. What the hell is going on?"

I tell her in as much detail as I can. There's silence on her end when I finish.

"I can't believe it!" Julia whispers. "Dead men? Shooting? And now you're with this... this *man*?"

"He's safe," I say quickly. "I think so, anyway."

"You think so? Honey, you've only known this guy for a day. He's meeting with gangsters and gets caught in a shootout. And you *think* he's safe?"

"He saved my life, Jules. Then brought me to his house. To keep me away from the bad guys. Why would he do that if he wanted to hurt me?"

"Because..." Julia's voice trails off. "Hang on. You like this guy, huh?"

She's my best friend, and maybe she can read my voice—know what I've left unsaid.

"Jules!"

"Tell me what he looks like."

I touch my forehead and sit down on the porch steps. "I can't believe you're asking something like that now."

"Hmm. Sweetheart, considering what you've just been through, you sound far too relaxed. Come on, spill!"

"There's nothing to spill! Let it go, Jules."

"Where are you?"

"I can't tell you." After a pause, I say, "Look, tell the boss I'm on sick leave, okay? I'll know better in a couple of days."

"What if your dad calls?"

I sigh. "Don't worry. I'll call him myself."

I say goodbye to Jules, making her promise to keep all this to herself. Then I have to do the inevitable. I call Dad. I have to. If I don't he'll start calling me then Julia. Then, knowing him, he'll start a nationwide manhunt.

"Dora, is that you?" Dad barks on the phone. "You didn't answer my calls yesterday. I called you three times. Why didn't you call back?"

It's not "You didn't call. Are you okay, darling?" No. All I hear is disapproval. I take a deep breath. If I tell him the truth, he's going to flip. He hates where I work anyway. If he knows I followed a source and ended up in this mess, he'll kill me.

"Dad, I'm in Maine. By the sea. Living with a friend of mine. I'll be staying here for a few days."

I hate the fact that I have to lie. I hate that he makes me feel like a teenager sneaking out to meet some boy. I detest, despise the fact that someone I should love and trust has such a hold on my life.

After a long silence, he asks, "What friend? And what number are you calling from?"

One lie leads to another in a tangled web. "A girl I met at work. Her name's Laura. I thought the break would be good for me and—"

"What's happened to your phone?" Dad asks abruptly.

"Uh, it's out of battery. I left my charger at home." Lame, but what the hell. I just want to get off the phone. Strange as it may sound, I want to get back inside the warm, snug kitchen and have Richter show me how to make chorizo pasta.

"Dad, I have to go. I'll be fine, don't worry."

"I'm always worried about you, honey. You know that. You need to take better care of yourself."

I hang up, then hang my head between my hands. Why is it such an effort to speak to my dad? With every passing year, it gets harder. I can see a time coming when I'll just stop speaking to him, and I don't want to see that day arrive. After all, he and Harris are all I've had since my mother died.

So complicated.

I breathe in the clean mountain air, fresh and strong. My eyes open to see the bright sunlight, colorful butterflies pausing on blades of grass before they fly off to another, as if they're saying hello to their friends.

Life has gone down a strange path and brought me here. Now I have to follow that winding road to see what happens.

I get up and go back into the kitchen. Richter is sitting at the kitchen table, staring at a laptop screen. He glances up and closes it when I walk in.

"Your folks okay?"

I shrug and lean against the counter. He stands up, making the kitchen look smaller. He reaches out, and I hand him the phone.

"You didn't tell your folks about me, did you? Or where you are?" His eyes are sharp, searching my face.

"No, I didn't." For the first time I realize how much he trusted me.

"Good. If they try to trace your call, the trail stops at NYC."

"Uh-huh." A thought strikes me. "Your phone, does it do stuff like record calls?"

He goes still for a moment, his eyes searching my face again. Then he nods stiffly. "It does a lot, in fact. It has voice recognition, too."

"So did it record what I just said?"

"It records everything. But I didn't listen to what you just said."

We stand there, staring at each other for a while, before he breaks the silence. "I figured you're smart enough to know bringing trouble down here won't be good for either of us."

He's right, and we both know it. For some reason, this man I just met has learned to read me, and I don't know how.

He spreads his hands. "Shall we cook?"

"Okay."

He hands me an apron but doesn't wear one himself. I think he only has one but decide against asking. He's taken stuff from the fridge already.

"Garlic, ginger, tomatoes, and red onions." He looks at me. "Do you know how to peel garlic and ginger?"

"Uh…"

He opens a drawer and takes out a peeler. He grabs a tube of ginger and scrapes off the rough brown surface. Then he knocks the peeler on the sink until the bark falls off.

"Can you do that?"

"I can try."

Richter moves away, and I grab a raw ginger tube for the first time in my life. I have to apply more pressure with the peeler than I thought. After a few strokes, I get the hang of it.

"Have a seat," Richter says. "Once you're done, dice the tomatoes. Done that before?"

"Uh, no."

He washes then dices a tomato for me. I sit down at the table with the ginger and tomatoes while he stands and cuts the garlic and onions.

"You don't like eating out of a jar, huh?"

"Something I learned in the Army. You get sent to places where you might have to pluck the stuff from trees, kill a goat and skin it, then roast it."

"Eww." I crinkle my nose.

I can see he makes an effort to not laugh.

"So you were in the Army. Which division?"

The mirth vanishes from his face. A scowl appears, and the muscle on his jaw jumps to life.

"That's classified."

I finish the ginger and pick up one tomato. I slice it right down the middle then into semi-circular sections. "Classified like what happened last night?"

I don't have to look up to know he has stiffened. I finish with one tomato and reach for another. "Or classified like Jozdani's name?"

This time I look up at him to see he's staring into space. He glances at me and sighs. "You're not going to let this go, are you?"

"I might not be a great reporter, but I have to try."

He points the knife at me. "I'm sure you're a great reporter. But maybe you're chasing the wrong news."

I concentrate on the tomatoes again. I never knew cooking could be this relaxing. "Bad enough to get me killed. Guess that makes me dumb."

He drops the knife and sits down next to me. His presence is like a silent command, asking me to look up at him. His sexy mouth is set in a grim line, his bunched jaws stand out on either side.

"Why do you put yourself down? You're a smart, sensible person. Do you know how many people would come out alive from a situation like last night? Zero." He points a finger at my chest. "That makes you special. You have a talent for adapting quickly."

With that, he gets up. For a few seconds, I stare at the space he just vacated. Did he just say that? No man has ever paid me a compliment. Not in my adult life anyway.

"Thank you," I say meekly.

"You don't have to say that," he drawls in that low voice of his, a rumble from deep in his chest. He doesn't turn to look at me.

I finish dicing the tomatoes and move them to the counter, where he's chopped the onions, garlic, and some red peppers, arranged in neat, individual piles.

My hands brush against his forearm as I place the pot next to him. Static, like electricity, burns in the air. He turns toward me and reaches upward to the shelf. I inhale his scent again. I could easily reach out to touch him in this tiny kitchen.

"Grab the olive oil, please." He points to a cupboard underneath the counter, and I bend over, fully aware his eyes are on me as I do so.

CHAPTER 14
RICHTER

She's wearing a dress, a flimsy yellow thing that ends way above her knees. As she bends down, the dress rides up her creamy thighs. I get a flash of her full, pert hips, just the tantalizing start of it. I remember how my hand was resting on that hip a few hours ago, when I hugged her as she cried.

She stays bent down for a while, bending her knee further. The dress rides up higher. I can now see where the skin of her ass turns paler. My cock is done twitching. It's painfully erect, straining against my jeans.

"Found it," she says.

I turn my back to her, pretending to get something from the fridge. The cool blast helps. I gulp and breathe. Damn, this woman is driving me nuts.

There's a soft vulnerability to her, so gentle and somehow so appealing, every protective instinct in my soul is fired up. And the way she carries herself, that sexy, curvy way her hips move when she walks, makes my hands itch to roam all over her body.

I can't help it: this attraction to her is like a fucking giant magnet, pulling me with a force I'm desperately trying to fight against but losing.

Yes, that makes me a loser. After what I've been through, I can't go there again. I'd never forgive myself…

I barely know Dora. But I do know she deserves better than me. For the next day or two, I need to find ways to distract myself. I might start my early-morning runs on the mountain trails again. Or climb the damn rocks. Better than climbing the walls in here.

"What shall I do with it?"

She's standing there, legs crossed, back to the counter. Her right arm is crossed under her tits, pushing them up. Her left hand holds the bottle of olive oil. Sunlight streams in through the window, falling on her face, lighting up the brown eyes. She's naked from upper thigh down to the sandals on her feet. Her sleeveless dress reveals freckles on her shoulders.

There's an innocence on her face, something untarnished and pure, mixed with the erotic way her pink lips are slightly parted.

She looks so fucking sexy I want to grab her by the waist and pull her toward me. Feel her against me, move my hands down to her hips, then the front…

"Richter?" She dangles the bottle. "Hello?"

I need help.

"Uh, just put it down." My voice is a growl. I set the skillet on the fire and pour a dash of oil into it.

Then I look at her. "Ready?"

She nods and moves closer. She bought this perfume while we were out. It's not expensive, because she borrowed my money, and although our business does well, I'm not her rich dad. But the perfume smells like heaven. Light, airy, lavender, lush.

"You wait until the oil is heated then add the onions and peppers," I say.

"Yeah, that heating bit is what I got wrong the last time."

"Nah," I find myself saying. "Just an accident. Could've happened to anyone."

I've got another pan out, and I add the diced tomatoes, ginger, garlic, oregano, basil, and some water to it. Then I stir until the ingredients are well mixed with the water.

"This is for the sauce. Now let it boil on low, to thicken."

"Are you gonna add the chorizo to the onions and pepper?" she asks.

"Right on." I add the chorizo she's sliced already and put it into the skillet. It makes a satisfying sizzling sound, and the aroma of the paprika and chilies soon fills the room.

I open the back door and the window. The Sancerre is chilled in the fridge, and I show her the bottle.

"I have a Chablis as well, if you prefer."

"Whatever." She waves her hand. "I love Sancerre."

"Would you like red wine instead? I have a Chianti, too." I like my wines and personally would've preferred the Chianti. But I have a lady in the house for the first time in years. And I know ladies prefer white wine.

"Sancerre is fine," she says.

I get the wine from the fridge. Moisture beads on the dark-green bottle. When the pasta is done, I drain it. Dora is standing to one side, looking uncertain.

"Is the chorizo done?" I ask her as I uncork the bottle.

"Shall I check?" she asks with an anxious tone in her voice. When I nod, she lifts the lid of the pan and gives it a stir.

"Uh... I..."

"Yep, it's done. Let's eat."

I let her set the table then pour the wine into the old, heavy wineglasses I have from years ago.

Dora takes a sip of the wine and nods. "Lovely wine."

I put some pasta and sauce on her plate. We eat in silence for a while. The food is good, and both of us are surprised, I think, by how hungry we are.

"So," I say, wiping my mouth with a napkin. "Now you know how to cook a pasta dish."

She takes a sip of wine. "I wouldn't go that far. You did most of the work."

"It would've taken twice as long if you hadn't helped. You're the sous chef, at least." Her habit of demeaning herself is getting to me. "Can I make a request?" I ask.

She holds my eyes over the rim of the glass. "Go ahead."

"I want you to stop putting yourself down. You've got a lot going for you. I mean that."

"I will if you tell me what happened last night."

Sucker punch, and I almost grin at the way she led me into that. "I told you, it's classified."

"National secrets are classified. Is that what this is?"

I need to veer her off this topic. "Tell me about your childhood," I say, putting food into my mouth.

"That's lame." She grins. "Gotta do better than that."

"Right. Tell me what's up between you and your dad."

Her smile vanishes like a candle being snuffed out. She looks down at her plate. I feel like an asshole.

"I'm sorry," I murmur. It sounds like a growl. "That's none of my business."

She forces a smile, but there's no mirth in it. "I'll tell you my classified secret if you tell me yours."

I raise my hands. "Sorry, honey. No can do."

We eat in silence for a while, then she says, "It's complicated with my dad. I don't want to go into it now."

"Sorry I asked."

"Tell me about yourself. Where did you grow up?" Her tone is lighter.

I take my time before answering. My past is not something I open up about. Apart from the fact that even former Delta operatives should keep their personal lives secret, my childhood wasn't exactly smooth sailing.

But for some reason, those melting brown eyes are pulling me in deeper. I can't stare at them and not feel the stir of loneliness inside me.

"I grew up in Denver." I look at the wall opposite as I talk. "It was a typical suburban life, I guess. Dad got a job up in DC, and we had moved to McLean, Virginia." I can't tell her that Dad was a CIA agent. Not yet, anyway. "Cal and I joined the Army. Our grandfather was in the Marines, and I guess that inspired us. Then Dad died in an accident."

My eyes lower to the table, and I move the food with my fork, appetite suddenly decreased.

"Sorry to hear that," Dora says. "Is your mother…"

"No." I shake my head. "She died a few years ago, too. Cal and Sam are the only family I have left."

"Oh, Sam's your sister?" she asks, surprised.

I look up at her, and she looks so darned pretty, those huge eyes in perfect symmetry with her small nose and early-dawn-pink lips.

"Yes, she is. She works for us now."

"Aha. So you guys are like a family firm almost."

I shrug, reaching for the glass of wine. "Guess you could say that." I take a sip and put the glass down. "How about you?"

"My mom died when I was little, so I never really knew what it was like to have a mother. My dad remarried, but I was never close to any of his wives. They were much younger than my mom would've been, which didn't help."

Dora looks up at me, those melting eyes like a hammer to my chest. "But I guess I can't complain. I had a massive house, chefs, butlers, the whole lot." She makes air quotes with both hands. "I was the clichéd rich kid growing up."

Yeah, but were you happy? I ask myself in silence.

She carries on, surprising me. "My dad is controlling. But he's also my dad. You know?"

"Yeah. Did you want to be a journalist when you grew up?"

Dora smiles, and it's a genuine one. "I loved reading as a little girl. That continued when I was a teenager and all through college. Books were my escape. I wanted to write stories when I was older."

"Like a novelist?" I raise my eyebrows.

"Yeah. But I got into journalism while in college. A girl was raped in the football locker room. It was a big scandal. I interviewed everyone, including the jocks, coaches, all of them."

"Impressive," I say, and I mean it. There is the contradiction again. She's quiet, unassuming, but with a streak of toughness like iron ore in a clay mine.

She twirls a strand of her thick brown hair. "It made me realize there are people whose stories are never told. It's not just about getting justice. It's about awareness. About the truth. Know what I mean?"

Something about her words reverberates inside me. Truth. Justice. That's what I liked about the Army when I joined. What I got was something different. Not worth thinking about now. I have a beautiful woman in front of me, taking up all my attention. I'm trying hard not to show that, but hell, it's as if someone plucked the sun out of the sky and put it in this room. She has this air of brightness, of lightness, that reaches into the darkest corners of my soul. I can talk to her.

I have never talked to anyone about my childhood. Only Cal and Sam know. Charlotte did too. And after her...no one. There's only been cold winter in my life. It's what I've grown used to. Is the ice thawing now? Why do the bird songs in the trees sound so different today? Why is the grass a more luminous green?

CHAPTER 15
RICHTER

I'm not sure why. I don't want to analyze it too much. All I know is I feel a sense of peace, of being joined together after having several parts of me broken and fragmented like debris from two planets colliding. I might still be lost in space, but sunlight is peeking around the corner. I feel warm inside.

"Do you like your job?" I ask.

"Yes," she says. "I love uncovering stories and writing about them."

I don't want to pry, but curiosity wins out. Because this woman is a strange contradiction of coming from a very privileged background and still wanting to be herself. Like many in the private security industry, I've protected the rich for good money. In my experience, the adult children of these folk tend to follow their parents. They're spoiled and whiny. Dora is down to earth and practical.

"You can tell me to shut up. But didn't you want to work for one of your dad's companies?"

She entwines some pasta on her fork without eating any. When she looks up, there's that soft core in those liquid eyes again, as if they want to flow with unspoken words, invisible tears. I've never seen such eyes. They're so expressive my withered soul constricts in its old cage.

I swallow. But I can't look away. It's as if she's reaching inside my ribs and slowly caressing my heart.

"My dad and I don't get along. He acts like he needs to protect me all the time. But what he actually does is restrict me."

She looks down at her plate again, and I feel like shit all of a sudden.

"It's weird," she continues. "I wanted to do my own thing, you know? I didn't want to work at a news station."

"You gotta do what you want to. I'll tell you what. If you were my kid, I'd be proud of you. Happy that instead of relying on me, you're making something of yourself."

She smiles at that, a long, slow smile that lights up her eyes with quiet but sad happiness. Contradiction, I know. But happiness can be bittersweet sometimes. It depends on the price one pays to get happy.

I read that in her eyes, and I wonder what she has seen in her young years.

"It's nice outside." She suddenly changes the subject. "Shall we go for a walk?"

She's totally right. Montrose is made for long, hilly walks in the summer. We've polished off the delicious food. The wine bottle is only half empty, but I'm not much of a drinker in the afternoon. Judging from the one glass she had, I'm guessing she isn't either.

But I need to be careful. Viktor is still out there, and knowing him, he'll be looking for revenge. While Dora goes upstairs to get changed, I call Cal on the secure, encrypted line.

"Any news?" I ask when he answers.

"No. It's weird. Jozdani is hiding somewhere, but he's gone completely off the grid."

"You sure he hasn't left the country?"

"No one with his name or matching his description has. That comes from the NSA supercomputers, crunching billions of terabytes of CCTV images."

"He could be travelling under a false name or a disguise."

"Possible. But he landed in JFK with his own passport then went dark. That takes some doing."

"What about Viktor?" This guy's my main worry. Viktor has close links with the Russian mafia, also known as the Bratva, or Brotherhood. If they find out where I am, Montrose will burn.

"Nothing," Cal says. "It's like he's biding his time."

I think about what's happened so far. I have access to CCTV cameras all over this town from my laptop. I spend hours every day going through the footage. But I can't do it all on my own.

Cal seems to read my mind. "We have eyes on you. Samantha is going through the camera feeds as well. If we see anything unusual, you'll be the first to know."

I hang up just as Dora comes downstairs. She's dressed in a light cotton vest, dark pants, and walking boots. I give her one of my coats. We don our dark glasses and lift the hoods up to cover our faces. I go out the door first. There's no one on our street of one- and two-story houses. Many are holiday homes, and some are folk who live in Montrose. I see a family at the end of the road, loading into a car. Mrs. Carruthers's house is right at the end, but I can't see it from here. I check the Yukon then go inside to call Dora.

It's late afternoon, and I don't want to go too far. Summer light can last until early evening, and I've got my Maglite and a backpack in the car, not to mention my weapons. But we're out in the open, and I need to be careful.

We drive for ten miles, then I choose a parking spot that's known for its natural beauty. The mountain ranges open up across a valley way down below. A river runs through the middle of the valley, its waters glinting silver in the slanting sunlight.

Dora stands near the edge with her hands in my jacket's pockets. It's way too big for her, but she's managed to wrap it around her well.

"Wow. So pretty."

I lock the Wrangler and stand next to her. Both of us are silent for a while, appreciating what Mother Nature gives us without asking for anything in return.

"The path is up there." I point behind me. "It's a gentle slope, and I have a trekking stick in the car if you want."

"I'll be fine," she says and starts to walk up the trail. I hitch the backpack over my shoulders and do a last-minute check on my weapons: Colt M1911 in the shoulder holster, spare ammo in the beltline, and the hunting knife strapped to my ankle. Then I follow her.

It's a glorious day. The sun isn't too hot, as it's past three p.m., and the trail is nice and dry. Small rocks skitter down as we climb. There is dense woodland around us, hugging the slopes. Dora is walking ahead of me. I do mountain runs three times a week and trail walk with a 60-pound backpack the other days, a habit from my Delta days. With that and the weightlifting and swimming, I manage to stay in shape. That's when I'm not working. I like to stay busy. It keeps other thoughts out of my mind.

The trail gets steeper, and I can see Dora slowing down. She's done well so far. I see a jutting rock ledge and call out to her. She stops, and we both sit down on the ledge. Apart from the breeze sighing through the trees and the twitter of birds, there are no sounds. The mountains cascade in blue and green waves to the far horizon.

"You come here to get away, don't you?" Dora asks.

I jerk my head toward her. Those liquid eyes are focused on me. I stare at her for a while then look away. When I speak, my voice is ragged, loose.

"What makes you say that?"

"This seems like a good spot to be alone. But not lonely. If you know what I mean."

My head hangs. This woman has a way of pulling emotion out of me, coloring it with words I could never express.

I know exactly what she means.

And I have to wonder, why did I even bring her here?

I sneak a look at her. She's staring forward at the magnificent view. For the first time, I wonder if she knows more about me than she's letting on. No, that can't be. My whole friggin' life's been classified. And the personal stuff, well, no way any of my team could have told her that.

I don't say anything, and we sit together in that companionable silence. I take out a bottle of water and give it to her.

"I'm guessing your job gets violent sometimes. I can see why you live here when you can. Nice escape."

"Yeah."

I stand because I don't want to face any more of her questions. I put the backpack on and glance at her. "Couple of hundred yards to go. Can you hack it?"

She pauses for a moment as if she knows why I got up abruptly. Then she stands and hops off the rocky ledge into the trail.

We carry on walking. The summit is full of rocks, ice white during the winters, shades of dark brown in summer.

"Let's head to the top," Dora says.

"No. The rocks get steep there, and I don't want to fall in between. It's also a cliff face now. Too dangerous."

"Just a little more. I want to take some pictures." She's got her new phone with her.

"I don't think so, Dora."

But she's already moved ahead. Without looking back at me, she stretches her leg out to a rock that's covered in moss. Beyond that rock, there's nothing but air. There's a steep drop of several hundred feet to the trees below.

"Dora, wait!" I shout.

She stops and turns around. As she does so, her ankle twists. She loses balance right on the edge of the trail, and her hands pinwheel. If she falls against that sharp rock, it's going to hurt her back. But after that, she'll be hanging on to shrubs that will give way easily. My blood turns to ice.

She gives a yelp as she falls. I'm next to her in two long strides, but even so, I won't be able to grab her. I dive forward in desperation. My hand catches her coat before I fall to the ground, Dora landing on top of me. I'm winded but safe, and so is she.

Her eyes are wide, full of fright, but they swim with a light as she gazes at me. The scared look evaporates. My eyes move down to the red splotches appearing on her cheeks and the gentle parting of her pink lips. Her body feels soft resting on mine. Her eyes are focused on my lips. My heart is beating so loud I swear she can hear it. My breathing is fast and loose.

Her face starts to lower toward mine. I can't look away from her lips. Her face descends, and I feel heat in my lower belly, spreading to my cock, making it hard.

She lowers her face until it's almost on mine. At the last minute, her cheek brushes against my beard, and she nestles her face into my neck.

I exhale, closing my eyes. It feels so comforting, *so right*, just to lie here, her body resting on mine. I don't care about the rocks pinching my back. I don't care about anything but that sense of peace, like slipping under a warm blanket in the dead of winter, as she lies above me.

And the heat of her pliable, feminine curves. I need to control this, because I'm getting harder. I clear my throat, and she moves. Her head lifts, and she holds my eyes for a few seconds, an unspoken message passing between us.

I hold her eyes, recognizing this for what it is —a silent communion between two souls who feel it, this desire that's an aching, burning longing between them.

Strangely, it's her who seems to be in control now. Her face doesn't change. She puts two hands on my chest and lifts herself. I raise myself, dusting off my clothes.

"Thank you," she says. "I should've listened to you."

"It's all right. I know the rocks can look deceiving. Let's go up here. There's a safe spot."

It seems natural when she reaches for my hand, and I grasp it. But I still feel the electric jolt when her warm flesh meets mine.

CHAPTER 16
DORA

During dinner, I try my best to keep my eyes away from his mouth. If I stare at it for too long, I know I'll climb onto the table and start kissing him, and if he kisses me back, just like he almost did up in the mountains, I won't look back. His rough hands will slip underneath my shirt, under my bra, fingers squeezing my hardening nipples, and without letting go of the kiss, he's going to stand up and push me down on the table...

Dora, stop!

My mouth's open, and I've forgotten to breathe. Or eat. I feel like an idiot with the fork halfway between the plate and my mouth. A quick glance at Richter shows he's busy checking his phone and hasn't noticed my daydreaming.

We keep sneaking looks at each other. There is a weight in the room, sitting between us. It's not a heavy, difficult thing, more like a lingering tension I can cut with a knife. I'm so strongly attracted to this walking, talking man mountain I don't know what to do. I haven't been with someone for a long time, never mind with someone like him. Both of us are holding back, and yet I feel we cannot help being drawn to each other, like the moon pulling the tides of a restless sea.

And yet I need to think of the practicalities. The reality is that my life is in danger. When that danger is over, we will go our own ways. I'll probably never see Richter again. I'll go back to my boring life hunting for a scoop. But one thing I know: I won't be the same. Richter will always stay on my mind. I know he's hard as nails; one look at him makes that obvious. But I didn't expect how protective he would turn out to be. How considerate toward my feelings. How special he can make me feel—with nothing but a few words.

And I can sense a deep well of sadness inside him. I can't be sure, of course, and it seems weird to think I know anything about a man I only met yesterday. But I can feel it. Once I get past his tough exterior, I can feel it radiate from him.

"I'm going for a walk after dinner," Richter says, taking a sip of wine. "I want you to stay in the house. You'll be safe. Don't worry. I want to do some recon in the area."

"Sure you don't want me to come?"

He fixes on me. "Only if you'll be worried. But if we keep all the doors locked, there's nothing to be worried about. I can see anyone approaching the house on the cameras of my security app."

He hands me his phone, and I look at the open app showing live feeds from all around the house.

"I'll do the cleaning up," I say, standing once I've finished eating.

He considers this for a moment then nods curtly. I hear him putting on his coat and moving out the door. He locks it securely.

I clear the table then sweep the floor of the kitchen. I make sure all the utensils are in their correct places. Richter keeps his kitchen tidy, and I owe him enough to make sure it stays that way.

I go up to the bedroom and take my iPhone out. I search for the name Jozdani. I get several hits on Google, but many of the pages are in Arabic. I try to translate one using the Google button and realize the language is Farsi, not Arabic. Which makes sense, as Jozdani is not an Arab. He's Iranian, essentially Persian.

Amir Jozdani is a nuclear scientist and an expert on nuclear weapons. I see photos of him from when he did his PhD at Stanford, and in one photo, he appears with a woman and child. The woman is Caucasian, and I suddenly wonder if Jozdani has a family in the States. But he's Iranian, so how could he be living in the United States?

That guy, Viktor, wanted to know where Jozdani was. He looked as if he would kill for that knowledge. Only thinking about Viktor's cold, serpentlike black eyes makes me shudder. He would've killed me without a second thought if I hadn't blurted out some bullshit about where Jozdani was.

Questions circulate in my mind. Richter must be with the good guys. If Jozdani is being hunted by both Richter and Viktor, he must know something important. I do more digging on Jozdani online. He works at an atomic research facility in Tehran, where he's a professor. On Google, his name has several hits in connection with uranium enrichment and the Middle East. I read and make some notes.

I really want to call Julia, but I know I can't. My phone isn't the same as Richter's, and that encryption software isn't loaded on mine. But I do a search for U.S. military tattoos. I'm not that surprised when the Delta sign comes up on a man's arm—the same ink that Richter has. Was Richter in the Delta Forces? The way he moves, those stacks of muscles, I wouldn't be surprised. And those men who rescued us? They moved like a smoothly oiled fighting machine.

I don't know much about the Delta team and read on to find they are the elite forces in the Army. The Navy has a counterpart in SEAL Team 6. Delta Forces existed before the SEALs and have more history behind them. It's fascinating stuff, and I read for a while.

Richter won't tell me anything, so I'm left to my own devices. It's easy to figure out that Jozdani is hot property. Men like Viktor will kill to find him. And Richter's team want Jozdani to hand him over to the U.S. government, I suppose. There's a lot I don't understand, and once again, my reporter's instincts are humming. It's obvious our government wants to know all about Iran's nuclear program. And it seems Jozdani knows a lot about said program. It makes sense that Richter's team are looking for him. Questions swirl in my mind as I lie in bed, reading by the light of the table lamp.

The Sancerre from dinner is thick in my bloodstream, and with the wine, thoughts of Richter return to my mind. On that mountain trail, I was so close to kissing him. For three seconds, that vertical, rocky drop to the canopy of conifers way below flashed before my eyes.

Then his arm was around my waist like a lifeline, whipping me back to safety. I think of the agility, the ferocity with which he must've moved and of how stupid I was in not listening to him.

But when I fell on top of him and lay there, it took every fucking ounce of self-control to not sink my lips onto his sexy mouth, to feel the warmth of his tongue sliding into mine like a glorious invasion, touching, tickling, tasting, biting. My lips open suddenly, and heat fans between my legs. It's been too long.

I scoot underneath the covers, and the phone drops onto the bed. I undo the top buttons of my jeans. In my mind's eye, I can see Richter kissing me back, his hard hands holding me prisoner as I buck and twist against him. The mountains are deserted. No one but us, rocks, and blue sky. Like nature intended. I can feel the heat of his cock between my legs, straining to be free. I can feel it through the layers of clothing... I moan as my fingers slide down, rubbing my clit. I can't believe how wet I am. If only Richter was here, his length filling me full to the brim. If only...

There's a knock on the door. I hear it so faintly, but my imagination is so hyperactive it registers only on the periphery of my subconscious. Then the knock becomes louder, accompanied by a male voice.

"Dora?" The tone is softer, but it's Richter.

My eyes fly open. Volcanic fire lashes at my cheeks. My hands fly back up, and I make sure that I'm well covered by the sheets. I scoot back up against the headboard, sitting up but covered from the waist down. I put my hands to my sides then fold them across my chest. My nipples are still taut. I put my hands back down to rub my palms on the bedding.

"Yes?" I answer.

The door opens fully, and his broad bulk fills the doorway. He doesn't move in any farther when he sees me on the bed. But his eyes move down my body slowly, and I see him swallow. His face is unreadable. He's wearing a dark button-down shirt and black slacks. His feet are bare.

"I'm sorry," he rumbles in that deep way of his. "I saw your light on and wondered if you were awake."

"Yes. No, I mean getting ready for, you know, bed." I give a lame laugh.

He doesn't laugh back.

Nice. Really cool, Dora.

My words are tangled like the dull white heat in my brain. Why do I feel like a kid who's been caught at mischief?

"Was everything okay while I was gone? I mean, you didn't hear any sounds or anything?"

Apart from the moaning I was doing, which you might well have heard, I think.

Oh shit. He did hear me moan, didn't he? I didn't say his name. Did I?

Mortification is mottling my cheeks like Mount Etna, Vesuvius, all firing at the same time.

If he's noticed me blush, he's choosing to ignore it. Instead, he says, "It's quieter in the country, so small sounds can be amplified. Hope nothing bothered you."

I shake my head.

He steps back. "Fine," he says. "I'll leave you alone then. Goodnight."

"Goodnight."

He shuts the door on his way out. When his steps recede, I fling the covers back and get undressed quickly. Then I turn the light off and, despite the visions churning in my head, try to fall asleep.

CHAPTER 17

DORA

The alarm clock says 8:30 when I wake up. I didn't set an alarm, so I'm not surprised I overslept. But I feel better. It's weird to think how much has happened in the last two days. From chasing the scoop of my life to living with Richter in a remote, sleepy small town. Why do I feel so comfortable here? Is it because the constant rush and change of DC life is suddenly gone? There's no sound of traffic when I wake up. Only birdsong and a faint rustle of the breeze.

I get up and open the curtains. The mountains, shrouded in clouds, spring to life. I stare at them for a while then get ready to go downstairs. Either Richter is up and downstairs or still sleeping, which I doubt. He doesn't seem like a man who spends his time in bed.

As I'm coming down the stairs, I hear a rattling sound. I stiffen and stop. It's the front door. I hear heavy breathing and someone moving around. My heart is beating painfully, and a sudden fear gathers like a black cloud at the base of my throat.

"Richter?" I call out. Immediately, I feel stupid. I just alerted this person to my presence.

Thankfully, a familiar voice calls out, "Dora? It's me."

I come down the stairs, and Richter is standing in the middle of the living room. He's sweating buckets and panting. He's wearing running gear and is naked from the waist up. His top lies at his feet. Rivulets of sweat pour down his head and neck, pooling down the deep groove in the V of his heaving chest.

And this time, there's no mistaking that more-than-impressive package in his pants. His running shorts are soaked tight to his skin, the huge, corded muscles of his thighs swelling below them. The bulge below his waist is so obvious I can't help but stare.

Richter puts his hands on his waist. He puffs out his lips, and sweat droplets fly from his mouth and beard. He shakes his legs, making the sinews of his thigh muscles contract and expand. The cords of muscles on his shoulders ripple. The dragon tattoo on his chest seems to have a life of its own, snarling, spouting fire from its nostrils as the image drapes across his pecs and onto the expanse of his biceps.

Everything about this leviathan is brute strength and heat. It radiates off him, almost consuming me as I can't help but gape. But I also come to my senses. My hand scratches my left ear, tucks in a loose strand of hair, and I look away.

"You went for a run?" I ask, clearing my throat, trying my best not to look at him. Stupid question. *No, he just poured water over his head. He wears the running gear for fun.*

"I run most mornings. Five miles, no more. Do you run?"

"Hell no." I laugh, trying to lighten the atmosphere, to ignore the fact that Richter is standing practically naked six feet away from me.

"I should go for a shower," he says, heading for the stairs.

I'm standing right in his path, so I move toward the kitchen quickly. I surprise myself with my next words. "I'll make breakfast."

Richter stops. He has one hand on the staircase bannister and his back to me. He doesn't turn, but I can see the sheet of muscles on his back twitching.

"You don't have to do that," he says. His tone is odd, subdued. I can see the fingers tighten on the bannister. His head leans forward, like he's observing something at his feet.

"It's fine," I say, continuing to move toward the kitchen.

He stands still for a while. Then slowly, he moves up the stairs.

I've been watching some cooking videos. Plus, I cooked yesterday. I can do this. I get the eggs, tomatoes, ham, milk, and bread out of the fridge.

By the time Richter comes downstairs, I've made an omelet and buttered the toast. The only thing I haven't managed is coffee. I'm no good with a bean grinder.

I look up as Richter appears in the kitchen door. His beard is trimmed, and he's wearing a sky-blue T-shirt with dark jeans. He stares at me for a while, and if I didn't know any better, I would say he looked unhappy. But it passes as he bows his head and walks into the room. I bite my lower lip. Men can be territorial. Am I invading his space?

"Smells nice," he says. His tone is light, and I turn to see him leaning against the counter, arms folded. His eyes are still hard, and there's no smile on his face.

What's the matter with him? He seems to have lost his easygoing mannerisms.

"I didn't make coffee," I say.

"Yeah, I saw that."

He turns his back to me and starts fiddling with the coffee maker. I frown at his back. *Asshole.*

I was only making breakfast to say thanks. I don't know what he's uptight about, but it's annoying.

After he makes the coffee, we eat in silence. All of a sudden, there seems to be an iron curtain between us. Just because I offered to make breakfast? But he was teaching me how to cook last night. None of this makes any sense.

He stands abruptly, pushing the chair back.

"I'm going out." His tone is gruff, more of a growl than usual. "Stay indoors. It's for your own safety."

I swallow the anger that rises in me. Why the hell is he acting so weird? We were holding hands yesterday, in public.

"Where are you going?"

His eyes look at me, their grayness smoky, impenetrable. "Out."

With that, he gets up and leaves. He goes out the door and shuts it softly. I'm dressed already, so I hurry to the window to see where he's going. He walks past his car and onto the road. He's not driving. I watch as he takes a right and keeps walking.

I put on my shoes, check that I have my keys, and follow. He's walking at a fair clip, and I have to move fast. At the end of the block, where the fields begin, he takes a right and disappears from view. I break into a run.

A path leads through the fields on my right, and I can see Richter's tall figure following it. There's a bank of trees to my left, giving the path shade. The rest is farmland, some crop fields on my right, stretching to the horizon. I half jog, half walk, keen not to lose Richter again. I have no intention of finding myself in the middle of nowhere all alone.

His body is growing smaller in the distance. I see him take a left turn before I lose sight of him. Panting, I start running again. Part of me thinks this is a bad idea. Is this where he hides his weapons? Or is there something else going on? He did tell me to stay put, and I ignored it.

The other part of me is just curious. I need to see what he's up to.

I approach the turn, the fields and the waist-high plants around me still undulating in a gentle breeze. I can't see Richter anymore. I take the path on my left and head down to a clearing with a stream running next to it. On the banks of the stream is a little hut with two water pumps next to it. The hut has a window facing me, and I can see a shape moving inside. I'm too far away to recognize anyone.

I get closer. The hut is made of logs and is really like a hunter's or woodsman's cabin. The door is open, bright sunlight spilling inside. I swallow the apprehension inside me.

Will this be Richter or someone else? If it's someone else, what the hell do I say? *Erm, sorry, I got lost on your farm in the middle of nowhere?*

I creep up to the door and look inside. Richter's broad back is turned away from me. He's doing something with his hands on a table in front of him. I could smell the fresh earth already, but the room is filled with a strong, pungent odor of something else. My nose crinkles. Then I see the bags of compost stacked inside the room. I'm smelling fertilizer.

"I told you not to come," Richter rumbles, making me jump.

He hasn't turned around. Does this man have eyes in the back of his head? How the hell did he know I was standing here?

He keeps doing something with his hands. Well, now that I've been spotted, there is nothing to lose. I walk around to one side so I can see what he's doing.

Small baskets of soil are laid out neatly on the table. There's a bag of seeds next to Richter, and he picks a few out and presses them into the black soil inside the baskets.

His movements are calm, precise. Gentle. Soil darkens his hands, clinging to his fingers. With infinite patience, he presses a tiny seed into the soil, the seed almost invisible in his huge hand. Then he reaches into the bag and takes out another.

He doesn't say anything. I fold my arms across my chest. It's almost relaxing to just watch what he's doing with his hands, but I'm fed up with being ignored. I step closer.

His hands stop inside the seed bag. Then he resumes.

"Do you want to go first, or me?" I ask.

He sighs, and his hands still. Then he raises his head skyward, eyes shut. "What do you want, Dora? I told you to stay put."

"I've been shot at and almost killed. Then I'm basically abducted into this"—I make a circle with my arms—"countryside, forced to live with you, without any answers at all. So I'll tell you what I want. I want some answers."

He shakes his head, picks up another tiny seed, and, with great care, pushes it deep into the soil of another paper basket. Then he lifts his hands and walks over to a sink in the corner to wash them. He turns, drying his hands on his sleeves.

"Soon you'll go back to your normal life. Maybe another two days. No more." His voice is soft, but I can't help feeling it's also impatient.

"My normal life? What makes you think my life will be anything but *abnormal* from now on? You don't think I'll be looking over my shoulder every day, wondering who's coming after me?"

His features twist suddenly, so quickly it takes me by surprise. An expression of pain floods his face like a tidal wave. His eyes go glassy, staring right through me, and his head hangs. There's so much hurt in his face I can't help but move closer to him. I want to touch him, but somehow he seems just out of reach.

When he speaks, his voice is a ragged whisper. "I'm sorry. I didn't want this to happen."

Something in the way he speaks makes me wonder what he's talking about.

He lifts his head, and his eyes are still glassy, but his brows are lowered, lips downturned. He seems like a wounded beast, heavy, heaving shoulders sagging, knuckles clenched.

I come forward until I'm close enough to touch him. A wave of sadness engulfs me. Richter's jaws are clenched, a bunch of muscles twitching over them.

He's hurting bad. I touch his arm and lean into his space.

"What is it, Richter? Tell me."

His nostrils flare, and a light suddenly gleams in his eyes. Then he straightens, pushes past me, and strides out of the hut.

I follow. He stands on the banks of the stream. I can hear the gurgling of water over some rocks. A few felled tree trunks are dotted around, and Richter sinks down on one of them. I watch him for a while then sit down next to him.

We are silent, staring at the moving water slipping, sliding over small rocks.

His voice is a low rumble. "You being here wasn't part of the plan. Hell." He shakes his head, going silent.

I say nothing, giving him time.

"But having you here, around the house, it's just… Aw, hell." He sighs again. "I don't want anything to happen to you."

"I'm sorry I said that my life won't be normal again. I didn't mean it like that."

"No. You don't understand." He lets out a breath. "I can't believe this."

"Tell me," I say softly.

He cranes his neck upward then looks down at his feet. "I had a girlfriend. Charlotte. We were planning to get married after I came back from my third tour in Iraq."

After a pause, he continues. "She killed herself while I was away. Jumped off a cliff. I never knew she had depression. She hid it well." He cradles his head in his hands.

I can feel my fingers and toes turning numb despite the sunshine.

"I wasn't there for her. All I got was a lousy letter, then an interview with the medics in Iraq. I wasn't even allowed to come back for the funeral."

"I'm so sorry, Richter," I whisper.

We are silent for a while. Then I reach out and hold his hand. His fingers are lax at first, then they close over mine. I caress the rough skin on the back of his hand with my thumb. I think of the pain he's lived with. The guilt. Is that why he insisted on protecting me himself? Why he brought me to his own house?

"When did this happen?" I whisper.

"Four years ago." He takes a deep breath and lets it out. "I didn't know anything. Guess I hardly knew her. But if I could've been here, maybe it would've been different. She might be alive today."

"Richter, look at me."

He does. I grip his hands and stare deep into his eyes. "You don't know that. No one knows. In life, we all have to take responsibility for what we do. You were fighting for your country. Doing your duty. What happened to your girlfriend was waiting to happen. It might have still happened at some point in the future, even if you were here."

He gazes at me, his eyes searching my face. To be honest, I've surprised myself with what I said. But his pain is so solid, so palpable. It surrounds us like the sunlight, like the rocks on the mountains looming over us.

And I know what I said is right. Whatever happened, it wasn't Richter's fault.

I tell him that. He stares at me for a while longer, then his eyes screw shut.

"You know, I haven't spoken to anyone about this apart from Cal."

I wonder who Cal is then recall his brother's name.

His hand is gripping mine. I swallow hard. I don't know what to do here. I suddenly feel lost, adrift in a wild current. There's so much grief and remorse—an avalanche of pent-up emotions—and I realize how much this single event has shaped who Richter is today.

"Thank you," he says.

I smile at him. "Remember what you said when I thanked you? That I don't have to say that. Well, guess it's my turn to say it."

He sighs. "It's just... having you here has made me think."

We look at each other again, and this time both of us are searching. I'm the first one to look away.

"Did you live here? With her, I mean," I ask.

He shakes his head. "No. We lived in upstate New York. After my last tour, I came back here. My parents had a farm." He indicates with his arm. "What you see around you. I couldn't bear to live in New York anymore."

"I'm sorry," I repeat.

He shakes his head. Some of the shakiness is gone from his voice when he speaks. He seems oddly calm. "Don't be. It's all right."

I have a million questions. None of them seem right to ask now. In fact, I don't even know what to say. This was unexpected, but I did sense a heavy core inside him, a burden that seemed to weigh him down. It wasn't obvious, and I guess he's learned to wear his loss like many who go through grief and bereavement do—trying to live their lives as normally as possible but always putting a mask on for the rest of the world.

I wonder how I saw through that mask.

Or did he allow me to see through it?

A wind blows through my heart, desolate but warm, knocking open doors, bursting through windows. What *is* this thing we see in each other?

"How did you cope?" I ask. My question seems foolish, but I don't know what else to say.

"Well, working makes me forget things. It helps if I'm busy." He looks at me, and there's a strange light in his eyes. He opens his mouth to say something but then stops himself.

CHAPTER 18
RICHTER

I haven't talked about this to anyone but Cal. The others in my team know. But they don't ask, and I don't tell.

Truth is, I feel better for having talked about it, but not just with anyone. It had to be someone like Dora. She's this unique combination of being shy, demure, but remarkably perceptive. Like when we were up in the mountains and she asked me if I come here to get away from it all. That's exactly what I do. To be alone with my thoughts.

I'll never forget Charlotte, but I realize what Dora said is the truth. I couldn't have changed anything.

I glance at Dora. Why do I feel like I've known her a long time? How can she be so in sync with my thoughts? As if she can peer inside my head and look at my thoughts jostling around?

I feel like a dick for being a jackass over breakfast. The reality is I'm so drawn to her that I don't know where this thing is headed. And the last thing I want is for her to get hurt either by me or by that asshole Viktor.

I look down at our entwined hands then up at her. Her light-brown eyes seem to glow in the sun. Those pink lips are upturned and yearning, and beneath her shirt, the soft swell of her breasts strains the fabric. Almost begging to be touched. Her hand moves in mine, and this time she presses harder, and I feel blood roaring into my cock.

I don't know who leans over first, but I feel the pressure in my hand growing then her body getting closer. My eyes are fixed on her upturned lips and her smooth, flawless skin before my lips touch hers gently.

A shower of sparks tingles down my spine. I kiss the upper lip, then the lower, then my tongue slides against the smoothness of her teeth. Her mouth yields, and my tongue glides in, exploring every nook and corner of that beautiful mouth. She leans into me, and I feel her hunger and respond, my tongue claiming her mouth, entwining with hers in an unforgettable erotic dance. My cock is fully erect now, bulging against my pants.

She moans, a muffled sound deep inside her throat. My lips leave her mouth, and I nip at her lips and chin, making her whimper with pleasure. I trail kisses I know she'll love down the soft upper part of her neck. My tongue lashes against her throat, licking it in broad sweeps, claiming her skin as my own. She moans louder, and my hands move down, brushing against her breasts.

My head rests against her collarbone, and I stop. She cradles the back of my head. It's an incredibly comforting sensation. She smells of lavender, a sweet, light aroma that mixes with her own scent. My neck bends, and my face presses deeper into her chest. She pulls me in without hesitation, crushing my head against the fullness of her tits. My hands come around to grab her waist, and suddenly she moves onto my lap, pressing into me. Our mouths find each other again. This time it's harder, rawer, with a need we both cannot ignore. Our tongues dive, dart, caress deeply, tasting as far as we can go. I groan as her hand finds my erection and massages it. I'm on the brink of losing it. I don't want to stop. But I have to.

My head sinks back down from her mouth. She holds my head against her again, and I clutch her small, voluptuous, gorgeous body to mine as if I want to melt her into me.

Both of us are breathing as if we've just run a marathon.

Her hands are moving through my hair, and we're still holding onto each other. I move my head back to look at her. Those melting brown pools of light seem wet with a need I haven't seen before. I've never kissed a woman like this before. We search each other's faces, getting to know the lines and angles from close up. She lifts a finger and gently traces it down the side of my nose, past my lips, and to my jaw. I close my eyes; her trailing finger leaves a line of smoldering heat that makes me want to kiss those luscious lips again.

I let out a ragged breath. No words are necessary, and even if they were, I don't think I could utter any. Gently, she moves off me and then sits on my left knee, arm around my shoulder.

"So," she says, "you were in the Army."

I smile ruefully. "You got that right."

She rubs my left biceps. It feels good even through my shirt: her fingers sliding over my corded muscles. My cock twitches again. Whenever this woman touches me, I want to do sinful, lustful, ravishing things to her.

"So, judging by the tattoo you have on your biceps, were you in the Delta Forces?"

I stare at her with surprise. *Like I said, perceptive.*

She smiles with a mischievous twinkle in her eyes. "I'll take that as a yes then."

I sigh and pat her on the ass. My hand lingers there, my palm cupping the swell of her ass so nicely. I can't help but give it a light squeeze. What I really want to do is rip her jeans and panties off and sink my teeth into the soft lushness of her ass. My dick hardens again as if it has a life of its own.

We both stand. She holds my hand, and I take her back into the seedling hut. "You can help me plant some tobacco seeds."

Her enthusiasm is genuine. "Is that what they are?"

"Uh-huh. Tobacco was the main cash crop in Virginia. Less so these days. But we still have two acres of land, and we plant them in some patches."

I load the baskets of soil into a wheelbarrow with Dora's help. She walks ahead, and I follow, trying hard not to stare at the swing of her hips and the swell of her ass. The wheelbarrow handles are in danger of coming off in my hands.

I show her how to use a pick to loosen the soil and then lower the seed basket into the gap. There's a row of plants, and normally I hire one of my neighboring farmers to do the job for me. I take over when I'm here. The farmer sells whatever we produce, and we give him a cut. Cal and I share the profits.

On our way back to the hut, Dora says, "You didn't tell me if you were in Delta."

"I thought you guessed it already."

"Did I?"

I take one hand off the wheelbarrow and try to grab her, but she runs away with a squeal.

"Stop the games. You know I can't tell you any more."

"Classified, right?" She arches an eyebrow at me.

I love the way the sunlight falls across her hair. "Yup."

She leans forward. "Are we classified as well?"

It's my turn to raise an eyebrow at her. Then we both laugh. God, I haven't laughed in so long. Like, really laughed. Really enjoyed myself.

"I guess we are, sweetheart. Fucking classified."

She grins and looks away. I adore the bloom of scarlet spreading across her cheeks. "Fucking classified," she says almost to herself.

CHAPTER 19
DORA

We're in Richter's big GMC Yukon, heading to Montrose. I've felt drawn to him ever since I laid eyes on him, and now I can't stop thinking about our kiss, the feel of his hands on my body.

His presence is like a solid, dependable mountain I can lean on. I stare at his big hand, the scarred knuckles bunched over the steering wheel. For the first time, I see a scar going across the base of one thumb.

"What happened there?" I ask.

"Gunshot wound, sweetheart. Surgeons had to stitch my thumb back together."

"Oh." I don't know what else to say. I wonder how many scars he carries, hidden below the ink he wears.

"Were you ever wounded? In battle, I mean."

He is quiet for a while, but it's without the rigidity of before. There is a mellowness in his posture, an openness I haven't felt before.

"Several times, sweetheart. Mostly walking wounded. Surgeons patched me up."

I think of him out there, in the mess and hell of war. I shudder. I look up at his calm face, the beard neatly trimmed, his eyes focused on the road but taking a trip among memories I'm not sure I should've evoked.

"War is a clusterfuck, honey." He shakes his head. "Not worth it."

I can tell he doesn't want to talk about it. And I know the less he speaks, the more I feel for him, this man of flesh and blood who's felt his soul tarnished and ravaged by the dogs of war.

But he's a better man for it. I can tell. He is unruffled by danger yet compassionate to those in strife. I felt it that night in Dale City. And I feel it now, an aura of protection like a bubble that covers me as long as I'm with him.

*****

After shopping for fertilizer, I help Richter load the Yukon. He does most of the lifting while I position the wheelbarrow from the store close to the Jeep's tailgate. Richter is inside the Wrangler, stacking the bags in place. There aren't many people shopping, although this part of the strip mall is large. A few farmers are milling around, loading their cars and driving away.

Only one car—a gleaming black Lincoln Escalade—seems out of place among the pickup trucks and battered old SUVs. I don't know why my eyes are drawn to it. Then it hits me. It's the marks at the sides of the car. They've been painted over, but bullet holes aren't easy to hide.

A black curtain of dread rises in my mind, blocking out the sunlight. My throat chokes with fear. Didn't Viktor escape in a black Escalade? My memories are patchy, flashbulbs of screams in a night of darkness.

But I seem to remember being pushed toward a car just like this. Richter behind me. Our hands tied. Before he covered me, we fell down, and all hell broke loose.

The passenger door opens. A man of average height steps out. He's wearing a suit and dark glasses. Slowly he removes the glasses and stares at me.

My body is a block of ice. My eyes are bulging in shock.

Viktor.

He holds my eyes for a while then puts the glasses back on. He gets back inside the Escalade and reverses it out of its parking space. I can't help but stare as it bounces over the parking lot ramp and slowly disappears.

"Dora. Dora! *Dora!*"

I can barely hear. The shout from Richter registers across a long distance, as if he's leaning against a wind. Then it suddenly snaps as the Wrangler jolts when Richter hops off it, light on the balls of his feet. He's grabbing my shoulders gently and staring at me.

"Dora, what happened?"

I blink and focus on his face. Did that just happen? Was it really that creep, Viktor?

"That Lincoln Escalade from that night. It was here. Just now," I mumble and point. "Over there."

Richter's face turns ashen. He whirls around, head whipping from side to side and then up as well, I notice. He runs to where the Escalade was parked then comes back to me.

"Get in the car." The bite is back in his voice.

I can't believe this is happening. The sunlight is turning to rust.

We're back in the car and driving fast. Richter doesn't take the normal route. He slips down a dirt track, and we wobble our way around a long loop with farmland stretching out on both sides. Both of us keep checking the rearview mirror, and he stops twice to look up, shielding his eyes against the sun. Once he even takes out a pair of binoculars and checks the sky.

"What are you looking for?" I ask.

"Drones," he says. "Better for surveillance than anything else. Especially if they can fly high enough."

We keep driving until we see the stream. Richter follows the path alongside it, and soon we are back at the farm.

We saw no one the entire drive back. I'm sure Richter chose this place for a good reason. He kills the engine, but we don't get out.

"Tell me exactly what you saw," Richter says.

I tell him.

"Did you get the license plate number?"

"I'm sorry. He was gone so quickly."

Richter reaches out and holds my hand. His touch is warm, reassuring. "Don't worry, honey. It's okay."

He lets go of my hand and leans back. He reaches for his phone then climbs out of the car. I follow him. Richter is speaking as he walks to the edge of the stream. I go into the hut, fetch the wheelbarrow, and open the Jeep. The fertilizer bags are heavy, but I manage to get two into the wheelbarrow.

Richter comes back and takes over. His mouth is set in a grim line. "Just spoke to my brother."

He doesn't explain any further. We finish moving the stuff, then share a drink of water.

He narrows his eyes at me. "Did you surf the internet about anything to do with Viktor or Jozdani?"

I gape at him, breath suddenly leaving my chest. *Oh shit. That's exactly what I did last night. Just before you started to imagine him naked, Dora. Well done.*

Richter's looking at me with a frown, and I start stuttering. "Yes, I mean, why, you think—"

"Did you or did you not, Dora? I need to know."

I nod, eyes closed. I open them to see him rubbing his beard, staring at the ground. He walks off again with his phone pressed to his ear. I notice the antenna on the phone for the first time. I did wonder how he was getting reception in the middle of rural Virginia. Now I know: a satellite phone.

When Richter opens the car door, his face is set in stone. "Cal doesn't know for sure, but he's guessing they were using the same software as us. Checking for searches on Jozdani's name." He shakes his head, and his eyes darken. "We don't use our real names when we're operational. But Viktor's found out. The house is registered in my name. He must've put two and two together."

My shoulders slump. "This is all because I went online?"

I feel his hand reach out and his thumb rest on my chin. Gently, he lifts my face. "Not your fault, sweetheart. You couldn't know. If anything, it's my fault for not telling you."

He opens his arms, and I slide into his embrace. It's snug and warm, and he smells of wood spice and something smoky, an aftershave.

"Can we go back to the house?" I ask.

"Once I check it out first. You stay here in phone contact with me. Cool?"

I nod.

He gazes at me deeply. "You know I won't let anything happen to you, right?"

A fierce light dances in his eyes, and to be honest, it's kind of scary. And while I'm being honest, also kind of sexy.

I believe him. "Right," I whisper.

His face leans down, getting bigger. His lips touch mine gently, and tiny vibrations spread across my lips, dancing, tingling my skin. I open my mouth to let his tongue in, and it darts inside, hot, wet, and lustful as sin. His tongue is possessive, claiming mine as his. Heat builds between my legs, and I have to squeeze my thighs tight together. His hand comes down, cups my ass, pulls me closer into him. I like the way his hand touches my ass gently, then grips, kneads, massages.

No one else kisses like Richter. The width of his lips, the smooth moisture of his tongue, the warm prickle of his beard light my senses into a raging fire, turns my panties into a soaking-wet mess.

I want this man. Can he not feel it?

He lifts his mouth up from mine. His eyes are glassy, hazy with desire. *Yes, he feels it.*

I can feel the hardness of his cock. I'm yearning to touch it.

He clears his throat and swallows hard. "Stay here." He puts the phone in my hand. "Just press the green button. I'm on speed dial. Stay in the car, engine switched on. If you see anyone, take off down the dirt road."

His voice softens. He caresses my lower lip between thumb and forefinger. Then he leans forward to kiss me gently on the forehead. I shiver when his lips touch my skin.

"Don't worry," he drawls in a deep rumble. "They can't get to you here. All I'm saying is be careful."

I nod, and he moves to leave the car. I call him back.

"Richter?"

He turns. "Yeah?"

"Be careful."

He smiles. "I got practice in this shit." His smile fades. "Don't worry about me."

CHAPTER 20

DORA

Richter is back within half an hour. I spend the time biting my nails. It's such a relief to see him jog around the bend.

He was right about there being no danger. I didn't see a soul apart from birds and two deer who were more startled to see me.

We go back into the house. It's late afternoon, and sunlight is slanting across the fields.

Richter sets me up on his laptop. "This is where you do any research from now on. It's encrypted."

"Can I do research on you?"

He grins. "You know that's—"

"Fucking classified?"

"You bet your ass, honey."

Richter's bringing the shopping bags in while I unload and put the food in the fridge. I've been looking at some cooking videos and want to make a chicken dish with cumin, jalapeno peppers, and potatoes. Rooting around the kitchen, I find the ingredients apart from the peppers.

I've never done this before, but I'm definitely getting the hang of it. I start cooking, and soon the smell of food is filling the kitchen. Richter sticks his head around the corner.

"Smells good. What you making?"

"It's classified," I say. "You'll have to wait and see."

He comes in and slaps me on the ass then leans forward and inhales deeply. He stares at me, suddenly serious.

"God, I'm hungry."

His eyes hold me captive. I gulp. He reaches down and nuzzles my lips with his. "Don't burn the food," he says. "I need to make some calls. What wine do you want?"

We settle for a Chablis, and Richter puts it in the fridge. He goes out into the garden, and I watch him speak on the phone through the kitchen window over the sink.

*****

After dinner, Richter says he's going out for recon. "Don't answer to anyone. Only I have keys, and I'll let myself in. Got that, honey?"

I nod. We clean up together, then he goes out, locking the door behind him. I know all the windows are locked, and so is the back door.

I take the laptop upstairs to my bedroom.

I can't help but sneak a look at Richter's bedroom door. It's ajar, and I can see the bed. A shiver runs through me. What will happen tonight? He was quiet during dinner, glancing at his phone several times. But every time we look at each other, I can see we are waiting for the moment. There's unbridled lust in his eyes, and it makes me want to squeeze my thighs together.

I change into my camisole and shorts, not quite ready for bed yet. I sit down on the bed and open up the laptop.

A thud from downstairs pricks my ears. My door is open. Is that Richter coming back? It didn't sound like the front door. My pulse surges. I stand and put my slippers on. I tiptoe onto the landing and peer down the stairs. I can see a bit of the lounge, which is empty. I left the light on because I was scared. I don't like dark spaces. Staying on the landing, I call out.

"Richter?"

I don't receive an answer. I wait for a few seconds then put my foot on the first stair. A muffled thud sounds again. It sounds like it's coming from outside the house. I shrink back against the wall and scurry down the stairs into the kitchen. I turn off the light in the living room on my way. The house is dark except for the light on in my room. The kitchen is dark too, but I know my way around, and a faint evening glow spills in through the glass window.

The first drawer I open is the cutlery. Not finding anything, I shut it, and my eyes fall on the knife stand. It's one of those from which the black butt of the knife sticks out. I stare at it for a few seconds then grab one of them. It's a long one, and I only intend to scare an intruder, not actually use it.

I peer through the window into the garden. It looks empty. I creep out of the kitchen, knife in hand. The thud sounds again, making me jump. Fear scours my gut. My breath comes in gasps. I have the phone in my pocket, and I take it out. That's when I realize I don't know Richter's number.

Shit.

He's taken the satellite phone with him.

I feel like smacking my forehead, but I have a knife in one hand, phone in the other. The thud sounds closer. Someone's trying to get inside, I know it. Those sounds are from a heavy boot kicking around, looking for a weak spot somewhere in the windows or door. I crouch on the floor. I'm so scared I can barely breathe. What are my options?

What the hell am I going to do if someone comes in? Stab them? I've never even stabbed a dead chicken before.

Before I can think anything else, the thud comes again, distinctly closer, near the main door. I bite back a scream and hide behind the sofa. I raise my head, and what I see makes the hair on the back of my neck stand up.

There's a man looking in through the window. The streetlight is behind him, and I can't see his face. But he's tall with wide shoulders. He puts his hand to the window and peers in. I duck behind the sofa, sweat pouring down my face.

I start to pray for Richter to come back. If he's not back in time... visions of my dead body on the floor jump to my mind.

The tall figure is still standing by the window. I'm so scared I'm shaking. His head moves as if he's looking around. Then without warning, he raises a dark object, and a flashlight beam strobes inside the room. Shit, he's looking for me. I jerk my head below the sofa as the beam passes over my head on the wall. I cover my mouth, biting back another scream.

Fear makes me look at the phone in my hand. I switch it to silent, just in case. You know that scene in the movies, when the bad guy is looking for the poor girl who's hiding right behind him? And he's about to walk away, but the phone rings, giving her away? Well, that won't be me. However else I die, it won't be because of a stupid ringing phone.

Small comfort, I know. But it's all I can do with my brain going into complete meltdown.

Whispers. He's speaking to someone outside the window. I strain to listen. There's another voice, and it's clear there's more than one. Great. Just great. How many of those assholes are out there?

I suddenly think about Richter. I need to warn him. If he comes back and these guys are waiting for him...it's not worth thinking about. I stare at the phone, willing him to call me. It stays stubbornly blank.

I have to do something, or we both die. The light isn't flashing inside the room anymore, so I cautiously raise my head above the sofa. The man's shadow is gone. I creep out from behind the sofa on all fours and scramble for the kitchen table. The back door is only five yards away. If I can get to it and sneak outside, I can try to get around to the front. This might work. Unless they catch me out front anyway.

Whatever. I can't stay cooped up in here.

Getting out there is my only chance of survival.

Holding the knife in one hand, crawling to stay below the window, I make for the kitchen door leading to the back porch. I'm about to come out from cover, only two yards away from the handle, when another shadow looms up against the back door.

My heart freezes, and fear grabs my vocal cords and pushes out a scream. I suffocate it at the last second, and a weird grunting sound comes out.

I fall back against the kitchen counter, heart jackhammering, sweat blinding me.

I'm too scared to look out now. He's there. He knows I'm here. They're guarding both entrances.

I can't escape.

What the hell do I do? I know what Richter told me not to. But I have no choice. I have to dial 9-1-1. Richter didn't want the local police involved in this case for various reasons. Classified reasons. But fuck it. I'd rather be alive than have a *classified* death.

Trembling like a leaf in a storm, I crawl back to the living room and behind the sofa. My ice-cold fingers shake so much they drop the phone. I pick it up, and that's when I hear a sound at the door: voices again and the unmistakable sound of a key turning in the lock. The door rattles, and I hear multiple voices now, louder. But I can't hear the baritone growl I'm so desperate for. God, I'm so desperate I'm not even aware of the tears spilling out of my eyes.

Then the door is thrust open. Light floods the room, blinding me.

"Dora?"

It's Richter. He repeats my name, and I stand up shakily from behind the sofa. My nose is twitching, and I feel like an idiot as I dry my wet cheeks.

His concern is immediate when he sees me. His eyes widen, then the brows furrow, and his mouth gapes. We move toward each other, driving into one another's arms, and in a split second, he has me cradled against his chest, my hands trying to reach around his neck. Then my feet are off the floor, and I feel weightless. He clutches me to him like he'll never let go.

He's whispering in my ear, and through these silly tears I can hear him say, "Shh, baby, it's okay. It's all right." He says it over and over again. I inhale his familiar scent and bury my head in the crook of his neck as he pulls me closer.

CHAPTER 21

RICHTER

That haunted look on her face will stay with me forever. Those wide, frightened-as-hell eyes, the tears glistening on her cheeks. I would punch myself if I could. Hell, I want to shoot myself. She deserves better than this. Better than *me*.

I have no time to process my thoughts before I have her in my arms. My bones suddenly stop aching when she buries herself into me. I hold her tight, whispering in her ear, wishing I could take this all away.

I want nothing more than to be with her on a beach somewhere, living in a hut, walking in the sand. A vision of sharing a life with her suddenly springs to my mind, and it's so powerfully warm and enticing that it's like a sucker punch to my chest.

Cal and Brandon are behind me. I'm pissed with them for not waiting for me. I can understand why they'd like to check the house out, but at least giving me a call would've been the right thing to do. Without looking at them, I move into the kitchen, kicking the door shut.

Dora sits on my knee and dries the tears in her eyes.

"Who are they?" she whispers.

"My brother, Cal, and another member of our team. Don't worry."

Her head sinks to my chest, tucked under my chin. My arms are around her. Her creamy, smooth legs are folded at the knees, and she leans into me.

"I'm so sorry, sweetheart," I whisper. "I should've stayed. I didn't know they were coming down tonight."

She lifts her head. There's that tender, flowing light in her brown eyes that makes my blood suddenly stop. My heart constricts powerfully, lurching in its bony cage. I feel that space opening up inside me again, an empty field whose brown earth has lain desolate and cold for so long but now has the seeds of human touch enriching its hard ground. Her breath is warm on my cheeks, and it seems to pierce my skin and flow inside me, heating me internally.

I want to kiss her again so badly. And I don't want to stop there.

I'm in so much trouble.

"Don't be sorry," she says. "You were doing the right thing."

I clench my jaw. "Are you okay?" I feel stupid after asking it. She's obviously not okay.

A smile dares to play at the edge of her lips, like a butterfly dancing in the first light of morning.

"I am now," she whispers. Her arms tighten around my neck. Her forehead is touching mine.

Her words are so heavy with meaning it hurts me inside. My lips part. I cannot breathe. This immensely heavy emotion has captured my heart, washing my soul in swathes of colors I didn't know existed. Vermillion, crimson, thick as my blood, harking in my veins for an answer to the chaos inside me.

But I have no answer. I have no words. All I have is this beautiful woman, sitting on my lap like my modern Aphrodite, showering her sparks into the forgotten, forsaken corners of my soul.

So am I, sweetheart, I want to say. But the words are buried in the crevices of my mind.

We clutch each other, finding meaning in silence, solace in touch. Then I push her shoulders back gently. We look at each other, a new light shining between us.

"Let me speak to them," I say, stroking her lower lip with my thumb and forefinger. "Why don't you fix yourself a drink?"

"You got any whiskey?"

I can't help but smile. "Glenmorangie. Next to the wine rack. There's ice in the fridge."

She stands and brushes down her T-shirt. "I know that."

"Sweetheart, would you mind taking the drink upstairs, please?"

She's bending down to look for the bottle, and I realize she has this habit of keeping her knees straight and bending at the waist. Her hips stand up invitingly. Those joints must be so fucking mobile, those legs so easy to spread. My cock hums to life.

She leans one arm on the open cabinet door to hold her position as she turns to look at me.

Fuck me silly.

She's playing with me.

Just to drive the point home, she bends one knee, and her hips swivel. Those tight shorts grip her flesh just below the swell of the hip. Her toned legs look so damn sexy I have to bunch my fists and grit my teeth.

She grins. "Sorry, Captain. You were saying?"

She's gone from emotional to mischievous in minutes. She's like the colors of a rainbow, beaming on and off, light of my day.

I want to step forward. But I know what'll happen if I do.

I shake my head, a smile frozen on my lips. "Please, go upstairs with the drink."

"Aye aye, Cap'n." She winks at me and straightens, bottle in hand.

I leave her to it and step outside. Cal is standing by the window, looking out a gap in the drawn curtains. Brandon sits on the arm of the sofa. Cal turns around as I enter. His eyes fall behind me as Dora emerges with the drink in her hand.

She freezes for a minute, staring from Cal to Brandon then at me.

Cal drawls in his Southern accent, "Hiya. I'm Richter's brother. Sorry if we scared you."

Dora tucks a loose strand behind her left ear and shifts on one foot. I can see she's trying to look confident. It's adorable to watch, and so is the patch of pink on her neck and cheeks.

"Oh, no, it's fine," she says. Her eyes flutter over to me. "Guess I'll leave you guys to it."

She nods at Brandon, who smiles at her and does a mock salute. I watch the shapely hips wind up the stairs, and I don't miss the fact that the others are watching too.

There's a knowing look in Cal's eyes as he glances at me.

I spread my arms. "What the fuck? Couldn't you give me a call?" My growl comes out more harshly than I expected.

"Didn't know you had an appointment schedule." Cal smirks. "How does it look for tomorrow night?"

Brandon pipes up, "He might be busy playing house."

"Shut up, both of you."

My throat is so parched I feel like I need a drink myself. But there's a reason Cal is here, and that takes priority.

He speaks first. "You sure she saw Viktor?"

"She's called Dora," I stress, but the look on Cal's face makes me wish I hadn't.

"Dora. I knew that. Nice name," he deadpans.

I half grumble, half growl and sit down on the sofa. "What did you find?"

Cal walks to the middle of the room. He's as tall as me, wide shouldered, but he's leaner and clean shaven. With his glasses on, which he frequently changes for contacts, and his Oxford polo neck and slacks, he looks like the CIA agent he used to be.

"Viktor is here, there's no doubt. We picked up some chatter on the Bratva network."

I believe Dora, but my blood runs cold hearing it from Cal's lips.

He continues, "As to how he found out our real names, I have no idea."

"Anyone inside the CIA know?" I grunt. During my life in the Army, I grew to distrust the CIA. They play their own games, have their own agenda. We, the soldiers, are often put forward simply as cannon fodder.

Cal frowns. "Your files are redacted." He looks from Brandon to me. "Every time someone accesses your file, it's flagged on my system."

"And?"

"The last time it was accessed was by the CIA director, Derek Auster. But that's when our unit was first formed, six months ago. No one's looked at your files since."

"And do you trust the CIA director? Or any of them?"

Cal levels a gaze at me. I know better than anyone what he thinks of the CIA. He has inside knowledge, after all. He's helped set us up as a secret black-ops outfit that does deniable missions sanctioned by the National Security Agency.

"You know I don't," Cal says. "But it's kind of late, six months down the road, for your files to reach Victor's hands."

"How the hell did he find out then?" I growl.

Brandon speaks up. "While we find that out, we need to neutralize the situation here."

He's right, but I shake my head.

"The only way to resolve this is to haul ass," he continues. "We can't risk a civilian's life. Not when Viktor thinks she knows where Jozdani is."

"Any news on Jozdani?" I ask.

Cal shakes his head. "He's here but off grid. He's not using a phone or a credit card. If he's driving a car, he's paid for it in cash. Same for his home."

"He's got help. People with connections. This isn't good, Cal. The most senior Iranian nuclear scientist is hiding in the United States, and we don't even know where the fuck he is?"

"Don't you think I know that?" Cal snaps at me. His eyes are alive. "Sending you to meet Viktor was a bad idea."

"He did fall for it," I point out. We sent out word to Viktor that we knew where Jozdani was. In exchange for us telling him Jozdani's location, he was supposed to give up the names of active KGB agents in the United States. Years after the Cold War, there are still thousands of them. Hell, now the Cold War has started all over again. Even more Russian agents with fake Canadian and European IDs are flooding our country. The Russian Bratva acts as their unofficial support, helping as muscle when needed.

"And the operation was approved by the NSA. What happened was no one's fault."

Cal sits down opposite me and sighs heavily. "But it's still a clusterfuck of epic proportions. We don't know where the hell Jozdani is, and Viktor's running after us in a wild goose chase."

I tap my lower lip, thinking. "Maybe we can turn that to our advantage."

"How?"

"That depends on how confident you are of finding Jozdani."

"He has a son in college in Vermont. We're keeping tabs on the boy and his mother. She was married to Jozdani but remarried after he left. They live in Connecticut. I have a feeling he will surface in either Vermont or Connecticut. We've got eyes in both places."

"Once you have proof, send it to Viktor. Get him to meet me again. No fuck-ups this time. We lure Viktor in and get what we want. Then we finish him." My voice is quiet, but my words are the low rumble of thunder.

"That's dangerous," Brandon says. "Viktor won't go easy."

I arch an eyebrow at him. "And we will? Everything about this game is dangerous. If you have any better ideas, I'm willing to listen."

Both are silent, staring at me.

CHAPTER 22
DORA

I can hear muffled voices from downstairs. My ears strain, but I can't hear much. To be honest, I feel a little aggrieved. I was shot at as well. It's my life on the line, too. Why don't I have the right to find out what's going on?

Fucking classified.

Well, classified can officially go forth and multiply. My reporter's instincts are itching for information. Something big is going down here, and I'm caught in the middle of it.

Judging by the looks of Cal and Brandon, they are made from the same mold as Richter. Men of violence and action. I saw Brandon that night, but Cal is new to me. I can see the resemblance between the brothers. Of course, I only have eyes for Richter.

Curiosity wins out. I shuffle to the top of the stairs. Standing here, I can hear most of the conversation. When Richter asks them if they have a better idea, my hair stands up on end. I've been thinking about this. And damn it, I think I do.

I come down the stairs. The conversation stops abruptly as all three men turn to stare at me, causing me to swallow.

"Dora?" Richter asks eventually. "Is anything the matter?"

My mouth feels dry. I cross my arms over my chest and lean against the doorframe. "I guess you guys are talking about who I saw. That guy, Viktor."

All three look at each other. Richter fixes me with a soft stare. "Yes. Anything you want to add?" His tone is gentle; his face is serious.

"Yes. Viktor is here because he thinks we know where Jozdani is, right?"

"Right."

I notice Cal holding his head in his hands. He gives Richter a look full of reproach. Richter shrugs.

I turn to Cal. "I know this is classified information. But I know what's going on. There's no point in hiding it from me."

They're all silent for a while. Cal is the first one who moves to speak, but Richter puts his hand up. "I know that. But the point is men like Viktor will hound you for that information unless we kill him first."

"I get that. But do you think it's a coincidence that someone gave me information about Senator McGlashan and asked me to be at that spot?"

They look at each other again. Cal hitches forward on his seat. "Tell us about it."

When I do, all of them are deep in thought. Cal stands up and paces the room.

"I need to see if McGlashan knows anything about this. But any intel he gets is the same as the CIA, NSA, all government agencies." He stops pacing and looks at me. "And we need to know why that information was sent to you."

I nod. "Guess you can see why you need to keep me in the loop. Besides, I'm a journalist." I see the looks of alarm on their faces and explain quickly. "But don't worry. No word of this will break, I promise. But I can ask other sources if they know anything."

Richter's voice is firm. "No. You can't ask anyone or breathe a word about this, Dora. If the wrong person learns of this, you could get killed."

He stands up abruptly, eyes glinting fiercely, his broad bulk filling the room. He strides toward me, and he looks so fierce and intimidating that I almost consider taking a step back.

Almost, but I don't. Not when I know this massive man mountain is not going to hurt me in any way. Quite the opposite, in fact. He's capable of such exquisite tenderness it makes my heart warm.

He gets up close, and I stare up at the rugged immensity of him. It's not unlike standing at the base of a hill and looking to the peak. The slabs of muscles on his pecs rise and fall.

"Dora," he rumbles. "Give me your word. Do not conduct your own investigation."

I nod in silence.

I feel Cal and Brandon moving. Richter steps to one side.

Cal points outside. "The house opposite was empty. We took the, uh, liberty of moving in there."

"So we can keep an eye on you," Brandon says. "No way Viktor's coming anywhere near you without us knowing."

"Did you now?" Richter says. "You could have stayed in the field hut," he adds drily.

"Nah. Better off with a bed. Time for some shut-eye." Brandon yawns. "It's been a long drive from DC."

Cal comes forward and shakes my hand. "A pleasure to meet you," he says sincerely. "You're brave." He lets go of my hand then glances at Richter. An invisible message passes between the two brothers.

Brandon shakes my hands too, and they both leave.

Richter closes the door behind them. He stands there with his back to me. I go up to him.

"What is it?"

When he turns, I see a coldness that makes me gulp and step back. He stands in front of me, immovable, not looking at me.

Then he turns and walks to the kitchen. I watch as he pours himself a whiskey and swallows it quickly. Then he pours another two fingers. He doesn't acknowledge me. He opens the back door and walks out onto the porch, slamming the door shut.

I give him a few minutes then go outside to join him.

He's sitting on the porch steps, leaning against the wood of the railing. A sultry breeze ruffles the collar of his shirt. The sky is inky blue. Masses of clouds have merged with the granite shoulders of the mountains, more imagined than seen.

He moves away as I try to sit near him, and my heart breaks a little. He remains stone faced, ignoring me.

"Talk to me. What is it?" I whisper.

He chucks the whiskey down his throat then grimaces. He leans forward, hanging his head.

"I can't do this."

A chill slides through my veins. "What do you mean?"

He grabs his hair and pulls at it in frustration then smacks his hand down on the wood. "This." He growls like a beast. "You. Me. Bullshit."

Bullshit?

He might as well have slapped me. I hug my knees, rocking. I wish this wind could lift me up, fly me away from here.

He speaks roughly. "Can't you see what I'm doing to you? Putting your life at risk, that's what. Fuck."

"You're not," I whisper. "What happened, *is* happening, isn't your fault."

"If you had never met me, you'd be safe now," he says. "Getting on with your life." His voice breaks. I hear the silent sob in it, and my heart shatters into a thousand shards of broken glass.

"Look what I've done to you. Just like I did…" He doesn't finish. He gets up, throws the glass into the grass, and walks out into the garden.

There's pressure behind my eyes. I want to ease the tangled web of guilt in his mind, the dense, impenetrable darkness he is mired in. Like a whale caught in a giant net, the more he fights, the worse this gets for him. My eyes are burning. My throat feels raw. I want to touch him.

I get up and walk toward him. I reach out, but he moves away and shakes his head.

"No." His voice is a ragged whisper. "I can't do this to myself. Or to you."

"Can I be that judge of that?" I find my voice, and my control is teetering, losing balance. "I can look after myself, Richter."

"Then do it." His voice is cold. "Get away from me. Forget about me."

There's a note of finality in his voice. He turns and leaves me standing alone in the night.

I watch him step back into the kitchen then go after him.

CHAPTER 23
DORA

He's sitting down, reaching for his boots, when I move to stand over him.

"I need to get my shoes. Going to do recon." His voice is firm.

I crouch to face him. My nostrils are flaring, and my heart is aching, bursting. I'm hurt, angry, confused, pissed off. But damn it, I'm not going to let those wells of grief pooling inside my eyes spill out. Not yet.

"Oh yeah?" I say. "What will you find, Richter? Broken dreams? Graves full of guilt? If you can't let go of the past, you might as well stop living in the present."

His head snaps up, mouth agape.

"Life is unpredictable. Shit happens. What happened to your ex wasn't in your control. You being here wouldn't have changed anything. When will you get that?"

He's staring at me, eyes wild.

I raise my palm and put it on his chest. My voice breaks. "No one can control fate. Sometimes it's easier to just let things happen."

His eyebrows rise then narrow, a kaleidoscope of emotions rushing across his face. Blood mottles his complexion, and a vein appears in the center of his forehead.

His eyes move down my face to my throbbing lips. His own lips part, and I suddenly see a raw, primal hunger in his eyes, a wolflike, natural instinct that leaves me breathless.

His head bends lower as I lift mine.

There's no gentleness this time. There are no soft touches.

He growls deep in his throat as his lips crush mine, tongue demanding entry. I open my mouth, yield to him, giving my body up. His tongue ravishes my tongue, licking everywhere, just as his hands come around my waist and lift me into his lap.

I can feel the heat in his pants, the bulge of his rock-hard cock, and I grind against it. My panties are wet, and I swear it feels like his cock rubs against the flesh of my pussy. I tangle my hands in his dark hair, nails scratching his scalp.

His mouth leaves mine to trail hot licks of lust down my neck, and I bend backward, a moan escaping my throat. One hand slips under my shirt, brushes past my bra like it doesn't exist, and circles around my C-cup breast. Fingers squeeze one nipple as I move against him, riding him with my clothes on while he makes guttural sounds against my throat.

He's so big my legs are splayed incredibly wide, almost hurting. But I'm past caring, especially when his mouth dips down, his hands release one cupped breast, and he sucks a taut, pebbled nipple into his mouth.

Jolts of pleasure flood my spine. The hot, quivering mess between my legs makes me ache with the need to have him inside me.

He nips, nibbles, and sucks, taking his sweet time with the left nipple then the right.

Then he lifts his face to mine, claiming my mouth with his. When he draws back, I'm seeing stars, swirling black and blue clouds. Both of us are panting with insatiable need, locked onto each other.

"Like you said, honey, it's just easier to let things happen. Right?"

I can barely reply. His fingers dip into my jeans and expertly undo the top button. I shuffle back and feel his thick, warm hand slide into my wet panties to rub against my pulsating clit.

"Ah...huh," I moan, and my eyes drift closed. He licks my lips and growls at me.

"Right, Dora?"

"Yeah," I say, not sure if I'm answering him or just moaning. "Right. This is right."

His finger gently parts the soft folds of my flesh and then stays there, not moving, teasing. I buck against his finger, hungry.

"Oh, you want some, do you?"

"Yes," I pant against him. His tongue licks mine again, and I taste him, raw sweat and testosterone.

"Tell me what you want," he whispers.

"I want you inside of me."

He removes his hand and grips my waist before he stands up effortlessly, my legs still wrapped around him. Gently, he sets me on the ground. He rises above me, this dark, menacing sex leviathan. He stares at me with pure sinful lust and slowly unbuttons his shirt. He tosses it to one side then takes off his tank top and does the same.

The dragon tattoo on his immensely sculpted muscles seems to roar to life. He flexes his shoulders and gazes down at me.

"Take your pants off, sweetheart." Without waiting for an answer, he goes to the door and switches the lights off. The curtains are drawn, and suddenly the room is sunk in darkness.

I feel him kneel beside me. My hands move over his wide shoulders, the first contact with his warm muscles sending a riot of shivers tingling down my fingers. I arch into him, and our nakedness is complete. I am free of bra and panties. We crush against each other with pure animal passion. He molds my pliant body to his with hungry hands, massaging my butt cheeks with palms made to do just that.

"Richter," I gasp. "Is it safe here?"

"Honey, you're always safe with me," he growls.

He lowers me to the shag pile carpet, and I gasp as he spreads my legs. I see him as a dark, dense shadow, my primitive love god, an inchoate, raw force. His massive shoulders ripple as he bends down and kisses the insides of my legs. Each touch of his parted lips is like an arrow of fire, sending sparks inside me, wetting my pussy further.

He kisses, lashes my inner thigh with his tongue, stops, and kisses again. Slowly, he moves up, ignoring my writhing and calling his name.

Then he reaches my outer lips, and I feel like I'm going to burst and vanish into air as his smooth tongue delves into my silken depths. He licks, nips, bites, and then licks again. Then he moves up and sucks at my swollen clit while two fingers slip inside me. I arch my back, and my right hand comes down on his head, pulling at his soft hair.

He pulls, sucks at my clit as if he wants to swallow it whole. His fingers stroke in and out of my pussy as he sucks and teases. And dear god, I am bucking my hips as his tongue unleashes holy hell on my clit, burnishing brands of fire that shoot up my belly, consuming me whole. He's a devil, a monster who won't stop ravishing me with the sweet contortion of his tongue. My clit is throbbing so much I can feel it tingling now.

I am moaning his name, arching my back, all senses ripped out of me. I'm flying, fucking his fingers while his tongue is fucking my clit. A distance dilates before my eyes as a pressure grows in my pussy folds, and their walls start to tighten. He senses it too and increases the speed with which his fingers move. I can feel the tidal waves coming, a tsunami that gathers strength from deep inside my being, my belly, and I'm screaming, flailing, tethered to the earth only by his arm holding me down.

The distance pops, the waves bear down on me like an avalanche, and I shudder, twist, my pussy locking on his fingers like a vise. I'm all screamed out. All wrung out. My spine plops back down to the floor. I feel his mouth rise while his fingers leave my dripping pussy.

Then I feel his mouth on my inner lips again, breath hot, tongue warm, tasting my wetness, and it's incredibly erotic, cool sensations of liquid bursts popping, tingling on my skin as he slurps at my pussy like he's drinking from a fountain.

I'm gasping for breath. His naked thigh brushes against mine, then his tongue licks my cheek, and he kisses me.

He blows on my forehead, cooling me down. I reach down to find his wild dick, raging hard like a stallion in heat. My fingers play with his throbbing cock.

"You're hot and sweaty, sweetheart," he whispers. "Hope you're ready for what's coming next."

My mouth is upturned, and he kisses me again, a deep, slow dance of our tongues and fluids that pushes deep inside me, making me taste the confluence of me and him.

"Oh, Richter," I whisper.

"Get ready to say that again," he says.

Then he leaves my side and moves back to my feet. I'm aware I'm lying on a damp patch, and I suddenly feel shy that the wetness on his carpet is all due to me. I shift sideways and watch him move with me.

I see him again as an immovable shadow of black granite kneeling between my legs, muscles rippling as he opens a condom packet.

He bends down and kisses my swollen pussy lips again, teeth scraping the soft flesh. My head arches back, pressed to the side. It's beyond excruciating.

He kisses up my belly and hovers over me like a demonic but pleasurable cloud. What more will he do to me and to my frayed, taut-as-a-tightrope senses? Any more stimulation and I'll snap, recoil across a million miles into an explosion.

I have a feeling that's exactly what he has planned.

He kisses me before he says, "I wanted to taste you once again before I go in. I like the way you taste."

For some reason, his words send my passion flames shooting higher.

He moves back, and I feel him between my legs, and then the swollen head of his angry cock pushes against my labia.

"Ready, sweetheart?" he whispers.

"Please, Richter. Do it." I'm scarcely aware of what I'm saying, but I know I need this man inside me.

He says something, but I don't catch it. What I do feel is him grip the sides of my hips. Then suddenly, gloriously, gaspingly, he slams into me, filling me completely. The length of him is immense, stretching me to the limit.

I see stars. Hell, I feel stars as well. Black night sky and tingling of icy showers. He leans over me, mouth open, head thrust back. He stays like that, and we are locked, bonded, no space between us. My hands reach down to grab the corded muscles of his forearms, nails digging into flesh.

He holds me, pinning me to the center of my being, and slowly gyrates his hips, pushing his raging cock deeper into my belly, igniting nerves I never knew existed.

No words. No breath. No sigh. I am drowning, falling, mired in ecstasy so deep I might stop existing.

This is life, death, eternity.

He gyrates his cock in a circular motion inside me, keeping up the gentle pressure, grunting in pleasure as he does so. He withdraws then slams into me, making me whimper.

He's holding my hips now, pulling them up toward him. He does that gyration before he pulls almost all the way out and slams back into me. And again. Again. Faster. He picks up the pace until we're moving in a punishing rhythm, fucking me hard and fast.

He keeps going, barely breaking sweat. I feel the rain clouds piling up inside me again and the cyclone gathering strength. He increases his pace, leaning over me more, whispering my name.

I'm near the edge where there's no return, only a glorious leap into the whiteness of nothing. His balls are slapping against me harder as he bellows out my name and goes rigid.

I go over the edge screaming. He goes stiff between my legs, balls deep into me. He gasps and releases his load inside me. He jerks, twitches, that huge body writhing over mine.

Then he pulls out with a wet slosh and collapses next to me.

I cannot speak. He raises himself on one elbow and smiles as he pushes away the wet strands of hair plastered across my forehead.

"That was the main dish. Time for dessert soon, right?"

CHAPTER 24
RICHTER

Dora is curled up next to me, breathing softly. I'm awake next to her, hands folded over my head. I'm worn out from the three bouts of lovemaking we unleashed on each other. I had her on all fours, pulling her hair as I plowed into her. She rode me like a wild, bucking cowgirl, giving as good as she got.

And she got it, all right.

I gave her everything I had, while she milked every last drop of semen from my balls.

I don't remember feeling this satiated after sex—ever.

Dora stirs next to me, murmurs something incoherent, then goes back to sleep. I smile at her innocence. The smile hardens on my face, then fades.

This thing between us escapes easy definition. It's like the mistral wind fading from my hands every time I reach out to catch it. It's dangerous. Yet it's now oxygen to my deprived lungs. I see her face everywhere I go. I look at my hands and think of her touch.

I should know better. What she said just before we made love actually blew my mind.

If you can't let go of the past, you might as well stop living in the present.

She can read me like an open book. And we've only just met. But it feels like I've known her forever. How does that make sense?

Maybe it doesn't have to. Maybe it just has to *feel* right. Just has to *be* right, like a lock turning in a key, all the levers clicking into place.

I thought I loved Charlotte. Now that I look back on it, it was probably infatuation. I didn't really know her. Maybe she didn't show her real self to me, or I didn't take the time to get to know her. I was deployed, which took up a lot of our time. Whatever. Truth is, I never felt like this when I was with Charlotte. That's all I know.

As I stare up at the dark and blow out another sigh, I realize I'm tired of this shit. Tired of wallowing around in my sorrow, comparing my past to my present.

Sometimes it's just easier to go with it.

Dora's right. The realization causes goose bumps to spread along my limbs. Is she right for me? Hell, sure feels that way. Thoughts keep churning in my head.

A creaking sound cuts into my consciousness. My senses are like a guard dog's, and instantly I'm sitting up on the bed. We've moved upstairs to my bedroom.

The creaking sound comes again. It's in the living room downstairs. My bedroom door is ajar, but night sounds carry far, especially out in the country.

Another creak, and I gently remove Dora's arm and move off the bed. I shrug into my jeans and T-shirt. I open the drawer next to the bed, punch in the code for the gun box, and take out my Colt M1911.

Blood pumps hot in my veins, and rage sprouts inside me. The bastard who's broken into my house is going to pay for it. He must've cut some wires to deactivate the alarm. I tiptoe down the stairs. There's a shadow moving inside the room. I press myself to the floor. My only fear is he's not the only one. If he has backup, I'm looking at a firefight. I don't want that. But a quick glance into the kitchen tells me this guy is alone. The garden door is half open. That's how he must have snuck in after picking the lock.

I swarm down the floor in a commando crawl. He has no idea where I am. He's looking around the room, and by the time I'm close to his feet, he doesn't stand a chance. I pull his feet out from under him, and he falls against the wall. In a flash, I'm straddling his chest. He raises a weapon toward me, but I slap it away, and it skitters on the floor. Two punches to the chin rock his face from side to side.

I grab his collar and lift him closer. "Who are you?"

He looks dazed and doesn't answer. I'm not in the mood to mess around. I slap him forcefully across the cheeks then drop his head on the floor.

"Hey," I say in a gruff voice. I take the Colt out and press it against his temple, grinding his head to the floor.

"Don... don't shoot," he stammers.

Now he's found his voice. "Talk. Who gave you my address?"

"I can't...can't...can't tell you. They'll kill me."

Wrong answer. I've had enough of this shit. This guy might be a flunky, but he's also key to me finding out how the hell these assholes know my real name and my address.

"If you don't tell me, I'll kill you," I growl. "I'll count to three."

"One. Two."

He shakes his head. "Fuck you."

I hit him with the butt of the Colt, knocking out two bottom teeth. I reverse and hit him on the other jaw. He coughs, spits out blood. Rage is fanning in my veins like a sandstorm in a desert. I feel dry, brittle, ready to snap. My hand reaches out to grip his throat. I squeeze, and he makes a strangling sound. Veins pop up on his forehead.

"Answer me or die!" I growl.

"Richter?"

My world turns upside down at the voice. It's Dora. A light comes on, making me blink.

She's standing at the base of the stairs, hands gathered below her chin. She's shivering and watching me with worried eyes.

My heart shrivels, withers away and dies. This is what I was scared of—that one day, she'll see the beast in me, the animal I keep barely contained.

I turn my face away from her, feeling like a sixteen-wheeler just hit me. I get off the guy. He stays on the ground.

"What's going on?" she asks.

I take my phone out and scroll for Cal's number. "Nothing, honey. Just go upstairs."

She stands there, frozen, watching me.

Cal connects. I convey the situation to him. I keep an eye on the man and at the same time at Dora.

She glances at me one last time. There's confusion, concern, and more than a hint of fright on her face. It's as if someone put barbed wire around my heart and squeezed hard.

She's scared of me. I can see it in her eyes.

But I can't look for too long. The guy at my feet is trying to move. Dora heads back up the stairs.

I push everything to the back of my head and point the gun at him. "Move and you die, dickhead."

There's a knock on the door, and I let Cal and Brandon in. Brandon takes custody of the man, cuffs him, and puts a cloth bag over his head. He drags him across the road. Cal and I do recon around the house. Both of us have our guns out, scanning as we move in formation. I'm in combat mode, my senses on fire. This place is not safe anymore.

I'm angry. More than angry. I'm furious. I'm the dry earth that feeds the forest fire. When I find the bastards who turned my heaven into a hell hole, I'll squeeze every last drop out of them. They came into my house while Dora was sleeping. If I hadn't been there… it's not worth thinking about.

We check the back of the garden and then up and down the block. If Viktor is hiding somewhere, he's doing a darn good job of it.

Brandon is standing guard outside. "Guy's in the house. What shall we do?"

Cal looks at me and shrugs. "Can't take him with us. Call local law enforcement and let them take over?"

"Seems like the only option," I say. "Unless we make him talk."

Cal settles his eyes on me. "We could do that. Then leave him here. Either way, we need to get out. Too much heat. Let's regroup at HQ and decide on the next course of action."

Cal's eyes are still on me, and I know what he wants to say. I square up to him. "She comes with me. Stays with me."

Cal clenches his jaw. "Can I have a word with you? In the car."

Brandon goes off to practice advanced interrogation tactics on the man. He's the same as me, and I feel sorry for the guy. He should've just spilled the beans earlier.

I get inside the Yukon, and Cal takes the passenger seat. Both of us are silent, staring ahead.

He clears his throat finally. "How close are you to her?"

I rub my forehead. "What the hell sort of a question is that, Cal?"

"You know what I mean."

"Do I?"

"Stop it."

Cal turns to face me. Only he can talk to me like this and get away with it. He's younger by three years, my kid brother. We've looked after each other for more than thirty years. I know he means well, but it's rubbing me the wrong way today.

"Apart from the fact that I give a fuck about you and don't want to see you get hurt, this is also about operational security."

"OPSEC. Yeah, I know your CIA shit. Don't worry. It's all under control."

"Don't pull that tough-guy act with me, Richter. I know you. I know what Charlotte's death did to you."

Something drops and smashes inside me. I don't need this now. My right fist smashes against the door. "Then spare me the fucking lecture."

I open the car door, ready to get out. Then he stops me with his next line.

"I see the way you look at her. You look happy, bro."

My head sinks. Emotions tear and scratch inside me, leaving trails of hurt open and bleeding.

I'm silent while he continues, "I haven't seen you like that in a long time. Really long time."

I settle back on the seat, lean my head on the rest, and close my eyes. "I don't know what to do, Cal. Just don't."

We're silent again. I break it this time. "I need to protect her, Cal. She's my responsibility. Until this operation is over and Viktor is neutralized."

Cal nods. "Roger that."

I nod at him, and we get out of the car. Cal surprises me by pulling me into a hug. I don't usually do that sort of shit. But it's nice, and I do love him to bits.

"We move out tomorrow at first light." Cal thumbs toward their place. "Hopefully that canary will sing by then."

CHAPTER 25

DORA

I wake up not realizing where I am. Sunlight is streaming in through the cracks in the blinds. Memories of last night come back, and with them warmth to my cheeks. Oh my. I've never had a night like that.

A look to my left finds Richter's sleeping face. I'm in his bed, that's why I was confused. I lie back down, turning to look at him. The sheet is up to his waist. The stacks of muscles rise and fall as he breathes. The dragon on his chest and arms coils around his upper body. He looks beautiful in repose, mouth slightly open as he sleeps in total peace.

From the wide expanse of his shoulders to the massive bulge of his deltoid muscles and the deep grooves of his corded biceps, he gives off an aura of strength and invincibility. I find a scar on his abdomen, near his left hip bone. I move closer to get a better look.

It extends from the left hip onto his back. It's a long, ugly jagged line.

I think of what he has suffered, how much physical pain he experienced, and my heart melts for him. His eyes are shut, but I reach forward to touch his cheek.

He awakens suddenly and grabs my hand even before I can touch him. There's a wild look in his eyes, fierce and protective. For a second my heart skips a beat as he looks at me before his eyes soften. He sits up in bed and looks around the room.

Then he relaxes and flops back down, making the bed bounce.

He turns to look at me, his eyes wary. "You okay?"

I nod then move closer. I'm naked, and as my breasts touch his chest, his eyes go glassy. I detect movement under the sheets as his cock twitches. My lips lower to his, and he puts a gentle hand on the swell of my hip, moving me closer.

It's a slow, languorous, early-morning kiss, but I feel my thighs tightening with the promise of things to come. My breathing gets heavier.

Then suddenly, he pulls away. He studies me, the green flecks dancing in his gray eyes.

"I'm sorry you had to see that last night," he whispers.

At first, I'm confused. Then light dawns. "You mean that guy you caught downstairs?"

He looks down and sighs, his chest heaving. "I didn't want to scare you." He looks up, and his brows are lowered over eyes tender and full of hurt. "It's just who I am. But I'm not—"

I put a finger to his lips, stopping him. I lie down, head below his chin on his chest. "Richter, I'll never be scared of you." My hand moves across the plane of his chest into his shoulders. I love how warm and smooth his skin feels. "You can do nothing to scare me. Do you understand?"

The relief on his face is obvious.

"And you don't have to explain yourself to me."

He closes his eyes and then raises himself on one elbow. I'm spread out beneath him, and I'm suddenly aware of how naked I am. Feeling shy, I tuck the bedsheet up to my breasts.

He searches underneath his pillow and grabs his phone. "No calls yet," he sighs. "Cal must be asleep."

"What happened last night?"

He arches an eyebrow. "You screamed as you came on my dick, three times."

Fire fans up my cheeks. I smack him on the chest as he grins. "No, Mr. Classified. I mean that guy you caught downstairs."

His earlier pensive mood seems to have vanished. "Is Mr. Classified my new name, Miss Reporter?"

"It might be. Fucking Classified."

His grin is broader as his gray eyes dance with mirth. "Now I like that better."

"Will you tell me what happened, or do I have to go downstairs to find out?"

"There's no one downstairs," he says quickly. "Cal and Brandon have the guy." He turns to look at the bedside clock. I can't help noticing the fresh scratch marks on his upper back, and the scarlet fire spreads into my face again. *Did I do that?*

"Seven a.m.," Richter says. He dangles his legs outside and then hops off the bed. "We need to leave soon." He stands and stretches, still with his back to me. The taut lines of his shoulder blades jut out then merge into the muscles of his back as he rolls his shoulders. He's not wearing anything and just stands there with his back to me, brazenly naked. Thank god the blinds are drawn.

What happens next takes my breath away. He turns around, very casually, as if he does this with me every day. For the first time, I have a glimpse of his very impressive length. He bends one knee and gets back on the bed, leaning over me.

"We need to get out of here, Miss Reporter. Or I might end up in the news."

His face is hovering just above mine. I can't stop him when he touches my lips with his. It's another slow kiss, but I put my arm around his neck, and he lowers himself gently over me. The sudden heat of his body takes my breath away. We kiss deeply, and I feel my nipples firming as he pinches them into arousal. His cock fattens, the length pressing against my belly.

His lips leave mine and nuzzle my chin. "Nothing like a morning workout, right?"

"Which one did you have in mind?" I ask, my eyes half closed, lips parted.

He slides down the bed and starts kissing between my thighs. My legs part, and I groan as his mouth finds me, his tongue spreading me apart. He delves deeper, licks, pulls, making me squirm.

Then he lifts his face to me. There's a wicked grin on his face and lust in his eyes, hot as lava.

"You're about to find out," he whispers. His hands encircle my waist, and he lifts me off the bed. My legs wrap around his hips, and he nips and sucks at my sore, aroused nipples. I can feel his hardness on my ass, and I try to jiggle over it, eager to get my pussy on it.

He slaps my ass, making me squeal.

"Not so fast, honey bunny."

He carries me to the bathroom, and I stand as he turns the shower on, adjusting the heat. I go in first, the warm water cascading over my eyes, hair, and face. It feels invigorating. His hands run over my ass and my tits to cup them. Then he presses me against him and his raging hardness.

"Bend over, Reporter," he growls.

I moan as he gently leans me forward. I can see him kneeling behind me before his long, hot tongue slides inside me like a wet dream. I squirm as his fingers find my clit, knees almost giving way. He tongue-fucks me for a while then stands up and holds my hips. I hear a condom wrapper being undone.

"Time for the workout," he says with a gentle slap on my butt. I like it. Then I feel the top of his massive dick line up against my lips. I spread my legs for him, back arching, body aching for the throb of his dick. He fills me slowly, and holy fuck, it's the best feeling ever. Like I'm complete. Enclosed. Enraptured.

He slides in and out then holds on to my hips and increases his pace. I can't take it anymore and sink to my knees. He goes down with me. I'm on all fours, the water surrounding us like rainfall, warming my body as his deliciously hard dick reaches parts of me I never knew I had.

The momentum builds and builds until the collapse approaches again, and I can feel nothing but the slap of his balls against me, skin on skin, body on fire. He cries out my name like a wounded animal, hand reaching forward, squeezing my tits then finding my lips. I suck on his finger. This seems to get him off even more. He bucks wildly against me, pushing me against the shower enclosure as he pumps savagely until he suddenly goes rigid. I see white noise, an explosion, then I'm falling, limp, aching, gorgeous heat suffusing every pore of my being. He holds on, thrust inside me as deep as he can be, the silken muscles of my pussy clenching, milking his cock until the last drops are shed.

We spoon on the floor like fetuses, new beings of love who are finally satiated. He holds me close to his belly as we both pant, our breaths mingling with the warm water coursing over us like tropical rain.

CHAPTER 26
DORA

I'm wearing Richter's oversized bathrobe as I try to deal with my wet hair. I have to leave my shoulder-length dark curls the way they are. I can hear Richter on the phone, and although his voice is calm, I can detect the tension in his short, clipped sentences. They sound like commands.

I try not to think of what lies ahead as I apply mascara. It's the only makeup I've needed over the last three days. The days feel like a lifetime, though. I never knew my life would be totally upended in seventy-two hours.

He knocks on the door and then leans against the doorjamb, watching me. He's wearing pajamas, naked from the waist up. His forearms flex and biceps bulge as he crosses them over his chest.

"Hi, honey," he drawls softly. I see his eyes move down my length, a little smile playing at the corner of his lips. It vanishes quickly.

"What's up?"

His lips are set in a fixed line. "We're hauling ass. You're coming with me, *naturally*." He says the last word with an emphasis. I'm not sure if he meant it to come out the way he did. There's a tone of possessiveness I've not heard before.

"Cal and Brandon will follow us. Another team will meet us halfway, and we're going up to our headquarters in DC."

"Where in DC?"

"You'll soon find out."

"Fucking classified?" I pause, looking at his reflection in the mirror.

"Yes, Miss Reporter."

When we're ready, Richter takes my bags and stashes them in the Yukon. It's a nice summer day, and the Virginia sun is bathing the blue sky in swirls of bright light. Distant white clouds move slowly like majestic sailboats. The undulating peaks all around me, shades of green and blue, are like a garland around the horizon. I'll miss this place. That might sound weird given the circumstances. But I did find peace here. Its rural simplicity was quiet, unassuming. All my life, I've been to lovely places my dad's money bought. Here, instead of a sprawling mansion or resort, I had a farmhouse. I didn't need anything more.

Across the road, I can see Cal leaning against the driver's door of a black SUV. He lifts his hand in greeting, and I acknowledge it. He has black aviator sunglasses on and wears dark jeans and a button-down shirt. Brandon is packing the car.

"Ready?" Richter says.

I nod and head for the passenger-side door Richter opens for me. We set off while the others wait.

Richter pokes on the satnav, setting a course for DC.

"What about the man you captured last night?" I ask.

Richter doesn't say anything for a while. I glance at him, and he knows I'm waiting.

"We'll hand him over to the cops. He's a gang member of the Bratva. Deserves to be in jail."

"Bra—what?" I frown.

Richter goes silent again then smooths his beard with one hand as he drives.

"I know most of what's happening, Richter. You might as well tell me the rest."

He shakes his head, and I can feel the stiffness in his posture. Then his shoulders slump, and his jaws clench. I reach out and rub his shoulder.

"Hey. It's okay. I know you want to keep me safe, not drag me into this. I've been a part of this since that evening we first met. Right?"

He glances at me with a strange look in his eyes. My own words reverberate around my head.

Been a part of this. Have I now become a part of him, too?

And if I have, what does this mean?

Richter chews his lower lip then nods. "I guess you have. And I guess you have a right to know what's going on." He pauses before he continues. "But honey, this is stuff that can't find its way into the media." He lifts one hand. "I know you won't do it. I'm just saying. Be careful who you speak to."

"I got that. How do you think reporters get scoops anyway? They find a mole or a leak. Someone who's willing to rat on the big guys. Someone the big guys have pissed off."

He ponders this in silence.

"And when we find that leak, those sources, as we like to call them, we keep their identity secret. In fact, reporters often keep their own identity a secret. It's the newspaper or magazine that takes the blame. That's why having a good editor is so important. Someone who has your back."

"Whatever. What I'm about to tell you can't go to the media. Are we clear on that?"

"Whatever you tell me stays with me." I pause then look at him. "You should know that by now," I say slowly.

His mouth opens, and he lets out a shaky breath. "Oh, Dora."

I say nothing. We both know what's on each other's mind. This thing we started, this warm, mellow bond that connects us—where is it headed?

I shake my head. "We share things that no one will ever know. Right?"

When I look at him, his knuckles are white on the steering wheel. He doesn't say anything. He doesn't have to. I know this rugged, growling man of steel by now. I can figure out what he's thinking.

I reach out a hand again and rub his thigh. He relaxes and flashes me a quick grin. He, too, is thinking about how much we share and how it happened so quickly.

"But I have a right to know why I was called to that place in Dale City. What that source wanted to tell me."

Richter chews his lower lip again. "I've been thinking about that. It can't be a coincidence, can it?"

"The source called me about Senator McGlashan. I don't know what he wanted to tell me. But it was something important, obviously."

"How do you know he wasn't a crackpot?"

I shrug. "I don't." I look at him. "And why were you there?"

Richter pauses, and his eyes slide over to mine. "Remember what I told you? We fed Viktor false news to flush him out. We know he's looking for Jozdani. The Russians want to work with him, maybe to help build Iranian weapons, we think."

"So you told Viktor you know where Jozdani is?"

"Correct. Then we get to grab Viktor." He stops as if he wants to say something more but can't. He looks straight at the road, winding over a yellow central line.

"What were you going to say?" I ask softly. "It's about Viktor, right?"

Richter shakes his head. "Damn, woman. How do you know what's on my mind?"

Because you're on my mind. Always. But I can't say it out loud.

When he speaks, his voice is flat, hard like the road. "Viktor killed my father."

The words are like a slap to the face. His voice is quiet, but I can see the iron will in his eyes, fixed on the road.

I wait for him to speak. Eventually, he does, telling me what happened to Julian Blane and who Viktor is.

I listen, spellbound, trying to digest what I'm hearing. I'm clear now why Richter was there that night. But I can't figure out the connection between my source and Richter's mission.

I tell him that. He nods, deep in thought.

"Cal is looking into Senator McGlashan. So far, he hasn't found anything."

"His campaign for the House was financed by some shady people. I thought this source had more information on that."

"Uh-huh." Richter turns to watch me fleetingly. "That sounds interesting. What sort of shady people?"

"Businesses that hide their money in offshore accounts, and no one knows what sort of business they run or who they represent. Like holding companies run by a trust, and the trust is run by lawyers."

Richter grimaces. "An onion."

"Yup. One that keeps adding layers to itself."

We're lost in thought for a while. Finally, he says, "I wonder what this source, as you call him, had to say."

"Me too." I see a sign on the road. "Can we stop by my home?" I ask brightly. "I would love to pick up some stuff, and you can see my place as well. It's in the old quarter, by the river."

"Would love to, sweetheart, but it's risky. Chances are Viktor's following us. Don't want to lead him straight to your crib."

"Right." I fight to hide my disappointment. I love my apartment. Dad offered to pay for it, but I refused. I pay the rent on it, and although it's half my salary, it's worth it. So worth it, in fact, that I might just let Daddy buy it for me.

"I'm sorry," Richter says. "But we have to be safe."

I look out the window at the forest rushing past us. I need to contact Julia and Dad. My brother as well. I'm sure they have all tried to call me. I just hope they haven't called the cops. I take out the phone Richter gave me, my phone, and stare at it wistfully.

"You can't have any messages, 'cos no one has your number, right?"

"Right," I say. "But a girl's gotta message her friends. Know what I mean?"

He raises his eyebrows. Then he fiddles inside his pocket and takes out his phone.

"Here, use mine. Who is this to?"

"Oh, thank you! It's to my friend, Julia." I need to speak to Dad too, but right now, in the car with Richter, doesn't feel like a good time.

"You know the drill," Richter says. "Nothing about the classified stuff."

I nod and fire off some texts to Julia. She's ecstatic. For the next half hour, we text each other nonstop, since Richter says it's best not to talk.

"Can I tell her to meet me in DC? Please?"

Richter thinks for a long time. "Negative. Maybe you can later, but I need to speak to Cal first."

I can't help feeling annoyed. "I don't even know where we're going."

"Anywhere we go, you're going to be with me," he says. "That okay with you?"

CHAPTER 27
DORA

The Wrangler slowly drives down the concourse to a basement parking lot. It belongs to a hotel close to downtown DC. We stopped en route, and I met two new guys from Richter's team, Ken and Oliver. I stayed in the car as instructed by Richter, and they came to shake my hand. Apparently, there's only one member of the team I haven't met yet—Samantha.

The Meridien Hotel occupies half a block. Ken's car is ahead of us, and Cal's is behind us. I get the feeling we're being escorted. Richter's even more watchful. His easy demeanor has vanished. He keeps looking around at the parked cars. He's taken his gun out and is resting it on his lap. I'm trying not to think what's going to happen if he needs to fire it. My seat is lowered and inclined backward so I can crouch in case of a firefight.

But we park the car without incident. Ken and Oliver walk into the hotel first, taking the stairs. I emerge last, flanked by Richter and Cal. Quickly, we move to the elevators. I can't believe I'm standing between two large men with drawn weapons I know they will use without hesitation. My heart is hammering against my ribs, and my mouth is dry. But I also feel well protected—these two will go down shooting before anything happens to me.

Ken is outside the elevator when the doors ping open. We march down the wide hallway into the double doors of a suite, held open by Oliver.

I walk inside to find a pleasant marble-floored lounge with comfortable-looking sofas and concertina doors opening to a balcony. There's a bar area to the right and a TV and open-plan kitchen area to the left.

Most of the open-plan kitchen, however, is taken up by desks, wires, laptops, and other machines. A screen hangs in one corner with a projector beaming on it.

Richter puts a hand on the small of my back and leads me inside.

"Welcome to our HQ," he says.

A woman gets up from a desk. She's about five seven—my height. Her blond hair is tied back in a ponytail, and she's dressed casually in a T-shirt and slacks. The belt holster with a weapon in it is hard to miss. She's pretty, with hazel eyes and a small, prim mouth.

"Hi, I'm Samantha. You must be Dora." She sticks her hand out. I shake it, and she smiles. "Glad to have you here." She indicates the men standing around us like silent statues. "Now I don't feel so outnumbered. You must be tired. Coffee?"

"Thanks," I say, relieved. "That would be nice."

While Samantha goes to make coffee, Richter shows me the balcony. I want to step outside, but he shakes his head. "You don't know who's watching." He's standing away from me, his posture stiff.

From the glances I have received already, especially from Ken and Oliver, I know they suspect something. And every time Richter looks at them, I see sly smiles appearing on their lips, something Richter chooses to ignore.

Cal is the only one who acts casual. I wonder how much he knows.

Samantha brings me coffee, and Richter strides to the middle of the big lounge. The others face him, including me. It's time for a debrief.

"You guys know the operation to grab Viktor went south. But we learned something important in the process." He stops and takes everyone's eyes in. He dwells on mine at the end.

"Viktor will take the bait. Jozdani is important to them for whatever reason. For us, it's a matter of national security. Both the NSA and Office of the Director of National Intelligence are counting on us to find Jozdani and hand him over to them. It goes without saying we do the same with Viktor."

Ken says, "So, where is Viktor?"

Richter turns to him. "Don't know. But he found us in Montrose. Dora saw him. That's why I had to call Cal and Brandon."

"How did he find you?"

Richter hesitates before replying. I shrink back into the sofa. Part of me thinks I shouldn't be here. This is not my life; I don't belong here. The men and Samantha are listening with hard frowns on their faces, and I can see by the tension in their postures that this is life and death to them. This is their life.

I don't fit in.

Then I look at Richter's face. Those deeply glinting eyes, the chiseled jawline, the sumptuous expanse of his addictive mouth. That's where I belong. My eyes close momentarily. Should I even be thinking about this? What Richter and I have shared over the last three days has been special—for me, life changing. But when this is over, life will go back to normal. My heart sinks as I realize there will be no space in Richter's life for me.

I barely hear Richter's voice over my heart-shattering realization.

He says, "A search was made on a civilian phone for Jozdani. Viktor's crew have supercomputers searching for any signal on Jozdani's name, just like we do. I guess they found our location from that search. And Viktor had my real name, and the farmhouse, unfortunately, is registered under our parental last name. Viktor must've put two and two together."

Ken lowered his brows. "But who would search for Jozdani's name like that? None of our crew, I hope."

Silence. Richter looks out over the balcony, avoiding looking at me or at anyone else. Ken's eyes are roving around, and Samantha is doing the same, perplexed. Oliver also looks puzzled.

I can't take it any longer. This was my mistake, and it should be me owning up to it. "It was me," I say. "I had an iPhone, and I searched for Jozdani's name on that."

There's an audible intake of breath. My voice is shaky, and I try hard to keep my tone confident, but I guess everyone can see I'm faking it.

"I didn't ask to be in this position. I have a right to know what's going on. Richter wouldn't tell me anything because it's classified." I glance at his face, noting it's carved from granite. But there is understanding in his eyes, and he nods as I carry on. I feel a rush of heat knowing he's on my side.

"I'm sorry, but I did search for his name," I finish.

"No need to apologize," Richter says. "I gave you the phone, remember? Some of the fault is mine."

Oliver is leaning against the wall, and he speaks from that position. "So, did Viktor follow you guys all the way back here?"

Cal speaks up. "We don't know. If he did, he kept himself hidden well."

Ken and Oliver throw their heads back and sigh. Samantha and Brandon don't look happy. There's an oppressive weight in the room, a stickiness that won't go away.

Everyone avoids my eyes but Richter. I know what all of them are thinking.

I am the problem here. If it weren't for me, Viktor would probably have been captured by now. By being there that night, I blew their operation wide open.

CHAPTER 28
RICHTER

I knew this could happen. And as the leader, I need to take the initiative. I lock eyes with Cal, and he gives me a slight nod.

I stand straight, and all eyes converge on me. "Dora being there was an accident. These things happen. You know every operation you go on carries unforeseen risks. Right?"

I look at each and every one of them, forcing them to meet my eyes.

"It was necessary to tell Viktor that Dora knew where Jozdani was. That's why he didn't kill her. If Dora had been killed—" I swallow, my mouth suddenly dry, as a horrible image of Dora lying in a pool of blood flashes across my mind. I speak quickly. "If that happened, we would have the death of a civilian on our hands. There would be a federal investigation, we would get heat, and to cap it all off, we would have killed one of our own citizens. That doesn't help anyone."

Ken and Brandon have the hint of a smile on their lips, but there is also something else. I know what they think. Hell, Brandon saw me hugging her when they all but broke into my house. Even these battle-hardened men can take a hint of what's happening between me and Dora.

But what bothers me is their faint disapproval. None of them look like they want to accept this.

I agree it's awkward. We never have a civilian in our midst. But we have to make the best of a bad situation.

The biggest problem, however, is that my own feelings are a mess. I can't be emotional in this, for Dora's safety if nothing else. I know I'll protect her to kingdom come. Take a bullet to the head, chest, anywhere to save her life. But I'm in deep with her. When she's with me, alone, all my senses are awash with her. It's not just about the sex, although our sexual chemistry is so unique it's like experiencing a side to myself I didn't know existed. I have never felt so satiated after being with a woman, so complete that her body feels like a part of mine.

And when I talk to her, it's like speaking to a long-lost friend I never knew I had. She knows what to say and guesses what's on my mind before I even say it.

Does that sound bizarre? Maybe, but it's the way it is. I can't even extricate myself from this quagmire I'm sunk in right now. My feet are in quicksand, and I'm slowly sinking into this delicious feminine softness that is Dora Simpson, and I can't do anything about it.

I don't want to do anything about it.

All I know is that I have to keep her safe.

I clear my throat. "So Dora is our number-one priority right now. We keep her safe and get Viktor."

Dora clears her throat, and everyone looks at her. Her chin is up, and her eyes look defiant. She is no longer the shy and uncertain girl I saved that night. She's changed in the time I've known her. Or maybe this is an aspect of her personality that's always been there and is now coming to the fore.

"There is something you are missing about me," Dora says. "You're forgetting why I was there in the first place." In the silence, her voice is soft but has everyone's attention. "It was about Senator McGlashan. The man who is the head of the Senate Intelligence Select Committee."

She stands and looks at everyone. I feel an immense amount of pride in her. She knows she's out of her depth here, but she's trying her damndest to make this work. And she also has a great point.

"We know that McGlashan financed his campaign with money from offshore funds. No one knows what or who these funds represent. Don't you think it's a little bit weird that the night you chase down Viktor is the same night someone wants to rat on Senator McGlashan?"

Silence reigns as everyone looks at each other. The thought has occurred to me already.

It's Samantha who speaks up. "So, you're saying there's a connection between McGlashan and Viktor?"

Dora shrugs. "I don't know. What if these offshore companies are how the Russian mafia launders their money?"

"So your informant had a score to settle with McGlashan?" Samantha asks.

"Possibly. He had something on the senator, or why would he risk his life to be there?"

Samantha raises a finger. "But he wasn't there, right? He didn't turn up. Or he lost the nerve."

"Or Viktor's men found him first," Dora says.

"Either way, we won't know till we find him." I switch my attention to Dora. It's hard to be objective when those large, soulful brown eyes look back at me with rapt attention.

Just like she did when... *Focus, man, focus!* Deep breath. Get rid of that image of her lying beneath me as my cock is buried to maximum depth inside her.

I ask Dora, "Did anyone see this person who dropped the note off? Do we have him on camera?"

She shakes her head. "No. But the security guard who took the package saw him. He was slim, no taller than me, wore dark glasses and a hoodie. He didn't get a look at his face."

"And you don't know anyone who fits that image?" Cal asks.

Dora thinks to herself then slowly shakes her head.

Something about this whole setup smells fishy to me. "There must be CCTV on the street, right?" I address Cal then look at Samantha. These two are our analysts, after all.

Cal nods, and he and Samantha exchange a quick glance. "Yeah," Samantha says. "I can hack into the city networks and get some images for you. I need the address of your office though." She turns to Dora.

"No problem. I've got it here."

Samantha takes the address down from Dora, along with the date and rough time the notes were left.

My phone keeps beeping, and I pick it up to check the number. It's not one I recognize. I scroll back to see numerous texts from the number and realize it's Dora's friend.

When I look up, Dora is staring at me anxiously. I smile at her, watching her smile back nervously. Unexpectedly, my heart lurches. Poor little thing. Through no fault of her own, she's been cast into this crazy, violent world. My jaw clenches as I feel the resolution burning inside me. She will not be hurt or harmed in any way.

"So what do we do now?" Brandon asks.

"We stick to the mission," I say. "Find Jozdani. Get Viktor. We're waiting for new intelligence. Cal?"

My brother clears his throat. "Totally. We're crunching all the data we got on Jozdani and his contacts. Something's gotta give soon."

The meeting breaks up.

I go out onto the balcony. DC traffic stretches out below us. The building opposite is an office block, and we have cameras trained on every room in it. I don't normally come out onto the balcony for security reasons, but now I have no choice. It's the only place to have a quiet conversation with Dora.

I gave her a silent signal as I walked past her, and she joins me soon.

"Your friend's been trying to contact me. Didn't leave a message."

I hand her the phone, and she scrolls through. She bites her bottom lip then blows out her cheeks.

"Something's happened. It's not like Julia to keep calling me. Can I call her back?"

"Yeah. But don't tell her where you are."

She nods, and I leave her alone.

Inside, Cal and Samantha are hunched over a screen, and Brandon and Ken are having coffee. The others are outside. We have two suites in this place and two double bedrooms.

I make myself a coffee and, without speaking to anyone, stare out the French doors leading to the balcony. Dora is speaking on the phone, and her face is pale, nervous.

A sense of unease is spreading through me like wildfire. What if Viktor's men are onto her friend, Julia? How far will this web spread before someone gets hurt?

CHAPTER 29

DORA

Julia's voice is loud on the phone. "It's your dad. He's going crazy."

My heart sinks like a stone. The last thing I need is my dad kicking up a storm. But I can't blame him for being worried. However, Dad worrying about me is another aspect of his controlling nature. He always has to find out where I am, who I'm speaking to. It's intrusive and annoying.

Regardless, he is still my father. He may be distant, aloof, and possessive, but he has given me the lifestyle I have grown used to.

"I'll call him back. Don't worry."

"I told him you were in Maine, at some small town whose name I don't know."

I clamp my lips together. I hate lying and hate the fact that I made Julia do the same for me. "Sorry you had to do that, Jules. I really am."

"Don't be. Sounds like you've been for quite a wild ride. In more ways than one."

The double entendre of her words is obvious, and I can feel my cheeks heating up.

"I don't know what you mean."

"Sure you don't. That's why you've been living with this sexy man for the last three days. I can hear it in your voice, girl. Don't hide."

"Jules, stop it. Look, I've got to go. And by the way, any more messages for me? Any letters?"

"Nope. I am keeping an eye out. You be careful, right?"

"You too."

I hang up, staring at the phone and thinking. I need to call Dad, if only to let him know I'm fine. I know he's going to be angry. Furious even. I realize how odd it is.

I'm a twenty-five-year-old woman. Am I not allowed to have my own life? Why should I tolerate my father's relentless interfering? Add to that the constant put-downs because I didn't choose the path he selected for me.

It's only now that I see how sheltered and cosseted my life has been. I've been living in a bubble all these years without even realizing it. Being with Richter has changed my life for good. It's been a crazy whirlwind, and it's not over yet. I don't know what's going to happen, but one thing I do know. Richter helped me to see a part of me that had lain in darkness all my life. It was *there*.

It's me who possessed it.

But I either chose to ignore it or didn't have the strength to face it.

The part of me that is bold, confident of what I think and say, that believes what I think is right. Why shouldn't I think that? Why can't I say what I think is right, and the rest be damned?

Why can't I *do* what's right for myself?

I did this when I chose my own career at the magazine. But after that I fell back into my old ways. Pensive and worried Dora, always looking for someone to help her and guide her. These are character traits my father and brother have reinforced in me all my life. They're the only authority figures I have known, and because of my nature, I have been molded by them.

It's funny that it took another man to show me how wrong my family has been. How *dependent* I have been on my father and his money.

I've been like a blind woman groping for the switch in a dark room. Richter took my hand and put it on the switch, helped me to flip it, and allowed the light to shine on me.

I think back to the way I've just spoken to a team of highly trained, ultra-secret military operatives whose business it is to kill without a second thought. I pointed out things to them they're now working on.

That felt good. It felt *really* good.

I'm changing. I can feel it. It's as if the sunlight on my face is warmer, leaving my skin more tingly. The summer breeze lifts my spirits to the blue sky, whispers in my ears. Whatever happens in life now, I have to bear it. Not my dad. Not Richter. Not anyone.

Only me.

I dial Dad's number from memory. It rings several times before he picks up because I'm calling from a hidden number.

"Who's this?" he barks.

"Dad, it's me, Dora."

"Dora! Is that you? Where the hell have you been?" He's shouting angrily. I don't hear concern in that voice. I didn't hear a *Honey, are you okay?*

"Answer me, Dora. Where are you?" His voice hasn't softened.

I'm speechless for a moment. The drumbeat of my heart is pitching higher and higher. I'm anxious, nervous, but my heart is also drumming to a different beat: the beats you hear on a battlefield as an army goes to war. The sound of battle drums.

"If you don't stop talking to me like this, I'm going to hang up, Dad," I say with quiet steel in my voice.

There's a sudden, total silence. I can hear static and heavy breathing. Then he speaks.

"What? What did you…" His voice trails off as if he can't believe what he's hearing.

"I've been busy. I have a life of my own. I'm not just someone you can push around."

Silence again. I can hear him collecting his thoughts and mentally prepare myself for the backlash.

"What's gotten into you, Dora? Are you on drugs? Are you wrecking your life? It's that damn stupid job of yours. All these artsy types—"

"It's got nothing to do with my job, Dad. It's about you understanding that I have a life of my own. That I can make my own decisions, meet with who I choose to. I'm not a teenager who needs to be told what to do."

I hear him gasp. "Teenager? You think that's what I think of you? Who raised you, Dora? Who gave you the life you have today?"

"You did." An alien pain slices into my heart, like the knife of an invisible assassin. Did I choose to become the person I am today? Or is it his fault I am this way?

Or is it both?

Either way, it's time for me to wake up and smell the real world and see it for what it is.

"You did, Dad, because that's what fathers do. But no dad I know hangs on to their adult daughter like she's a teenager who knows nothing."

"I think you're suffering from a mental disease. What's got into you?"

"Common sense, Dad," I say, my voice breaking despite my best effort. "I wish you could see it too."

He shouts something again, but I hang up. I turn around to face the afternoon sun, closing my eyes. The sound of traffic filters into my senses, drifting up from below. The summer air is light on my face, but I smell the exhaust fumes from the street. There is no perfection in life. Something will always taint it. But I have to make the best of what I have.

"Penny for your thoughts," a familiar voice growls behind me.

I bow my head then turn to face Richter. He's standing with his massive arms folded across his chest, eyes smoky and dark with passion as he stares at me.

"Is your friend okay?"

"Yes."

The look of relief on his face is surprising. "And your family?"

I sigh. "My dad's fine. Just worried is all."

He comes closer. "We'll get to the bottom of this soon, I promise."

"But I have to meet with my family. I need to, uh, tell them things." The conversation I want to have with Dad isn't possible over the phone. The thought of meeting him does fill me with dread, though. He is that kind of a man. Intimidating. But I know I have to, come what may. If he loves me, which I think he does, then he'll come around to my way of seeing things.

"Things, huh?" Richter says, his tone almost a whisper. He's standing so close now that I can feel his warmth. I want to reach out and touch him. But I know I can't.

"Yes, things." My eyes are prisoners to his, and I can't stop myself from looking at his chiseled jawline and the sexy turn of his lips.

He says nothing, and I know he knows more than he's letting on. The few words I have spoken about my family are enough to paint a picture in his mind. Maybe one day I'll tell him the rest.

"I need to go home, Richter. I need to get my things. I can't live like this."

He considers this for a while, brows lowered. He rubs the beard on his chin and opens his mouth; I can see his pink tongue, stuck against his cheek. Thoughts of what that tongue has done to me suddenly rise up in my mind. Heat fans across my face, and I look down, cross my legs at the sudden pressure between my thighs. When I look up, he's staring at me, his face serious, but eyes soft, hazy.

"Okay." He nods. "I can't see the harm if we're in and out quickly. Can you do that?"

I beam at him. "Sure thing."

CHAPTER 30
RICHTER

My mind is in turmoil. What am I doing? I'm taking a civilian who is in danger back to her home. A civilian who's deeply embedded in this operation. A person to whom I'm so strongly attracted that the white heat of that magnetism drowns out every rational thought in my head.

This is dangerous.

I cannot have Dora so exposed. But at the same time, I can see her point of view. She can't be a prisoner, either. She's in her hometown. Getting her stuff and then coming back to HQ seems like a reasonable idea.

I just hope nothing happens on the way. I tell Cal where I'm going and leave Dora's address with him. She lives in an apartment in

Georgetown. We should be back in a couple of hours. Cal knows what to do if we're not back in time.

"You sure you'll be okay without backup?" Cal asks.

"It's not far. Should be fine," I say.

But it's not fine. I'm going through the motions here, but I know every step I take is putting Dora's life in danger. And no matter what she says, she's in this position because of me. I also know my team isn't happy having her here. I don't think it's personal resentment against Dora, but I get it. We've never had a civilian be a part of our operation. She's not trained the way we are. That said, the way she's handled herself so far has been nothing short of incredible.

But how far can we go before something happens and she gets hurt?

I care about her enough to know it would destroy me. What happened with Charlotte has kept me away from a meaningful relationship all these years. I stop myself. Is that what this is, a meaningful relationship?

I can't deny it's deeper than anything I've had so far. She's reached right into me and, with a careful hand, plucked out the thorn wedged deep inside my heart. I was like a wounded beast, hurting from the injury, unable to help myself. The wound is healing, and she's given me strength to live again.

And what have I given her? A life of insecurity? The need to bring an armed guard or a weapon every time she steps outside, scared of getting ambushed?

She deserves better than that. A whole lot better. This is no life for her. And it will always be my life. Which means... I'm saddened by these thoughts. I feel heavy, worn down. Dora is the sole ray of brightness in my dull, gray life of relentless work and duty. Fire in my cold nights. Flesh to my bones. How can I live without her? Crazy as that sounds, it's true. But in my heart of hearts, I know the answer.

We're in the elevator, going down with Brandon. He escorts us to the car then stands by the entrance as we move up the ramp and out.

"You did great," I tell Dora once we're moving. "Now we can focus on McGlashan. Find out how he fits into this."

"Glad I could help." She seems quiet but happier. "Can we take a detour and stop by my office?"

I frown. "Why? I don't want you to go inside."

"Sure, but I'd like to take a look, just from outside. Maybe the source is hanging around somewhere."

I know she's making sense, but my sixth sense is buzzing. I sense danger without knowing why. I turn on the two-way radio and call Cal.

"Send Brandon and Ken to our location. Just in case we need an extraction."

"Got it," Cal says. "ETA fifteen minutes, your location."

Dora doesn't say anything, but I can see the apprehension on her face. I try a smile, knowing she can see through my bluff. "Just a precaution."

In response, she does the most heartwarming thing ever. She folds her knees and slides over to me. We're separated by the console. Her hand reaches over and rests on my thigh. She rubs it up and down. I know she's doing it for comfort, so I cover her hand with mine, driving with one hand. But when I put both hands back on the steering wheel, her hand on my thigh starts to inch upward. Her fingers slide down to between my thighs. My cock jumps to life, hardening in an instant.

Her hand moves upward, and my mouth opens as she starts to massage the hardness straining against my trousers. It feels so good I don't want her to stop. But I know she has to. She has to, right?

But she doesn't. Goddamn, she keeps massaging my cock with an expert hand through the fabric of my pants till it's harder than a baseball bat.

I'm breathing faster, holding the steering wheel so tight it might just come off in my hands.

"Dora. What are you doing?"

In response, she leans closer. "The windows are tinted, right? No one can see in." Her voice is a sultry whisper.

"Yes, I know but we can't...Uhh!"

My words get lost as she reaches down with both hands and unzips my fly. My cock springs to life, and her hand is around it, pumping the hard, erect shaft. I can't breathe. My hands will rip off the steering wheel any moment now.

She whispers in my ear. "Don't tell me you're scared."

"Dora, please." I try hard to focus and turn to look at her. To be honest, I'm surprised. I didn't expect this from the shy and soft-spoken girl I've gotten to know. But I must admit, she has changed subtly over the time I've known her. She showed that at the HQ. Now, as I look at her hooded, sexy eyes and feel the breath squeezed from my chest, blood rushing to engorge my dick, I realize she's ready to push some boundaries.

"Not now," I say, my voice weak.

She smiles at that while the hand holding the base of my dick moves up and down. My mouth falls open at the exquisite feeling, fanning fire into my belly.

"Sure you don't want to?" she teases, the other hand rubbing my thigh again.

I know what she's doing. She's in control. She's showing it, and I am powerless to stop her.

The lights ahead turn red, and I press on the brakes. As soon as the car stops, Dora leans over and kisses my cheek. Before I can do anything, she slides down.

Stars burst in my eyes. A delicious coolness drowns my senses as sparks of fire from her tongue encircle the head of my dick. She keeps up the pressure on the base of my cock while her tongue swirls around the head without going any lower.

My head is thrust back. I'm gasping. The sensation is shooting sparks of pleasure down my spine, jolting every fiber in my body. Without conscious thought, my hand moves to the softness of her hair, putting light pressure on her head. She obliges at the slightest touch and engulfs me whole.

Oh my god. I'm pressed so hard into my seat I think I'm going to break it.

Her gorgeous mouth moves up and down, her hand sliding as well.

Blood is rising up to my neck, and I feel my head will burst open with the tingling, electric flames shooting up into my skull. And she's doing it slowly, taking her sweet time. She lifts her head, and her tongue swirls round the top again, hitting that sensitive part on the underside of the head.

She curls the tip of her tongue around it and rubs it.

That's it. I stiffen, go absolutely rock fucking rigid. I'm losing control. If she carries on, I'm going to start fucking her mouth, then come deep inside her throat.

The light turns green. I don't see it because my eyes are hazy with a mad rush of desire. I'm seeing double and triple. At a busy intersection.

In fucking DC. Getting the blowjob of my life.

The cars honk behind me, getting louder. I press on the gas and start to move with the flow.

So does Dora. Her sweet mouth has increased the pressure, and so has her hand. I let out a gasp as my hand slips on the steering wheel, and the car swerves.

Shit, I'm going to crash.

I put gentle pressure on her shoulder, and she eases back. With a plopping sound, her mouth comes off my dick, and she gives it a last lick before letting it go. It remains upright like a pole, ready for action. I scramble to put it away, but the damn thing stays hard. I turn the window down, and thankfully, Dora moves away. She does the same with her window.

The cross-current of air and traffic fumes cools my ardor. I breathe heavily. Sweat blooms on my forehead.

"What's the matter, soldier?" Dora asks in a husky voice. "Heat getting to you?"

CHAPTER 31
DORA

I can see from the look on his face he's taken aback. I can't help but laugh. He's driving but keeps looking over at me. He shakes his head then finally grins.

"Well, I never," he growls softly. He reaches out with one hand. His hand is big enough to grip my thigh. My panties are wet already, and as his thick fingers move up, I moan softly.

I'm aroused like never before, and it's because I've never done anything like this. I don't want to think too much about it. It was an impulsive, spur-of-the-moment decision, and I don't think either of us regrets it.

"There's unfinished business, honey," Richter growls. "It's my turn now."

I squirm as his knuckles rub against my clit, and I move against his hand. But he's driving, and I can see it's too much of an effort. He puts both hands on the steering wheel to straighten the car.

"You like playing games, huh?" Richter asks.

I look at him askance, and we both laugh. His is more of a low rumble.

"We finish this later, right?" he says.

"Anytime," I say, lifting an eyebrow.

Richter drives for another five minutes through the traffic before we're at the south side of Dupont Circle. I can see our office at the corner of the next block. Richter stops opposite the entrance.

"Now what?"

The blue sign of DC 24 hangs over the double doors. The windows on the second and third floors are open. We share the office floors with two retail clothing and fashion businesses. As I watch, a man comes out, dressed in a suit, followed by a woman with blond hair. My heart leaps in joy as I see Julia. She's speaking to the man, and they're both holding cups of coffee. They go for a walk, and it's clear from the way they move close to each other that there is a degree of intimacy here. I narrow my eyes. Julia never mentioned a man. Maybe she's just started dating him. And to be fair, I never asked her.

"That's my friend, Julia." I point for Richter's benefit.

Julia and the man walk around the corner, and we can't see them anymore. I notice Richter is looking closely at our office, craning his neck up to see the floors above.

"Looking for something?" I ask.

He shakes his head then reaches for his radio. He turns a knob, and it crackles to life.

"Zero, this is Charley 1. In position behind you."

Richter looks at the rearview mirror. "Roger that, Charley 1."

I look behind to see a black SUV like the one Brandon drove parked a few feet behind.

Richter puts the radio down and focuses on me. "Shall we go to your place?"

I nod, and we set off. The traffic lessens as we get closer to the green spaces of Georgetown. I've always enjoyed living here. The old parts of this town are truly historic and give the city a unique charm.

We come to the maze of streets that lead to my apartment. As we get closer, I see a shape run out from behind a dumpster opposite my apartment. The figure is thin, my height, and has a hoodie pulled over its head. My blood runs cold. Richter's seen him as well, and he slams on the brakes, bringing the car to a stop. He pulls over to the curb and gets out.

"Stay here," he barks at me. I want to run with him but realize the danger. With both of us out in the open, anything can happen.

Richter sets off, sprinting after the figure, who has a head start on him. Brandon pulls up behind us. He comes out of his car and runs over to me. I lower the window and explain what's happening.

"Okay," he says. "Stay here." He opens the back door and gets inside.

I turn to look at him. Brandon is more than six feet tall with reddish hair and a close-cropped fiery beard. Freckles cover his nose and cheeks. He's a good-looking man, one who would turn heads.

"Will Richter be okay?" I ask anxiously. "Maybe you should go help him."

"No." He shakes his head. "One of us stays behind as backup. And don't worry about Richter. If anyone knows how to handle himself, it's him." He smiles. "In fact, it's the guy he's chasing that I feel sorry for."

He looks at me curiously. "I looked at your file. You're Michael Simpson's daughter. Your dad's a big shot in the media world, right?"

I frown, not sure if this is the right time to make small talk. But he's right that we have nothing to do while we wait for Richter to come back.

"Yes," I say, sitting forward again.

Brandon doesn't say anything for a while. I'm only too aware of this handsome man sitting behind me.

He coughs. "Hope you don't mind me saying. Richter's quite taken with you. Never seen him like this."

Warmth blossoms on my neck. I look down at the twisting fingers on my lap. "Really?"

"Oh, yeah. I've known him for years. Anything happening between you two?"

"Now, Brandon. You should know better than to ask a lady that question."

He grins. "Thought you might say that."

"Are you Delta as well? Army?"

Brandon hesitates before replying. "Did Richter tell you that?"

I shake my head. "No. He didn't. But I kind of guessed."

He narrows his eyes then smiles. "You got it out of him, right?"

I'm about to reply when I see Richter jogging back. He's alone. I don't wait. Opening the car door, I step out onto the pavement.

"Are you all right?" I say, moving toward him.

He's sweating, shirt sticking to his chest and shoulders, accentuating the ripple of his muscles. He wipes sweat off his brow with one hand and nods at Brandon, who's standing behind us.

"He escaped. Vaulted over some gates, and I lost him after that." Richter sighs then looks around the block. "He was very quick," Richter adds. "Faster than I thought he would be."

I look around my neighborhood. It's a nice, safe street, with two- and three-floor Georgian houses. I like living here, but right now, it's giving me shivers. I draw my arms around myself. Richter's hand touches my shoulders.

"Hey." His voice is warm. "Don't sweat it. We'll get this sorted out. Shall we go in?"

"No." I shake my head firmly. "No way are you guys going in before me. I need to see what state I left it in first."

Richter says, "What if this is an ambush? How do we know they haven't been inside your place already?"

I meet his eyes, fierce with protectiveness. "Richter, I need to do this. You can be one step behind me. I don't mind. But please, I go in first, on my own."

I can sense his reluctance but give his forearm a squeeze and move past him. The two men follow me as I cross the road. The house that contains my first-floor apartment looks the same as before. The men behind me split up, walking to either side of the property.

I put the key in the slot and push the door open. I can sense Richter behind me. I turn the alarm off, which is reassuring. No one's tampered with it.

I half turn to Richter. "Gimme a minute."

"No problem," he says, his eyes hard. "But leave this door open, please. And if you don't call us in five minutes, we're coming in."

"Okay," I say.

I check the living room and dining area. It seems to be in the same shape I left it. I have wooden sculptures from South America and Africa, and none of them have been touched. My artworks hang in their frames. My Roche Bobois sofa sets haven't been slashed open. The kitchen is still the same. Upstairs, in the bedroom, I pick up some underwear I'd left in the bathroom and put them in the wash. The spare bedroom hasn't been slept in, as expected. I breathe a sigh of relief. From what I can see, the place hasn't been searched.

"Come on in," I call out, leaning over the bannister.

Richter is in immediately. I see the drawn gun in his hand and gasp. His face blanches. He puts the gun in his belt.

"It's just for protection," he says then grins. "I wasn't planning on using it."

"Don't think you'll have to," I say. "The place is clean."

CHAPTER 32
RICHTER

Dora's right. The place is clean. I can't help but admire how tastefully decorated the house is. This is clearly her home, and she's given it her own unique stamp. The living area is wide and spacious, the furniture retro chic, in keeping with the art deco, original-looking artwork. Read: expensive. From the designer sofa set, TV, art on the wall, this place cost money, and a lot of it.

I guess Daddy's credit card has its uses.

Through the Sub-Zero kitchen, I see a back door, showing the garden. It's not huge, but it's big enough for a nice BBQ.

"Come up here, Richter," I hear Dora say from upstairs.

"Coming," I say.

I can't help but compare her place to mine. I shouldn't, but I do. My house back in Montrose is a much plainer affair. Sure, I like to keep it neat and tidy, but it doesn't have designer stuff dripping off the walls. And that's the way I like it. I'm not a pretentious person. Could I afford it? Hell yeah. The farm we have makes a lot of money, and after we pay the farmers, what we have left over comes to Cal and myself. Not to mention the big contracts we keep picking up for the security firm. I have no dearth of money, but that doesn't mean I have a need for this kind of shit.

All of a sudden, I'm starting to realize what sort of a person Dora is. The social circles she mixes in. The things she probably expects a future boyfriend to have. I guess there's some truth in the saying you don't really know a person until you see where they live.

Am I being a judgmental asshole? Shit, maybe.

But I also understand one thing: I can never give Dora this stuff. I would never buy fancy masks from tribes in Uruguay. I would never have Lichtenstein hanging from my walls.

I could never uproot her from this life.

The heaviness in my heart grows, a black shutter slowly closing over the sunlight.

Forget about the money. This is what she finds comfortable, stable, ideal. Or why would she have her apartment like this?

And can I give her these things? Can I come home to her every night, like a normal, everyday man does?

Oh god. Stepping inside was a bad idea. Coming here has really driven the stake deep into my heart. Driven it home, so to speak. If there was ever hope in my mind that we could make it work, that's now completely vanished, like clouds melting in a desert sky.

"Richter!" Her voice floats from above.

I turn and slowly trudge up the stairs. She's standing on the landing, one arm bent on her waist, a puzzled look on her face. "Where were you?"

"Just having a look, that's all." If my voice is stiff, there's no point in hiding it. Yet when I look into those melting brown pools of light, an iron fist grips my heart and crushes it. How can I let go of that beautiful face?

Dora grabs my hand and pulls me close, which means she floats over to me. "What's the matter?"

I'm having trouble speaking. Being with her exposes me to these extremes of emotion. Pure, unadulterated sexual pleasure, the dizzying heights of an emotional happiness I never knew I would feel again, then crashing down to the bare bones of the rotting carcass of my hopes and dreams. My heart feels like an arid desert. Vultures are circling overhead. Vultures like Viktor. Maybe I was born to fight bastards like him. I'm hard, rough, a man of violence.

I'm as alien in here as a rosebush in the Sahara.

And my ardent, voluptuous rose, red as the blood in my veins, now stands before me, eyes full of a mild question.

Who am I to pluck this rose away from her home?

All I'm going to do is cut myself—and her—on the thorns. Hell, I've done that already. No point in bleeding any more.

If she bleeds because of me, I will never forgive myself.

Sounding repetitive? Boring?

Hell yeah. Because it's the one nightmare that keeps circling in my mind. The one sound, like raindrops lashing against my window, that wakes me up at night, bedsheets soaked with my sweat. I couldn't be there for Charlotte, and I won't be there for Dora. But I've bonded with Dora like with no woman before.

No woman—fuck that, no human being—has reached inside and touched me like a cool benediction, like a soothing balm to my fevered, wounded soul. She did that. This beautiful rose, my sweet Asphodel, who taught me how to let go of the past and live for myself again.

And if I cause her harm, like I have already, I won't be able to live with it.

No, I am an impostor in this lovely, cultured apartment. A home. The kind of home that Dora will want one day from her man.

It's laughable, a joke that I thought I could be that. As if I could buy her works of art. Take her to the opera. Talk about the latest shows on Broadway.

The thoughts rush through my head like a cyclone moaning between stars, a desolate, derelict space. I can't stop thinking about it, and I can't stop looking at her, drinking her in with my eyes: her small button nose, those generous, fulsome pink lips, and her swirling brown depths.

I can't believe I'm doing this, but I have to. There is no other choice. If I delay this any longer, all I'll be doing is making it worse.

She deserves someone better than me.

A frown appears on Dora's face. In three days, she's gotten to know me better than anyone. We're attuned to each other's feelings, body heat, stance, posture. How crazy does that sound? In such a short time, how is it possible to get so close to someone you feel like you've known them all your life?

I don't know. Maybe someday I'll understand. Maybe I'll go back and tell it to the mountain whose peak I climbed with Dora, who lit up that evening like she was the sole star in the sky, shining her silver sparks on me.

But whatever. I can't let my life ruin hers. I need to step away now so she can live hers to the fullest.

I owe her that much. Hell, if I could only tell her how much I owe her, what she has done for me in these seventy-two hours, whose minutes and moments I'll never forget.

The frown is spreading across Dora's face. Her hand has reached out to touch mine. The feel of her skin is soft, mesmerizing, and when she steps close into my personal space and looks up at me with those swirling chocolate browns, I just want to scoop her into my arms again. She lifts a hand and places it on my cheek. Desire, duty, and the fear of losing her battle in my heart like it's intergalactic warfare. I'm coming apart like an exploding supernova in slow motion.

I feel the lusciousness of those full breasts on my chest, and blood stirs in my dick.

"Talk to me," she purrs, lips close to my ear.

My mouth is open, eyes closed. Without knowing what I'm doing, my hands reach down to cup her round, voluptuous ass then pull it into me. She moans then whimpers as she rubs herself against my hardness.

The house is very quiet, and small sounds are magnified. I don't hear it at first, what with our fevered breaths mingling in my ears. Then I do: a loud click from downstairs as the door shuts. I kick into action immediately. With one arm, I shove Dora behind me, shielding her. The Sig P226 is in my other hand. I lean over the banister and see a redheaded man walk into the hallway. The gun relaxes in my hand.

"Brandon?" I say. He looks up, and his face blanches when he sees the gun pointed at him. I holster the weapon. "Did you do a recon outside?" I ask him.

He's still standing in the foyer, looking up at me.

"Yes," he says. "All clear."

"Wait in the car. I'll be down soon."

There's a spark in his eyes as his lips twitch. "Exactly how long are you going to be?"

I guess Dora and I are an open secret now. "Not long," I drawl, deadpan. "Just get back to your car and keep watch."

Brandon grins and does a mock salute. I watch till he shuts the door on his way out.

Dora's questioning eyes are on me again. They're like laser beams scanning my mind, searching for answers. I can't help but look back at her, mesmerized.

"I want to show you my bedroom," she says huskily, and when she leans forward, I can't resist kissing those soft pink lips. They taste like heaven. Her tongue runs along the inside of my lips, and when she opens her mouth, my tongue darts in, lashing against the inside of her mouth. She groans and rubs against my hardness, and my hands are on her ass again, drawing her in hard.

She breaks off to whisper against my ear, "Remember what happened in the car? We have unfinished business, right?"

CHAPTER 33
DORA

"Unfinished business, huh?" Richter growls softly against my ear. His hand slips down, unbuttoning the top of my jeans with two practiced fingers then slipping down to my panties. Within seconds, his thumb is on my clit, and I feel another finger dip inside my soaking entrance. His thumb circles, and the thick finger moves in slightly then comes out again before playing with my wet folds.

I'm gasping, grinding myself on his fingers. One arm is thrown around his neck, his mouth buried in the hollow of mine. Somehow we walk backward till my back hits the wall. He trails kisses down my jaw and then the side of my neck. The finger slips inside me fully, stroking up and down, his thumb still circling the electric, engorged knob of my clit.

"Let's go inside," I manage to gasp. "Into my room."

It's almost impossible to break off. We seem glued together. He licks the base of my throat, then his hand comes up to cup my breast. We kiss again, and I put my hands on his shoulders. Grabbing his hand, I take him to the bedroom. I have a four-poster bed, and drapes hang at the bed head. Two sets of windows face the street and the back garden, and Richter helps me to pull the blinds down. The room is almost dark. We collide softly, in slow motion, with an unspoken urgency that has set our bodies on fire.

His hands are all over me again, lifting my top over my head then pulling down the straps of my bra. I unhook the bra and then groan as his hot mouth sucks a nipple, sending warm currents of pleasure radiating into my body. He scoops me up and puts me on the bed.

I lift my knees as he pulls the hem of my pink lace panties over my ankles then tosses them to the floor. I feel the wide expanse of his shoulders nudge my inner thighs apart. His hot breath is at the center of my pussy, then I feel his tongue lashing my clit with lick after hot lick. One finger is playing with the folds of my center, now so wet, but deliberately, he refrains from pushing it in. His mouth does the main work, sucking, nipping, and biting at my clit, teasing it with his tongue, sending quantum waves of pleasure rippling into my lower belly. Heat undulates from low down in my body, radiating upward in hot red blooms of pleasure and joy. My mouth is open, fingers clutching the bedsheets as if I'm going to rip them to shreds. My hips rise and rock, wanting more of his mouth, practically begging his fingers to thrust inside me.

When he does so, the feeling intensifies and takes me over. Two fingers thrust in and out of me in rhythm to the lashings of his tongue. He speeds up, and I'm moaning, sweating, writhing, floating, becoming a wet, slippery mess of pre-orgasm excitement as I call out his name and buck my pelvis wildly in his face. My hands are on the soft brown curls of his head, pushing him into me. Richter has a jaw like a machine, and the speed with which he lashes and laps at my silken folds, then alternates with flicking his tongue on my clit, all the while finger-fucking me to oblivion, brings the giant waterfall closer and closer. The heat gathers like rainclouds low down in my belly. I cry out his name one last time, and then I'm falling, flying, losing myself in the warm cascade of another glorious orgasmic Niagara.

Wet hair is plastered to my forehead, and my chest is heaving. I open my eyes when I hear the sound of a condom wrapper being ripped. Richter smiles and waves the condom at me.

"Gotta carry a spare one when you're around." He winks, the sultry grin on his face making my cheeks heat up again, thinking of what that mouth has been doing to my sex.

I watch his impressive length bob in the air, thick with veins, as he sheaths himself. He positions himself between my legs, and I feel the insistence of his raging erection pushing against my folds. But he doesn't slide in. He leans over, and we kiss passionately. My hands caress his chest and shoulders then grip his bulging biceps hard. He kisses down my neck into my chest then sucks on a nipple as he slowly enters me. The combination of him sliding slowly in as his wicked tongue circles my nipple is intensely pleasurable, sending sparks of fire to my center. He increases his rhythm slowly, then sits up, holding my ankles up on his shoulders. He strokes into me hard and fast, kissing my legs, grunting with pleasure. His mouth opens and his eyes close as he slides his gorgeous dick into me, plunging deep inside my belly, branding me.

The speed grows, the heat spreads, and I feel the nebulous storm building to a crescendo inside me again. He starts to buck wildly, growing more inside me, and I feel his head bulging inside, stretching the condom sheath. He shouts my name and hammers into me so hard my butt is lifted off the bed. He buries himself in me one last time, and I can feel him spasming inside me, my pussy muscles doing the same to his dick as we come together in wave after wave of endless sexual delight.

He collapses next to me, gasping. We lie speechless for a while, sweaty but sated. My body feels light and airy, like I'm lying on a hot water bed. He's the first to talk, raising himself on one elbow to look at me. Then he leans over to kiss me, and I love that moment after heated sex with Richter, when his tongue gently tastes mine, somehow cool and refreshing yet warm and saline at the same time, the taste of me still lingering in his mouth.

"Is there coffee in your kitchen?" he rumbles.

I run my hands through his hair then pull his face down for another kiss.

"Yes. But the milk might've gone off."

He gets up and hops off the bed. The washboard muscles on his abdomen ripple and tense as he bends to find his clothes. I get dressed while Richter is downstairs. It's nice to be back in my own home. Nothing replaces the comfortable sense of familiarity of being in my pad, where everything is arranged just the way I want it. I open the windows to let some fresh air in. The clothes inside my dresser are the same as I left them. Same with the shoe rack. My laptop hasn't moved from its place on the table.

As I sort the room out, I smell cooking. The aroma of pancakes comes wafting up from the kitchen, and I grin to myself. I want to go downstairs just to see Richter in my kitchen, but I stop myself. He's planning this as a surprise, so I might as well let him.

I still can't use my phone, but I can use Richter's. I power up the laptop to check my emails. Richter comes in, and when I turn around, he's holding a wooden tray with two mugs of coffee, two plates heaped with pancakes, and a bowl of maple syrup. Cutlery gleams on the tray. The smell is heavenly.

"Breakfast is served," my man says with a smile on his face that rivals the sunlight.

Did I just think *my man?*

Oh, why does this overpowering sense of happiness suddenly crush me? Seeing Richter standing in my room, holding that delicious tray of warm food, takes me deep into a mellow, fuzzy place. My heart aches all of a sudden. Richter stands there like a vision, bathed in a glow that seems to make my room brighter than it's ever been.

What would it be like if Richter was living here? With me?

My head can't even believe I'm having these thoughts. So far out they belong in an undiscovered galaxy. But I guess my heart has a way of stepping across different worlds as if the space between them didn't exist. Right now, I'm there, basking in the dream of seeing Richter here all the time, always mine…

I blink and stare down at the floor. This feels like a dream, and I need to wake up. True, I've grown closer to him than I am to any other person except my best friend, Julia. My heart lurches against its ribcage. The emotion I feel right now is so true. So real. Like the goosepimples that rise up on my arms.

Could Richter be in my future? My throat seizes up with emotion as I watch him set the tray down gently on the table. He's close enough to touch, and his strong, clean smell drifts over to me. I know the answer to that question. I can hear it like I can hear the air rasping in my lungs.

Yes.

And for the first time, I feel something stronger, deeper. It opens up inside me, like watching the sunrise over the ocean. I have no words to describe it, but the feeling is so strong I can't ignore it.

When Richter kneels at my feet and looks at me with his gray eyes like smoky fire, I know what the feeling is. It's undeniable, a pull that's more than magnetic, a bond that is still new but more durable than the toughest diamond.

I'm falling in love with Richter Blane.

He rubs my thigh with one hand then kisses me lightly on the lips. I savor his touch, closing my eyes. It just feels so right.

"Hey," he drawls, in that low rumble of his. "Hope you're hungry."

I nod happily. He puts the trays out, and he's even got white napkins, which I store in the kitchen cupboard.

The first mouthful of pancake and syrup melts in my mouth. It's delicious.

"So good," I say between mouthfuls as we both tuck in. It's a good thing there's a heap of pancakes, as we're both hungry, and Richter puts it away faster than I can.

"Can I call my family and Julia from your phone?" I ask when we're done.

He thinks about it. "Letting them know is risky. If they're under watch, then they could lead Viktor's men straight here. I'd be keeping an eye on them if I was Viktor."

I raise an eyebrow. "What if I tell Julia to follow a surveillance evasion route on her way down here?"

He barks out a laugh, throwing his head back. But then he becomes serious very quickly. The soft glimmer evaporates from his eyes, and his nostrils flare.

"This isn't your world, sweetheart. And I don't want it to be," he says in a low voice. He tears his eyes away from me, looking out the window.

I reach for his hand to find it knotted into a hard fist, the veins rising on his skin. He doesn't relax it when I touch him.

"Richter," I say softly. "Look at me."

When he does so, his grays are restless, and the irises darken. I strengthen my grip on his hand.

"I'm in this now. This is about me as much as it is about you."

He sighs, shakes his head, and rolls those massive shoulders as he leans forward. My table creaks as he puts his large elbows on them.

"I know, darlin'. But this business is messed up. It always is." He stares at me pointedly. "It's like a can of worms that only opens from the inside. And often, you don't know your friends from your enemies."

I don't know much about Richter's work. But I am a journalist. I have some idea about how corrupt politicians can get and how people in power will do anything to forward their agenda. People like Richter lay down their lives for their country, but the people who send them to war are never who they seem to be.

I nod, stroking his hand. "You can't trust anyone, right? Apart from your own group."

A flicker of a smile crosses his lips. "Something like that. My men are like Cal to me: we're all brothers." The smile vanishes. "But we have a job to keep this country safe, and for that, we need to trust others as well."

"And sometimes the lines can get blurred."

He shrugs. "Yes. As long as—"

The phone on the table pings and vibrates. Richter looks at the number and frowns. "I gotta take this."

He answers, listens, and the frown spreads down from the knot of his eyebrows to his tightening jaws.

"Coming over now," he says then hangs up.

When I look at him expectantly, he shakes his head. "Guess you have a right to know. Samantha managed to find out where Jozdani's son is."

My eyes widen. "That's great news, right? Now you can track down Jozdani's ex-wife."

He lays his palms on the table and stands, then looks at me contemplatively. "When I said found, I didn't mean physically. They know who he is, but not *where* he is right now. But it's new intel, and I'll learn more at the office."

I stand too. "I'm coming with you."

He raises both hands. "Whoa. Easy. You're safe here for now. Brandon will keep watch outside, and I'll get another team to help him. I'll be back as soon as the meeting's over."

I cross my arms across my chest. It doesn't escape me that his eyes move down my chest as my arms accentuate the bulge of my breasts. It's totally unintentional, but the lustful light that springs in Richter's eyes is unmistakable. He has a slightly glazed look when he drags his eyes back up to my face.

"No way," I say softly. "I'm coming too."

CHAPTER 34
RICHTER

I can see from the defiant upward tilt of her chin that she means business. This is a new side to Dora that I'm beginning to see more of. I like it. She's confident, sassier. And it makes her sexy as hell. Just the way she stands, hips swung to the left, arms folded, full breasts invitingly raised, makes blood percolate all around my cock, making it twitch. I stare at her smoldering browns and swallow.

All I wanna do is pick you up and put you up on that bed. Again.

But I can't think like that. Hell, thinking is hard when she stands so close to me. When she strikes that pose. I stare at her like an idiot, drinking her in with my eyes. Then I shake my head.

"Don't make this difficult for me, sweetheart. I'll let you know what's happening, but I need to find out first."

She lifts an eyebrow. "Why can't I be there? Not like I don't know what's going on already."

"True, but that knowledge also puts you in danger." My teeth clamp down when I think of just how much risk she could be facing right now. It doesn't bear thinking about. And there it comes again—that horrible feeling that turns my desire to ash and dust. *It's me who dragged you into this mess. No one but me. If it hadn't been...*

Dora interrupts my thoughts by stepping closer. When our eyes meet, she leans into me. It's just so comfortable to feel her body against mine, softly cushioned against my chest. Her arm goes around my waist, and she hugs me, head tucked under my chin.

My eyes close. This feels so right. And that feeling—the thought of Viktor and his men now out there roaming the city for her—is so wrong. A cold hand wraps around my heart, and my eyes flare open. Anger and frustration suddenly burn in my bloodstream.

I wish it wasn't this way. But it is. Because this is what I do. Every day of my life, I've dodged bullets and hunted animals like Viktor.

How can I expose Dora to this life more than what I've done already?

Somewhere deep inside me, a voice whispers like a lonely echo in a deserted house. When I'm with her, I feel happiness that brings me a peace I've never known. My life has been one of strife and restless action. No woman but Dora has made me feel complete, safe, secure.

So am I holding on to her for my own selfish reasons?

Because if I really wanted what was best for her, should I not let her go?

Once Viktor is eliminated, so is the risk to her life. And once that's happened, she needs to return to a normal existence.

I owe her that much.

The sadness comes over me suddenly, like shutters drawn against the sunlight, and leaves me in a dark, cold place.

For her own good, I should let her go.

The words knock against my skull, reverberating in the empty corridors of my bare heart.

My eyebrows crease up, and I feel intense pain stabbing me, cleaving my heart in two clean halves.

My body must feel stiff, because I feel her moving against me.

"What's the matter?" she asks, her eyes now soft again, that mellow, melting chocolate that draws me deep into her soul. It's as if I can see into her mind, and with that frank, questioning stare, she can untangle the knots in mine. Before I know it, her hands come up and cup my face.

She smiles slightly and just looks at me.

I swear to god, I can feel teardrops in the backs of my eyes. I'm drowning, sinking slowly, throat closing with emotion.

I'm a hard son of a bitch, right? Give me a gang of terrorists to hunt down out in the deserts of nowhere. Give me days without water, nights without food, only the desire for danger burning like molten lava in my blood.

But don't give me this beautiful woman, a heaven-sent angel who has transformed my life. She's my sunset, my evening breeze, my blue sky and dappled diamonds that twinkle in the night sky, eternally out of reach. She's become my work and my rest, the sigh that settles down my pain. She's the dream in my sleep.

No, I don't deserve her.

I squeeze my eyes shut. My hands are like claws, shaking, as they reach up to cover hers. With light pressure, I drag them off my face.

What can I say?

I'm so damn scared of losing you in the future that it's best if we lose each other now?

Does that even make any sense?

What I do know is that the longer I leave it, the worse it's gonna get. Soon, I need to tell her. If someone shoots at me one day and she's in the way, it'll be worse than me taking a bullet. I can't have that, no way, no how, not while my heart beats.

I let out a deep breath then lean forward till our heads are touching. Her lips are so close I can feel them. Dear god, I want nothing more than to taste them again.

My voice is hoarse when I speak. "Sweetheart, let me go and see what Cal has to say. I'll be back soon, I promise."

I do mean that. No way in hell am I leaving her till all this has been sorted out. I don't know how to explain what's in my mind, and I have a feeling it's going to hurt her. But if I get blown up someday, in some forsaken corner of the world, she's only going to get hurt more.

No, I need to do what's right for her.

Her face lifts, and the warm invitation in her lips makes me groan. When our lips touch, it makes waves of heat unfurl slowly in my belly. I flick my tongue across her teeth, and she opens her mouth to let me in. Pretty soon, our tongues are entwined in a familiar electric, erotic dance, and she's grinding against my dick, moaning softly in her throat. A whimper. A catch. Shit if my hands don't reach down to knead the flesh of her butt, pulling her into the vortex of the heat that's suddenly claiming us.

Because this is what happens. We come together like an explosion in reverse, all bits and pieces, fragments of insecurity, wild emotion and pain, unspoken tears and loneliness, and we slowly fit together into a whole. Our sexual chemistry makes us inseparable, like a glue that binds us together, mind, body, and soul. It makes me complete.

Suddenly, her legs are up on my waist, and her arms are hooked around my neck. One of my hands is under her shirt, touching her breast, and as my forefinger and thumb pinch her nipple, she moans into my mouth.

I put her down on the table, her butt just missing the food tray by inches. Her hand is inside my shirt, pressing hard on my abdominal stack, and the touch is so full of heat I just want to press into it, into her.

We break the kiss to stare at each other for a few breathless seconds. Our mouths are open, panting. Just savoring the interlude because anticipation heightens the pleasure.

And that's when my phone pings again. Its insistent rattling on the tabletop is like a dog pawing against a door. Cal's number is flashing on the screen.

"Sorry," I mumble and reach for the damn thing.

"Not interrupting anything, am I?" my snarky brother says. I can feel his smirk down the line.

"I'm on my way," I growl. "All right?"

"You better be," Cal says, and I can detect the amusement in his voice. "Because there's like a national security issue that needs resolving? More important than your—"

"All right," I bark. I've moved away from Dora, and I give her a wink as she looks at me questioningly. The frustration in her eyes is plain.

"Hold your horses," I say to Cal. "I said I'm coming."

"Are you now?" Cal laughs down the line.

"Shut up, Cal," I tell him tersely. "I need a team down here while I'm gone. Brandon alone isn't enough. But not our guys. Is Team Onyx available? Or Team Cobalt."

Both Team Onyx and Cobalt are groups of ex–Special Ops Army guys, made up mainly of Army Ranger and Marine Recon, just like we are made up of ex-Delta guys. We worked together in black ops and now in this new venture.

Cal takes a moment to reply. "Yes. Shall I send three operatives from Onyx down?"

"ASAP. I'm hanging around till they arrive," I say. When Cal starts to object, I shut him down. "Too risky, Cal. If something happens, Brandon, good as he is, can't hold the fort on his own."

"I've got the National Security Advisor on live video link in ten minutes," Cal argues. "It's gonna take longer than that to send Team Onyx down, even if I send out the order now."

"Tell the NSA to wait," I say. "I ain't leaving till they're here. Got it?"

Cal's still grumbling as I hang up.

I've moved away from Dora and am leaning against the doorjamb with my back to her as I put the phone back in my pocket.

I feel her behind me and turn.

"What happened?" she asks.

I tell her then glance at my watch.

Dora says, "Call the other team back. I'm coming with you."

CHAPTER 35
DORA

I can sense a struggle in him. There's a dullness in his eyes that tells me his thoughts are far away. I know he's worried about me, and although he doesn't say it, I can see the tension lines etched on his face. It seems inexplicable to me, because I feel so safe when he's around. He's my shield, my aura of defense that can deflect any weapon. The way he walks around, it's impossible to think Richter could be worried about anything. But I guess he is, about me.

Secretly, that gives me a thrill. It shows that he cares. And I love that about him. Yes, I just said that. I'm not going to fight this warm bloom that spreads through me when I look at him like the first blush of spring in my wintry heart. I've not felt the depths of true emotion like I have with Richter. I've gone to new places with him, and it's made me a stronger person. Strange to think *so* much has happened in the last four days. It almost feels like my life got turned over, up and around, and the woman I see in the mental mirror is not the woman I was one week ago. Or maybe I *was* this woman, but she was hidden beneath my fears and insecurities.

I clear my throat. "I'm not going to sit here while you decide what's happening with my life, Richter. I have a right to know. Besides." I move closer to him and put a finger lightly on his chest. "Thank you for looking after me, but I can do that myself, too." I lean in and kiss his lips.

He passes a hand over his face then lifts his chin and rubs his beard. He steps away from me, head lowered.

"You saw firsthand what Viktor and his men were like." He looks up at me, and he must see the jolt of panic in my eyes. He comes over and puts both hands on my shoulders.

"I'm sorry. All I'm trying to say is, these guys are playing for the highest stakes. They won't stop until we stop them. And it's going to get bad before it gets any better."

I keep my face straight and ignore the drumbeat of my heart. "I know that. But I can help you, right? It was me who told you guys that there had to be a connection between Viktor and McGlashan. Otherwise, why would we both have been there that night? Who called us?"

Richter's long, meaty arms fall to his sides. "I don't know," he says, a note of frustration creeping into his voice. "I get what you're saying. I really do. But it doesn't change the fact that you'd be safer here."

"Maybe. But I could also be a sitting duck. After all, that's why you're getting reinforcements to guard the house. I can help you. I'm a journalist. I might know something that makes a difference."

His eyes narrow slightly. "Is there something you haven't told us yet?"

"No." I shake my head. "But I can help you make sense of this. Let me come with you, Richter. You know it makes sense."

He puts both hands on his hips, and his ropelike forearm muscles flex. "You don't have security clearance," he says quietly. "We don't allow civilians into our operations. These are deep state secrets, Dora. Men are killed for knowing what's going on."

The frisson of danger in his words makes me shiver.

He continues. "Some senior figures of the intelligence community will be calling in via video link. We can't let them see you."

"I could be in another room while you speak to them," I say with a shrug. "And I figure they must know about me. Your operation went wrong that night. Didn't they ask you for a reason why?"

Richter's mouth opens, and his sexy lips form an O as he rubs his chin. Then, unexpectedly, he grins.

"You're a smart cookie, you know that?"

He comes forward, holds my waist, and pulls me towards him. I put my head on his broad chest as his arm goes around my back. It feels snug, comfortable, like I belong. I can hear the thudding of his heart. He sighs once, deeply.

"Okay. I guess you're safer where I can keep an eye on you. Let's go."

CHAPTER 36
RICHTER

When I push through the doors of our top-floor suite, the place is a hive of activity. Sam and Cal are arguing in front of a laptop, pointing at the screen. Ken and Oliver are both talking on their phones, and four TV channels are on live—Al Jazeera, a Chinese state news channel, one Pakistani, and CNN. The TV screens hang from the wall and are on low, but the human voices are louder. All sounds die down as Dora and I enter the wide space.

I cough into my hand before speaking. "You guys know Dora from last time."

Only Samantha's voice breaks the silence. "Hi, Dora," she says with a wave.

Dora waves back. It's awkward, and I know the unspoken question in everyone's minds. Dora being present once was not okay, but they went with it. But is she now a part of this outfit? Will she be turning up on a regular basis?

We're a tightly knit group. Without question, these guys will follow my orders, and they know I'll lay my life down for them. It's not just Cal who's my brother; the rest are too. And Sam will always be my little sister.

I know how they feel about an outsider—which Dora is to them, I guess—coming into our fold.

Cal walks over to me. "What happened with Team Onyx?" he asks, eyeing Dora.

"They arrived. But I thought Dora would be safer here. Last-minute change of decision."

"I see." Cal's hard blue eyes move from me to Dora before settling on me again.

"Douglas and Preston will be on the video link soon," Cal says. "Dora can't be here when that happens."

Douglas and Preston are the heads of NSA and the ODNI, respectively.

"I know that," I say. "Dora will wait in the side room while we debrief them. What's the sitrep with Jozdani's son?"

Cal frowns. "Can I have a word with you?"

I notice Samantha has appeared behind Cal. She catches my eyes and gives me a brief nod. Sam can read the situation and the tension in the room. I'm grateful for her intervention.

Sam says to Dora, "Will you come with me? Let's get a coffee."

I glance at Dora and incline my head. She holds my eyes for a few seconds then agrees. The two women walk away. Cal stalks off towards the office, and I follow. He's standing in the middle of the room, arms folded, when I walk in and shut the door behind me.

Cal raises his voice. "What the hell are you playing at? I know she had to be here the last time because Viktor might've been chasing you. But this time, I even called Team Onyx out of a mission to be at her house. And after I did all that, you just bring her here?"

"She's involved in this as much as we are, Cal, can't you see that?"

"I know. But this is classified information, Rich. She doesn't have creds."

"She might know something that we don't." I hate the defensive tone in my voice. "You know a lot here doesn't add up. It was Dora who pointed out that there could be a link between McGlashan and Viktor. Why else was she there that night?"

Cal puts his hands up and shakes his head. "I totally get that. She's got brains, and she's more than useful. But…" He puts his palms by his sides, arms down. He communicates silently with his eyes. I know exactly what he's saying.

You know how badly this is messed up. Can we really risk a civilian getting hurt too?

My shoulders slump. I shove my clenched fists into my pockets and kick a chair. Cal watches me in silence. I can feel his eyes on me, so I look up eventually.

He's the same height as me but wirier. Cal has tensile strength in his limbs, while I have bulk. I've seen him take down men my size with ease. I could never match the grace with which he fights, but we can go at each other, round for round, and he knows he'll never beat me. Cal rolls his shoulders, the hardness melts from his eyes, and his jaws relax.

"You care about her."

His words hang in the air. His steely blues are fixed on me as he steps closer. When I say nothing, his eyes widen.

"Shit. It's more than that, right? You got it bad."

He's bending his neck, trying to look at me while I avoid him. He parks his butt on the edge of the long, rectangular twelve-seater table and folds his hands across his chest.

"You're in love with her," Cal says. It's a statement, not a question.

My head jerks up, and I stare at him, eyes wide. My heart knows the meaning of his words, even if my brain can't get it.

She's in everything I see, all I do. I guess that's why I've brought her here, into a highly classified meeting, unknown to even the Pentagon. Into a situation rife with risk and danger, just so I can keep a close watch on her.

Because I love her.

There, I just said it.

Sometimes that's the hard part, right? Being honest with oneself. To bare one's soul not to anyone else but to one's own scrutiny. For so long, what I've seen there isn't good. It's dark, cold, deserted. But when I look now, all I see is Dora and her light laughter, flowing like tendrils of fog rising from misty mountains.

And I smile. For the first time in many years, I smile to myself. Then I look up at my brother.

"I think I do."

Cal's face is alive. I know he's been worried about me slipping down a dangerous stream. It happens to many soldiers. We see things no one should see. Death, destruction on a scale that doesn't bear thinking about, never mind seeing with our own eyes. As a result, we can't talk about it to anyone. We carry scars no one can see.

In Cal's eyes, I see the hard glint, like he's trying to appraise me.

But not now. His eyes shine with happiness. He reaches out and clamps a hand on my shoulder.

"Good on you, bro. If she makes you happy, that's all that matters." His face changes. "That still leaves us with a situation here."

I stand and roll my head to loosen my neck. "Okay, let's do it this way. Let's keep Dora out of the way while we do the video con with Douglas and Preston. Sam can stay with her for company. Then we can fill her in."

Cal nods. "Cool."

"Now give me a sitrep."

Cal sighs and slides a hand down his face. "The boy is called Andre Asher. Asher is the mom's name. That's why we couldn't find him. None of the Jozdanis in the United States live around here. They're mostly around Los Angeles, where there's a large Persian community. And all of the Jozdanis there are law-abiding citizens, as far as we can see. None of them even visit Iran anymore."

"What about Andre Asher?"

"His birth certificate states his father was Amir Jozdani. But it's possible Jozdani had already left the country when the boy was born." Cal pauses for a beat then continues. "Maybe that's why he took his mom's name. He goes to college in Vermont. He's been missing for the last week. No one told the police or the FBI."

Something stirs inside me. I stare back at Cal. "That's weird, right? What about the college or his roommate?"

"The college was sent a note with a doctor's certificate saying that he needs time off for his mother's illness. Sam's got hold of all the documents online."

"And that's all true? So the boy is with his mother?"

Cal shakes his head and brings both hands up to emphasize his point. "No. That's where it gets weird. The mother's gone missing too. The medical certificate, which is from Sloan Kettering Hospital, stating she has cancer, is fake."

I frown. "How do you know the medical certificate is fake?"

"Sam rang Sloan Kettering and spoke to the medical director. He wouldn't give out confidential patient information, of course. But when the ODNI's chief of staff joined Sam and explained this was a matter of national emergency, he agreed. They don't have a Joanne Asher on their records. We got her photo from her passport and driver's license. Sam ran a face recognition check on their database. There's no match."

I digest this in silence. "Why would she do that? Make a fake certificate just to get her son out of college, I mean?"

Cal stares at me, his eyebrows lowered, blue eyes glinting. "We should speak to Sam. She worked the Sloan Kettering angle."

He picks up his phone and calls Sam. Within seconds, she knocks on the door. When Cal asks her to come in, she stands at the threshold.

"What're you doing?" I frown.

Sam looks from Cal to me. "Dora's with me," she says quietly. "I think you should hear what she has to say."

Cal stiffens immediately. I glance at him, giving him a curt nod. He clenches his jaw and waits for a beat but then nods back eventually.

"Bring her in," I say.

Sam's features sag with relief. Dora walks in behind her, and she shuts the door. I automatically walk up to Dora, giving her shoulders a squeeze. A light smile appears on her lips before vanishing just as fast as it came.

"You okay?" I ask.

She inclines her head in silence.

The four of us are standing. I offer Dora a seat, but she refuses. She's being brave, I can tell. This is a new situation for her, and seeing the way she looks at Cal quickly before averting her eyes back to me, I know she's aware of the tension radiating between us.

"Don't worry," I say softly, putting her attention back on me. "Everything we do is classified, right? Hence the need for secrecy. But we can count on you. I know that."

Even as I say the words, I wrestle with their meaning. I'm dragging Dora deeper into this. Is that what I want?

Hell no.

But right now, what other choice do we have?

Dora's voice is steady and clear when she speaks. "Yes, you can." She gives both Cal and Sam a meaningful look. I see Sam smile back.

I keep my hand on the small of her back and face my siblings. Cal's features are soft, his eyes wider as he stares back at us.

I address Sam. "We were talking about Joanne and Andre Asher. Joanne's medical records are definitely fake?"

Sam nods. "For sure. The director at Sloan Kettering said it takes planning to make fake documents like she did. Even he was fooled at first. It seems like Joanne Asher had been preparing to do this for a while."

"But why?" Cal asks.

I hold up my hand and tick off the points on my fingers. "We can't answer the whys right now. But let's see what we do know. Jozdani appears in the United States, travelling on a fake passport. Then he goes underground, but presumably he's still in the country. Around the same time, Joanne Asher fakes an illness. She uses that to get her son out of college, and I'm sure she takes time out from work as well, right?" I address the question to Sam.

In return, she lifts an eyebrow toward Dora. Something passes between my sister and Dora, and it's noticeable.

"You think Jozdani being here at the same time was a coincidence?" Cal's voice is steely, jaw tight.

"This is weird," I say, trying to think. "Jozdani is a key figure in the Iranian nuclear industry. He divorced this woman a long time ago, right? Hasn't he married again in Iran?"

Sam speaks up again. "He has, but he doesn't have any children from the second marriage."

"So this is his only son? And he's now vanished?"

It's Dora who replies, and all eyes turn to her. "None of this is a coincidence," she says.

CHAPTER 37
DORA

I take a deep breath. Sam's looking at me, encouragement in her eyes. I take heart from it. We've been talking for a while, and when she realized I know a lot about the case, she opened up to me with some details. She's a nice girl despite the tough exterior. A lot like her brothers, I guess.

"Go on, sweetheart," Richter says.

Our eyes meet, and my heart fills as I note the proud smile on his face.

"Joanne Asher worked for the *Washington Herald*," I say, indicating Sam. "We checked her out. I have a friend who works for the *Herald*. Joanne hasn't been to work for the last two months because of her illness."

"Which we now know is fake," Sam adds.

I continue. "My friend also gave us access to what Joanne was working on before she took time off: a story about Senator McGlashan. He's former CIA and was stationed in Moscow in the 1980s. There are rumors of McGlashan being close to members of the KGB, and she had made some contacts in Brighton Beach, Norfolk, where there's a big Russian immigrant community. One of the families there knew McGlashan when he was stationed in Moscow."

They are listening to me with rapt attention. I continue.

"And he has presidential ambitions. Again, these are whispers in the corridors of Capitol Hill that my friend is aware of."

Richter's broad forehead muscles are contracted. "So, hang on. You were called to that house in Dale City for some dirt on McGlashan, right?"

I raise an eyebrow. "Too much of a coincidence that Joanne Asher has disappeared now?"

"That's what I was thinking. It's possible that Joanne called you to that house but didn't turn up."

Richter narrows his eyes, and his head swings from me to Cal. He says, "I was there before anyone arrived. I checked the place out, all three floors of it. It was empty."

I say, "So Joanne definitely wasn't there."

Richter says, "More importantly, I didn't find her dead body."

A shiver crawls up my spine, chilling my bones. Richter sees the look in my face and comes close and puts an arm around my shoulder.

"I'm sorry," he murmurs in my ear. "Just thinking aloud."

I guess he has nothing to hide from his siblings, both of whom are staring at us. Cal and Sam exchange a glance, and from the smirk on Sam's face, I can see they both know about us.

We're silent for a while, only the ticking of the clock on the wall tracking our thoughts.

Sam says to me, "Tell them the rest, Dora."

I fold my arms across my chest. "I know she wasn't at the house, but it's still possible that Joanne was the informant. For whatever reason, she's gone into hiding. But she knows something about McGlashan, and she wants me to know about it."

Richter asks, "And you've never been in touch with Joanne? I mean, from a professional point of view?"

I shake my head.

"It's McGlashan's Russian connection that I'm worried about," Richter says, a forefinger tapping his chin, eyes on his boots. He raises his head to look at me then at the others.

"And the fact that he might have threatened Joanne, hence she had to disappear."

Sam adds, "And took her son with her. Might have threatened him too."

I say, "To keep Joanne's story from leaking out. If McGlashan does have Russian connections, that could scupper his presidential ambitions."

Cal speaks up. "Where does Jozdani fit into all this?"

I've been thinking about this too, and I tell them what I figure is logical. "Maybe Joanne Asher sent him word that his son's life was in danger. That brought him here."

Richter shakes his head. "Jozdani hasn't been back to the United States for more than twenty years as far as we know, right?" I point to Sam, and she nods.

Sam says, "But if he came on a false passport, we might not have known. Just like he did this time. We only have data on his real name from the State Department. Maybe he stayed in touch with his family here and visited them occasionally on the same fake identity he used now?"

Richter nods, his slate grays hard and glinting. "It's his only son. He might have made the trip. Also, he wasn't famous till the last two to three years. It's only with facial-rec software that the CIA managed to pick him up in Heathrow and JFK."

I complete the thought for him. "So if he made the trip earlier, no one detected it."

Richter passes a hand over his beard, a movement I like making myself, feeling his soft bristles on my hand. Mind you, those soft bristles have also tickled my....see, that's the problem with staring at his sexy face for too long. My cheeks grow warm as I look to the floor.

Richter says, "First things first. Sam, find everything you got on Joanne Asher, her son, and McGlashan. Andre Asher must have a phone, and cell phones send out a signal for five days from being switched off. Have we tried to find it?"

Sam nods. "Yup. And no, there's no signal and no location from Andre's phone."

Richter curses under his breath.

I say, "I think we can get more clues from McGlashan. He's at the center of this."

Cal says, "I agree with Dora."

There's a brief pause as my eyes meet Cal's. He's as intense as Richter is, but physically, he's different. His vivid blue eyes are arresting, and in the slope of his angular jawline, I can see the similarity with his brother. He's definitely a looker, and I'm sure he's broken a few hearts. Of course, I only have eyes for Richter.

Cal's words are significant, however, because right from the start, I think he's been skeptical about letting me into their fold. I know the reason, and I understand it, too. He smiles at me then shakes his head.

"I never thought a civilian could make a difference to our investigation. But you have, Dora, and I guess I have to thank you for that."

My heart warms, and I sense Richter step closer to me. I feel a weight of emotion in my throat as he stares down at me, that familiar heat settling low in my belly as he hooks me with his eyes. His hand reaches out and touches me gently on the shoulder.

He whispers, "You don't even know how much you've helped us, sweetheart." He's leaning dangerously closer, considering we're not alone, when there's a knock on the door.

Richter straightens. "Come in," he barks.

Another guy comes in. He's the blond, good-looking guy they call Ken. He's younger than Richter and Cal. Ken shuts the door behind him. He's got a swagger in his gait, hot as hell, and he comes to a stop right next to Richter.

I'm surrounded by three ridiculously hot alpha heroes, all sexy eyes and bulging muscles, trying to keep my eyes off all of them and toward Sam. How does she manage to get any work done around here?

As if she knows what's on my mind, she grins and winks at me, making my cheeks warm again.

Ken addresses Richter and Cal. "Douglas is on the video link."

CHAPTER 38
RICHTER

Patrick Douglas is the head of the National Security Agency, and together with Derek Auster, the director of National Intelligence, is one of the two men we take orders from. It's not a good idea to keep him waiting.

But I feel bad about leaving Dora. I meant every word I said. She really has no idea how much she's helped us. As the others file out, she sits down on a chair.

"Give me a minute," I say to Cal, who nods in silence then shuts the door on his way out.

I kneel before Dora, putting my hand on her thigh. She covers her hand with mine, and it's so soft and warm. Her touch spreads up my arm, into my chest then my heart. I tilt myself upward and kiss her lightly on the lips.

"You did so well, honey. I'm sorry I have to leave you here, but believe me, Douglas can't know about you."

She reaches out a hand, and a finger trails down the side of my face. Sparks fly down my spine, and my eyes close.

"I know," she says in a husky voice. "Go and do what you have to."

I hold her hand and kiss it. Then I stand and salute. "Yes, ma'am."

Dora laughs, and it's a pure, crystal, musical sound, like the pealing of church bells on a summer morning. I just want to hold her again, but like she said, I have a job to do.

Giving her a quick smile, I step outside. Cal is standing to one side, just out of view of the video screen, where I can see Douglas's face. It's a three-way video conference with the ODNI in his office. Once we're done, the DNI will brief the president, and then we get final approval for all our missions. For reasons of security, we never have direct contact with the DNI or the president.

Cal's face is pinched and tight. He doesn't waste his words. "McGlashan was working for the CIA in Moscow when Dad was stationed there."

My jaw clenches, feeling the dark poison suddenly poured into my soul. "Exactly what I was thinking. Not sure if there's any connection, but we need to grill McGlashan, right?"

"Damn right." Cal speaks between tightly clenched teeth.

"Let's speak to Douglas first and deal with this later," I say, moving toward the screen, where the others have gathered.

Patrick Douglas is in his sixties, with white hair and glittering black eyes. He's a DC veteran, and not much escapes the wily old operator.

I explain what's happened so far, including our recent discussion with Dora. I omit Dora's name, of course, and mention only our team.

Douglas thinks about it for a while then gives us authorization to chase Andre and Joanne Asher if it will lead to Jozdani.

"But we don't have jurisdiction to arrest on U.S. soil. Nor can we shoot anyone unless in self-defense," I remind Douglas.

"Yes," the older man says in his gravelly voice. He's a straight-talking son of a gun. "Like the time you missed out on getting Viktor."

"That was different." I feel my hackles rising, but I control my temper. "If I have Viktor in my sights again, he won't escape. You got my word on that."

"Sorry if that's a tad unfair," Douglas remarks impassively. "You had the civilian there. Where is she now?"

It's my turn to remain deadpan. "In a safe house."

"She's the daughter of Michael Simpson. The media tycoon. Right?"

Douglas's eyes are boring into me. Not much goes past this guy.

"Yes, sir. We've taken her back home, and she's in contact with her family. She'll be protected."

Douglas nods. "Make sure of that. Regarding Viktor, make good on your word, Richter. Our patience is wearing thin. Get Viktor and Jozdani. I'll get you authorization from the State Department."

Cal says, "Sir, what do we do about Senator McGlashan?"

Douglas frowns for the first time. "From what you've told me, it's all speculation. As far as I know, there's no rumors about McGlashan having Russian connections. Joanne Asher is a journalist, and she can investigate what she wants. But just because she was investigating this frankly bullshit story about McGlashan's past doesn't mean her disappearance has anything to do with the senator."

He glares back at us for a while. I have a disturbing sensation at the back of my mind, and for some reason, the hairs rise on my neck as if I sense danger.

Douglas says, "The main person of interest is Jozdani. Get him, and the rest falls in line. Find out why Viktor is chasing after Jozdani, too."

"Yes, sir," I rumble, and then the line cuts out, leaving the screen blank. I stare at the white surface, thoughts screaming around my head. Cal turns to me.

"Was it me, or did it sound like Douglas is tight with McGlashan?"

"They're both politicians, so anything is likely."

"The DNI's going to be involved as well. Maybe both of them will vouch for McGlashan."

"Fuck them all," I say through gritted teeth. I hold Cal's eyes. "Someone sent you a letter saying Viktor killed Dad, right?"

I watch as a smoldering fire leaps into Cal's eyes. "Yes."

"And we still don't know who that was, but I think we're getting closer to the answer. Dora is right. We don't know where Viktor, Joanne, or Andre is. So McGlashan is the only person within sight. Let's get closer to him."

CHAPTER 39
DORA

I'm safely ensconced inside Richter's GMC Yukon. I've got my legs drawn up, chin on knees, staring out the tinted windows as the lights on Franklin Avenue flash past. He says nothing, but the way he sits, back ramrod straight, eyes fixed on the road, one hand gripping the wheel tightly, I can tell he's preoccupied.

But I don't get why he's been so quiet since we left the Cyborg Security office. Cal actually shook my hand as we said goodbye. From the genuine smile on his face and the warmth of his handshake, I could tell he was more relaxed with me, and it was a major thaw to the initial icy reception I got. Sam gave me a hug, and I've got her number now. Whatever happens, I think Sam and I could be friends.

All of which makes Richter's aloofness harder to fathom. I sneak glances at him, and normally we would catch each other's eyes and start laughing, but that's not happening now.

I decide to break the silence. "Are you angry with me?"

The words seem to penetrate his ears slowly. He frowns then shakes his head before glancing at me.

"Sweetheart, whatever you do, I could never be angry with you."

"Then what is it?"

He shakes his head. "I don't know who to trust. Whose word to take. As a soldier, I'm used to following orders. But in this world, it's all smoke and daggers."

I'm relieved that he's not upset with me. I reach out and rub his arm. He reaches out and we hold hands. We drive in companionable silence for a while. I cherish these moments I have with him, when neither of us needs to speak just for the sake of it.

Eventually, he does. His voice is lower, harder. "And I'm also worried about you. Caught in the middle of this mess."

"We're almost through it," I surprise myself by saying. "I can feel it."

Richter's looking at me, and I meet his eyes before he switches attention back to the road.

"I'm not so sure," he says. Then a note of bitterness creeps into his voice. "But I wish we were."

"What do you think about Joanne's story with McGlashan?" I ask.

"I think it's important," he says. "Despite what Douglas said. Can you get hold of the story Joanne was doing?"

"I can try. Daphne, who works for the *Herald*, is Julia's friend actually. I've met her a couple of times, no more. But I will ask her."

"That's great. For tonight, I might go and stake out McGlashan's office then his home. See what I find."

"Sounds like a good idea," I say. We've arrived at my apartment, and he pulls over. "What time are we leaving?"

His eyebrows turn north. "We? There's no 'we' here, sweetheart. Just me and Brandon."

We're sitting in the car, and our bodies are half lit by the yellow streetlights. A drizzle has started, and the roads are turning slick with rain. I open my mouth to protest, but it becomes a gasp of fright.

A black shape streaks out of my house. It runs across our car, jumps over the hood of another parked vehicle, then vanishes. Richter's seen it too. His movements are lightning fast. Before I can say a word, he's out of the Yukon, sprinting across the road in pursuit. He yells something at me, but I'm still in the car and can't hear him.

It all happens so quickly. Richter's big body is a blur as he runs to the opposite side, dodging a car, then disappears between two parked ones. I can't see the black shape that came out of my building. I can barely see Richter. Farther up the street, I see the headlights of a car spring to life. It moves out then takes off with a roar of its engines. I strain my eyes, searching for Richter. All of a sudden, I'm afraid. I didn't hear shots, but what if a silenced weapon was used?

The thought of Richter being wounded is too much for me to bear. I know he's armed and more than capable of taking care of himself, but he still might need my help. I open the door and step out into the drizzle. I run across the empty road, reaching the bank of parked cars. I slide between two SUVs to the dark pavement. In the distance, there's a tepid glow from a streetlight, but otherwise the street's in darkness. I can't see a body lying on the ground. The car that left must've been the getaway vehicle, and it was about thirty yards away, I guess. I start to run, my eyes peeled for a dark shape on the ground.

"Dora!"

The shout comes from behind me. It's Richter's voice. He runs up toward me, and we hug each other. My forehead touches the wet surface of his jacket, and I feel his chest rising with rapid breaths. His arms are around me, holding me in place.

He gasps when he speaks. "We need to get out of here, sweetheart. Why did you leave the car?"

"I came to look for you." I look up at him, his face shadowed in the half light.

An inscrutable emotion flits across his face, twisting his lips downward, pulling his eyebrows low. It's as if he's in pain. His jaw hardens, and he pulls me closer. His head lowers till we're touching.

"Don't worry about me, darling. I'll be okay. It's you I'm worried about."

I can feel warmth radiating from him, surrounding me in a halo. He's holding me close to him, and he doesn't want to let go. I'm more than happy to stay molded to him, but I feel unrest in him, a disquiet that he won't give words to but that I can sense nevertheless.

"When I didn't see you in the car…" He leaves the sentence unfinished. He pulls me tighter, and his face lowers farther, till our lips touch in a light kiss. He kisses my closed eyes, then my forehead, and it's so tender, so beautiful, I feel myself melt inside.

"Never do that again, darling. Never come out to look for me, okay?" His voice is gentle. I look up, catching a glitter in his eyes as he stares at me.

"Okay," I whisper. "Glad you're okay."

He straightens suddenly, his head whipsawing around as if he's heard something. He touches his left ear, and I become aware of the black object embedded there.

"Yes, moving," he says tersely, obviously speaking to someone else. "Had to find Dora first." He winks at me then pulls on my hand. I run to keep up with him.

"How far is he?" Richter says to the person on the other line.

We're back in the car, and he fires the engine up. I see a screen appear on the dashboard. There's not much to see at first, but then I see traffic, stopped at lights.

"Yes, I see him," Richter says, pulling out. "Stay on him, I'm a couple of miles behind."

CHAPTER 40
DORA

Richter puts his microphone feed into the loudspeaker. He points to the screen on the dashboard.

"That's the drone feed from above your house. It stays up there 24/7 now. Unfortunately, no one was looking at the footage earlier today, or we would've seen that man go into your house."

Sam's voice comes across on the speaker. "Dora's apartment is clear. Logan from Team Onyx just checked it. No break-in."

"You sure?" I ask, clearing my throat.

"Positive," Sam says. Then her voice changes. "Dora, are you all right?"

"I'm fine. I left the car to make sure Richter wasn't hurt."

Sam's voice has an edge of reproach to it. "You shouldn't have done that. Something bad could've happened."

I don't know what to say. I acted on impulse. I went out without thinking, because the man I love could've been hurt.

I stop, stunned. All thoughts crash together in my head, leaving me in the sudden blinding light of a silent explosion.

Did I just think that? *The man I love?*

It's almost as if I said the words out loud. But the admission, even to myself, is breathtaking. But it's not surprising. I'm closer to Richter than I've been to anyone in my life. My mother died before I had any memories of her. My brother and father have always been cold to me. Has Richter filled a void in my heart?

I feel a lightness in my head, a glow that makes me tingle all over, like the ends of my fingers and toes are lit up, shining in the darkness.

"....not advisable, even if you were armed." Sam is still speaking, and I've barely heard her. I catch the last few words.

"Hello, Dora? You still there?" Sam asks, her tone quizzical. Richter turns slightly to give me a funny look.

"Yeah, I'm here. Gotcha, no sweat." I'm speaking faster than usual, and I can feel my heart beating wildly.

Sam signs off. I glance at the screen and see the car we're chasing clearly for the first time. The drone feed has zoomed in. It's a Ford sedan, an old model. The feed zooms out again, giving us a wide-angle view of the road. The car's makes a right turn off the ramp into a quieter road, and Richter speeds up.

I see a sign for Mulberry Hills. There are only two cars ahead of us, and one is the Ford we're chasing. Large houses on secluded plots loom on either side of us, hidden behind tall security walls. I notice Richter has killed the lights already.

"Well, your stalker sure lives in an expensive part of town," he observes drily. One car ahead takes a turn, but the Ford stays on course, and now it's only us on this road.

The speaker crackles to life. "I've got news for you," Sam announces. "McGlashan lives in Mulberry Hills. And his mansion is half a mile away, on the right."

"Damn," Richter mutters.

"What's your plan of action?" Sam asks.

Richter's face is carved in concentration. His eyes are fixed on the car ahead. I see his jaw clench, and his forearm muscles bunch together in a hard pack as he grips the wheel.

He speaks to me.

"Get in the back, Dora." His eyes slide to me. There's a glint in them I haven't seen before. "Now," he says.

"What're you gonna do?" I ask. My hands are claws, digging into the seat.

"I need to stop him before he gets inside. Sam, how far are we from McGlashan's house?"

"It's a hundred yards up."

Richter touches the gas pedal, and the Yukon surges ahead.

"I've got no choice," Richter says through gritted teeth, addressing me. "I wish you weren't here. But how long can we let this guy stalk you? If we can get him to talk, we can blow this case wide open. He might even know where Joanne is."

I swallow and lick my dry lips. "Do it, Richter. Do it now."

He glances at me and blinks. I'm not sure what I read in his eyes, but the earlier hardness is gone.

He lets out a ragged breath. "I'm sorry. Get in the back, lie down on the floor, and cover your head with your hands."

I do as I'm told.

"Sam, I need backup," Richter says. "Where's Team Onyx?"

"They're still at the house, but Brandon's just coming off the ramp for Mulberry Hills. ETA two minutes."

"I haven't got two minutes," Richter bites out.

I lift my head from the spacious floor of the backseat. We're so close to the Ford even I can see the driver.

"Get down," Richter yells. I lower my head but keep a line of sight. The Yukon lurches to the left, overtaking the sedan. The two cars are side by side, and I get a glimpse inside the car. There's only one driver, and his head's covered in a black hood. I can see his white knuckles clutching the wheel tightly.

I almost fall to the floor as the two cars collide. There's a ripping, tearing sound as metal clashes against metal. The Yukon pushes the smaller Ford to the side of the road then comes to a stop. Richter jumps out of the car. Holding the gun with his left hand, he opens the driver's door. He drags the driver out, holding him by the scruff of his neck. The driver falls to the road, and Richter lifts him up like a rag doll, pushing the barrel of the gun to his head. He makes him kneel then frisks his pockets quickly. Then he makes the driver stand and shoves him over the hood of the Yukon, patting him down. Lastly, he yanks the hood off his head.

Richter freezes. So do I. My mouth is wide open, and my heart is slamming like a jackhammer against my ribs.

CHAPTER 41

DORA

The driver is a woman. Her honey-tinted hair falls in a heap around her face. She says something to Richter that I can't hear, but I can see he's even more surprised. He shakes his head, blinks, then looks behind her. I follow his eyes, not least because I'm drawn by the security lights that have suddenly blinked to life in the house opposite.

Richter moves quickly. He opens the passenger door and shoves the woman inside. Then he runs around the vehicle. As he gets into the car, I hear a swish, like air being let loose from a cycle tire. It comes again, and there's a thud on the window to my left. A spiderweb appears, spreading down the window.

"Shots fired!" Richter hollers into the speaker. He floors the gas pedal, and I'm thrown backward on the floor as the Yukon zooms off.

"Dora!" Richter shouts. "Are you okay?"

"I'm fine!" I scream back. "Let's get out of here!"

He needs no encouragement. I don't know how big the engine is, but it sure as hell is a big car, and it's moving so fast I can feel the windows rattling. I can't help but stare at the crack on the window, much larger now, and I'm just glad the glass is bulletproof.

*****

We're parked outside my building. Another Yukon is there, and I can make out Ken and Brandon as they come out of the car when they see us.

"Stay here," Richter says and jumps out. He speaks tersely to his buddies, who go into my house, presumably to check its safety. Richter waves at me then indicates that he's going to do a recon around my house. I give him a thumbs up.

Then my curious gaze falls on the woman in the front seat. Her head is bowed. When I touch her shoulder, she shivers then turns to face me.

I get my first proper look at her. She's in her late fifties, I'd guess, younger than my dad, but she looks older. No makeup, hair loose with bags under her eyes. She's thin as a rake, and her cheeks are sunken.

"I'm Joanne Asher," she says. She stares at me till her dark eyes narrow. She lifts a finger to point at me. "You're Dora Simpson, right?"

I'm too stunned to speak. Thoughts burst and crackle in my head like it's the Fourth of July.

"You...you're Joanne Asher?" I mumble, finally.

"Yes. Sorry for stalking you. But I was threatened after planning to meet you in Dale City. That's why I didn't turn up and went into hiding."

I shake my head, trying to clear the confusion. "But why didn't you just call me? Or arrange another place to meet?"

"I was pretty sure my phone was being tapped. And I started seeing a black Lincoln Escalade parked outside my house and following me around."

"Virginia plates?" I asked.

She nods.

Could be Viktor's men, I think to myself. *The car certainly fits.*

"Where's your son?" I ask.

Her face crumples. "I don't know. I was going to ask you the same question."

I shake my head. "Sorry, Joanne. I have no idea."

She rests her face against the seat and pushes her forehead into it before raising her head. "Bastards," she hisses in anger. "They took my son."

"Who? Who took your son?"

Joanne takes a moment to reply. Her nostrils quiver, and I see a shadow cross her face. "I don't know. But McGlashan played a part in it, I'm sure. My ex-husband told me he would try to kidnap Andre to put pressure on him."

I stare at Joanne's disheveled face, her haggard, pinched cheeks and ghostlike eyes. The trauma she's suffered is written all over her harrowed features.

But before she can speak further, Richter appears. He opens the driver's door and looks at me, then his eyes slide to Joanne.

He's breathing hard, and his shirt is drenched in sweat as if he's been running.

"We need to get inside," he says. "The house and this area are secure. If anyone suspicious appears within a five-mile radius, our ISR will pick them up."

ISR—that's a term I learned recently from Sam.

"Intelligence, surveillance, and recon, right?" I say.

He looks at me, his expression barely changing. His eyes are dark, glittery, wide, and he's in a world of his own, a world that I'm only getting a glimpse of. For some reason, his stare sends goosebumps down my arms.

"Yes," he says. Then he opens the back door, motioning me to get out.

I take his outstretched hand, and with a gentle pull, he makes me rest against his broad chest. He shuts the door so Joanne can't see. I'm so close our faces are almost touching. His breaths are humid and hot, and I can see the sheen of sweat shining on his forehead. A heady cocktail of danger and excitement radiates from him, heating up my core.

Why does a knot of desire let itself loose deep in my gut? I don't know, but when his hand slides down mine and grips my waist, I move closer to him. A need to be close to him unfurls in my belly, fanning liquid heat between my thighs. I silence the whimper that rises up in my throat.

"Are you all right?" His voice is hoarse. "I'm so sorry. That bullet hit the glass. It didn't come in, right?"

His whole body is coiled tight like a steel spring. His intense eyes are devouring my face. My mouth opens as his gaze slides down to my lips. But he raises them quickly, searching my face. He needs reassurance.

I put a hand on his chest, feeling the damp warmth and the loud thud of his heart.

"Hey, I'm fine," I say in my best soothing voice. "Nothing happened. Yes, the bullet stayed out. Don't worry."

Some of the rigidity dissipates from his body, but he's still on high alert. He holds my hand and places himself behind me. Brandon appears with Joanne. Ken and Olli are ahead of us, and we move in formation, Joanne and me sandwiched by a human shield.

Once we are in, Richter barks out instructions.

"Minimal lights. Shut the blinds. Hands over flashlights. Ken, look after Joanne, fix her a drink. Brandon, Olli, stay outside. Is Onyx Team still here?"

"Roger that," Brandon says.

Richter turns to me. "Will Joanne fit your clothes? Both of you need to change, right?"

I nod, and together we head upstairs. When we're in my room, Richter shuts the blinds then goes out and looks all over the top floor. It's been searched already, but he's being double sure.

"Can I put the table lamp on the floor and turn it on?" I ask when he comes back.

"Yes, sweetheart."

He comes closer. His eyes are ignited with a fire I haven't seen before. Flames are leaping in the light grays, burning like hot coal.

"You sure you're all okay? If something happened to you back there, I'd never be able to…"

Words are lost in his mouth as his gaze travels down my body, his hands sliding down my shoulders, back, hips, and thighs as if he's searching me. But I know he's making sure I'm not hurt or wounded anywhere. It's an infinitely tender, beautiful act, and when he kneels before me, checking my legs, my heart almost breaks.

I kneel to his level and hold his face in my palms. The pain is obvious in the twist of his lips and the vacant, hollow look in his eyes.

"I'm fine, Richter. Really, I am."

Our breaths are mingling, passions colliding, igniting heat and desire that fan into our veins like a forest fire of lust. His lips sink into mine, firing electric tentacles of heat that tingle down my neck into my spine. I arch my body into his and open my mouth to let him in. Our tongues entwine in naked passion, roaming, circling, playing with each other. His left hand is on my breast, sliding under my shirt. I whimper as he lightly pinches one rock-hard nipple. His mouth leaves mine. My back is against the wardrobe, and I sag against it as his hand expertly unbuttons my jeans while his luscious tongue licks my neck and his teeth nip my skin.

When his thumb touches my clit, an explosion of sensation shudders through my belly, weakening my knees. His hand slides down my sodden panties, and a finger enters my slick pussy. He slides it in and out, that wicked-as-sin thumb circling, teasing the hard nib of my clit like there's no tomorrow. His arm is hooked around my waist, steadying me, while his mouth comes back to mine, licking and sucking on my lips.

I'm seeing bright-yellow and white flashing stars, that geyser of heat blowing way down deep in my belly again, shooting heat into every pore of my skin. I'm breathing hard and fast, and oh god, it's coming, happening again, that glorious orchestra of clashing music, that enormous waterfall bearing me there, right there, over the edge. And I'm so glad his mouth covers mine as he stifles my scream, but I'm gone, washed over, shooting up and high over all the flashing, exploding stars in the bright open sky. My pussy contracts over his fingers as if it wants to hold on forever, and the spasms shudder through my body.

I sag against his arm and the wardrobe. I'm spent, light, wavy, oh boy, whatever. I can barely breathe.

Did I just have the best orgasm of my life standing up?

I don't have time to think as Richter scoops me up in his arms and deposits me on the bed. He leaves me to check that the door is locked. My cheeks flame scarlet, and he grins at me as we both realize it wasn't!

He locks the door then rips off his clothes. The grooves and ridges of his hard muscles are lit up from below, and he seems like a

Hercules from another world. As he slides off his pants then his boxers, his dick springs free. The thick, impressive organ bobs in the air as he approaches the bed. I come off the bed and kneel in front of him. I want to taste him.

As I lick the precum then slide my tongue over the head, he moans. When I engulf him in my mouth, he moans louder, and his hand rests on the back of my head. I slide my mouth along his length, using the tip of my tongue to tickle the underside near the head. He grunts with pleasure when I do that.

"Right there," he gasps. I feel his knees bend when I flick that sensitive spot under the head with my tongue again.

He sits on the bed, and I lick his shaft then engulf him again.

"Stop, darling, you're gonna make me cum." His hands are on my shoulders, and I rise. We kiss as his fingers unbutton my shirt. Within seconds, his mouth is on my nipple, even as his other hand is pulling down my panties.

He breaks off to scoot over to his jeans and take out a condom. I'm lying on the bed as he comes back, covering my body with his gently. The feel of his whole body on me sends shivers of warm delight everywhere. He takes care not to crush me then kneels by my feet. He puts the condom on, then kisses up my leg into my upper thighs. When his shoulders gently nudge my legs apart, I gasp. Can my soaking-wet pussy take another delicious onslaught from his ravishing mouth?

I might just melt—oh god, he just dives in!

No messing about this time. His tongue is just lapping at my folds like a hungry love monster, spreading my lips, diving inside. Then his mouth rises, and his tongue tickles my swollen clit, causing the earth to jerk, fractalize, move under me. I moan, my right hand clutching the back of his head. His tongue is relentless, moving from my clit back to my silken folds in repeated movements. Then he rises and leans over to kiss me. The smell and taste of myself on my lips almost sends me over the edge.

"My turn, sweetheart," he says huskily. I feel him settle between my legs, and the head of his organ pushes at my center folds. Then he slides inside me, that delicious, all-encompassing sensation of being warm and fulfilled shooting all over me. I hold his elbows as he pushes himself to the hilt and holds himself there, buried balls deep. I lift the small of my back and wriggle down, greedy for more of his erect manhood.

He slowly pulls out, then slides back in again. Slowly he builds up a rhythm. He's slamming into me soon, with deep, satisfying grunts from his enormous chest. He speeds up, and my legs come up on his shoulders. He's fucking me fast and furiously soon, bending over me.

I'm quivering, melting, seeing the stars appear again as the ceiling rocks and shakes in my eyes. The heat builds and builds till my pussy clamps down hard on his dick, and I cry out, arching my back off the bed.

Seconds later, he grunts out my name and thrusts once, twice, then goes rigid. I can actually feel his dick elongate and spasm, rippling inside me, through the condom. We cling to each other for seconds, for eternity, suspended in that white-flash moment of pure ecstasy between life and death as we come together in a mind-bending wave of orgasm.

Then he rolls off me, collapsing in a heap. We rest awhile, getting our breaths back.

Then he raises himself on one elbow and leans over me. We kiss gently.

"Where did that come from?" he says, a teasing smile on his lips. With his thumb, he rubs the corner of my lip. "Don't tell me you get off on dangerous situations now." His eyes are hooded, and there's a smirk on his lips.

"Never been in a situation like this," I say. My fingers flit over his neck and shoulders. "But then again, I've never been with—"

"Someone like me?" His eyes become darker and his face more serious.

"Yes," I whisper.

He stares at me for a while, then lifts my hand and kisses the fingers. His voice is tight with emotion when he speaks. "If I could only tell you how much you helped me, sweetheart, you wouldn't believe me."

"Helped you with what?" I ask.

He doesn't answer for a while. A moment passes between us, heavy with the weight of suppressed words. Finally he leans over to kiss me and then whisper in my ear.

"With everything."

Then he looks around the room and gets off the bed. He gets dressed quickly.

"I better get downstairs to see if Joanne's all right. She's got a lot to say, right?"

I scoot off the bed as well, searching for my clothes on the floor. "Yes, she does. You go down first, I'll follow in a minute. In fact, do you want to send Joanne upstairs? She might find it easier to get changed here."

He smiles sheepishly. "Yeah, good point."

He vanishes down the stairs, and I can hear voices through the open door. I rummage in my dresser and take out a long skirt, underwear, and a blouse.

There's a knock on the door, and Joanne appears. She's tied her hair back and looks more composed than earlier. But the trouble in her dark eyes is deep, and staring at her gaunt face, I feel sorrow stirring inside me. From her red-rimmed eyes, I can tell she's been crying.

She's lost everything, it seems, but mainly her son. I pull her into a hug. Her cheeks are wet when we disengage.

"We'll find Andre, okay? You just need to tell us everything that happened, right from the start."

She nods and wipes her face on her sleeves. I give her the clothes then show her the bathroom on the upper floor where she can get changed.

"Stay away from the windows," I warn her. "And lower the blinds before you turn on the lights."

CHAPTER 42
DORA

When Joanne is ready, we go downstairs. Richter is leaning against the doorframe of the kitchen, biting into an apple. He raises his eyebrows and smiles when he sees me. My kitchen and dining room are open plan, and Brandon is at the concertina doors at the back, staring outside. It's dark, so there's not much to see, but he's still staring intently. He turns when he hears us.

"Hey," I say to Richter and brush past him to the kitchen counter. He follows me.

"Are you hungry?" he asks, leaning over my shoulder. I don't miss the glint in his eyes. *Hungry for what? Second course?*

Seeing him and being so close to him makes my cheeks burn with the images of what we just did. I want to touch him again. What would it be like if we were alone? Would he lift me up on the kitchen counter, get between my—

Stop, Dora! I turn away from him, silencing my thoughts, suppressing the grin on my face.

"We could get takeout," I suggest. I haven't stocked my fridge in a few days, and it's mostly empty now.

"Sure," Richter rumbles from within his chest. "One of the guys can get it."

I ask Joanne and Brandon what they want, and we put an order out. Joanne is sitting at the table, sipping from a glass of water, and we join her.

I explain to Richter what Joanne has told me so far. Then I turn to her.

"Why would McGlashan put pressure on your ex-husband, Jozdani? And what could be so bad that he wants to kidnap your son for it?"

Joanne's eyes fall on Richter and linger there for a while before she drags them back to me.

"Because Mehdi—that's my ex-husband's first name—was a nuclear scientist in training at Moscow State University when he met McGlashan for the first time."

"Okay, and?"

"Mehdi became aware of a plot." She looks at Richter again, and her eyes don't leave his face this time. "At that time, a CIA agent called Julian Blane was caught spying on Russian submarines."

Color drains from Richter's face, leaving it white as a sheet. His eyes widen as his nostrils flare.

"That's my dad."

"I know," Joanne says softly. "It's me who sent your brother that message about Viktor."

She looks down at her knotted fingers. "Mehdi told me about this many years ago. We were always scared this day would come, and now it has."

Joanne sighs then looks up at us.

"In the early nineties in Moscow, McGlashan had become close to Viktor, who was then an assassin for the KGB. So McGlashan ordered Viktor to kill Julian Blane to stop him from talking to the Russians."

Richter's gaze is flat and cold, and he looks…dangerous. "What?" he whispers.

Joanne says, "It was sanctioned by the CIA. And Mehdi, my husband, knows, because he overheard the conversation between McGlashan and Viktor. Ever since then, McGlashan has tried to silence my ex-husband. Now that he's a leading nuclear scientist in Iran, McGlashan thinks he can kill two birds with one stone. He can tell the CIA he's doing them a favor by capturing a leading Iranian nuclear scientist. And he can get rid of my husband, thereby getting rid of anyone who can incriminate him for Julian Blane's murder."

I'm leaning forward, elbows on the table. My jaw must be touching the wood, but I don't care. Richter's eyes are almost popping out, and the look in them is one of pure rage.

"How do you know this for sure?" he grinds out.

"I applied for a job as the McGlashans' housekeeper before I wrote anything about him. Once I started, I sneaked into his study and copied files off his laptop. I found loads of stuff. He definitely has links to Viktor Megdinov still."

Joanne continues.

"In McGlashan's safe deposit box, hidden behind a painting in his room, he keeps one file labeled Top Secret. His instructions from the CIA are detailed there. His job was to develop assets inside the KGB. That's how he met Viktor."

Richter asks, "Does the file say the CIA ordered him to kill my dad?"

"No. But someone must've. I can't see him doing it on his own."

Joanne pauses and takes a sip of water. "Can you imagine the uproar this would cause if it was leaked to the media?"

When we don't answer, she continues. "But I had to do it, because he kidnapped my son."

I ask, "Where's your husband now?"

"I don't know. Either he's in hiding, or Viktor's men have gotten to him already." Her face twists in pain. "All I want is my son back." Her head sinks to her palms.

I scoot next to her and squeeze her shoulders. They shudder with pent-up emotion.

Richter catches my eyes. He gets up, giving Joanne and me a moment together.

While Joanne recovers and wipes her nose with a tissue, I pick up one long strand of the spaghetti junction of thoughts in my head and go with it.

"Hold on. You were the source who left the message to meet me in Dale City, right?"

"Yes."

"Why me?"

Joanne takes a deep sigh. "Because there are connections between McGlashan and your dad you should know about."

A cold fist sinks into the pit of my stomach. "Connections?"

"Yeah. Michael Simpson has just built a massive media park outside Arlington."

I frown. "How did you know about that?"

"Because your father was promised the rights to that land if he bankrolled McGlashan's senatorial campaign."

A numbness spreads across my chest.

Joanne's voice is softer. "I'm sorry. I took a gamble. I didn't know how you'd take it. But I felt you should know what your father was up to. I could see that you were ostracized from his company. I figured if I helped you, in turn, you could help me."

This is all too much to take in. But I also have to admire this woman. She's got balls.

"How could I help you?"

"By publishing the story about McGlashan kidnapping my son. Yeah, it'd be a big scandal, but one that would make you a star reporter. And I'd get my son back. Pretty desperate plan," Joanne continues. "But my options were limited."

CHAPTER 43
RICHTER

There's a maelstrom roaring inside my head, a blizzard of blind rage that's choking every thought. I stumble outside the front door, almost bumping into Ken.

"Get outta my way," I snarl then feel sorry immediately. Ken's done nothing wrong.

"Sorry, bud," I croak, then take off at a brisk pace. I need a walk to clear my head. The phone comes out in my hand, and soon I hear Cal's voice on the other end. I leave the sidewalk to enter a wooded area. My eyes are used to the dark, and I rest my hand on the butt of my weapon.

Then I tell Cal everything. He listens in silence without interrupting me.

"Joanne saw this Top Secret file? In McGlashan's safe deposit box?"

"Yes. She's got photos to prove it. This shit is real, Cal."

His voice is a whisper. "And it's dynamite. Can you imagine what's gonna happen if that file is ever leaked to the media?"

Something clicks in my brain. "Why do you think he kept it? I mean, he got his orders thirty years ago, right?"

Cal thinks for a while. "Maybe to blackmail the CIA in case they impeach him? I don't know. Whatever. Do you believe Joanne?"

"What reason does she have to lie? She wants her son back. And she put herself at great risk by sneaking into McGlashan's home as a cleaner. She wouldn't do that unless she was desperate."

"I mean what she said about Viktor killing Dad. And sending me that message."

"She did that so we'd go after Viktor, and that helps her. After all, he's got her son, right?"

Cal says nothing. I can't hide the urgency in my voice. "We need to get Andre out from their clutches. Joanne can send word to Jozdani. They have an email account they leave messages on. Once we have Jozdani, we go after McGlashan."

"Careful, bro." The warning in Cal's voice is clear. "You're talking about a leader of the Senate here. This ain't no common terrorist."

"We took an oath, Cal. Against all enemies, foreign and domestic. Don't forget that."

He says nothing, only breathes heavily.

"Get all three teams ready. We need to find that Lincoln Escalade. It's somewhere in DC. That gives us a location for Viktor, hopefully."

I hang up. There's a crunching sound behind me. I kneel and turn with lightning speed, weapon out, safety clicked back. It's a fox, trampling in the brush. It sees me then takes off in the opposite direction. I watch for a while, my senses on high alert. Then I stand but keep the weapon locked and loaded in my hand.

I walk back to the house, observing every parked car, every shadow in the trees. Ken waves at me, and I wave back. His voice arrives on my earpiece.

"All well, Lambda Zero?"

"Roger that, Lambda Three."

During operations, we have call signs for each other. Mine is Lambda Zero, as I'm head of Team Lambda, one of the teams that make up Cyborg Securities. Brandon is Lambda One, and Cal is Lambda Two.

As I walk past my car, I stop to check it over. When my eyes fall on the gunshot on the rear window, my heart freezes. The crack is large, a wide spiderweb radiating from the central hit zone. If any more bullets had landed in the same place....

A horrible vision suddenly appears in my head of Dora, lying on the backseat floor, face down, blood pouring from her head....

No. *No!*

My teeth are grinding together, fists clenched. The gun is back in my holster. I walk away from the car. Fast. I want to get as far away as possible.

I lean against the back wall of Dora's house. A security light comes on then blinks off after a few seconds, leaving me in darkness. My head hangs over my chest.

I shouldn't have gone after Joanne's car, not with Dora there. Jeez, what was I thinking?

When I think of Dora' sweet, beautiful face, those dreamy eyes, all I see is love and hope. Yes, I said it. I'm falling in love with her. I know I am. I'm as helpless as a piece of iron pulled by a magnet.

But then I think of the dangerous situation we're in and what could have happened tonight.

I shudder again, a whole-body tremble, and I'm not a man who shudders easily. Thoughts are a painful haze in my head.

I come off the wall and walk back to the house. Ken nods, and I give his shoulder a pat.

When I'm inside, Dora and Joanne are huddling at the dinner table. There's a bottle of white wine and two glasses between them. Dora sips from her glass and waves at me. I wave back. Brandon is in the living room, on the sofa, feet up on the coffee table. The TV's off, and he's staring out the window. He sits up when he sees me.

"What's happening?" he asks.

Brandon's almost the same age as me, a couple of years more than Cal. He's a Delta brother, and we go back. I sit down on the sofa.

"Whatever happens, we need to make sure those two aren't harmed." I hook a thumb toward the dining room.

Brandon is watching me carefully. "They won't be. Not while we're around. But I guess you know that."

I smirk at him then head back to the dining room. I nod at Joanne then eat Dora up with my eyes. She's left her hair hanging loose over her shoulders but put on some light mascara. She's got a glow to her skin that radiates across the room. I love her relaxed look, and I guess she's glad to be back home.

She returns my gaze unflinchingly. "Want some wine?" she asks.

I shake my head. "Not on duty, sweetheart. Got a job to do."

"You're doing it well," she says and right there, in front of Joanne, gives me a wink. I smother my laughter and walk into the kitchen. With a glass of water, I sit down next to Dora at the table.

Joanne asks, "Any news of Andre?"

"Not yet," I say. "But we know what Viktor's car looks like, and it won't be long before we find it. We'll get Andre, don't worry."

I can see from the expression on her face that my words don't have much of an impact. She needs to see her son, and for her sake, a wave of sympathy rushes through me. But Dora knows the score. She reaches out and squeezes Joanne's hand.

Dora turns to me. "Want something to eat? I can make an omelet with cheese and chorizo."

I suddenly realize how hungry I am. My belly rumbles. Dora is a whiz in the kitchen, and I just stand and watch. My heart contracts painfully every time she smiles at me. I think back to our house in Montrose, when we used to eat together. It seems so long ago, but in truth, only a few days have passed. I feel like I've known her for years.

After dinner, which is tasty as hell, we go upstairs. Joanne is sleeping in the room next to Dora. I check in with Brandon, Ken and Olli, then go back upstairs.

Dora has changed clothes and is waiting in bed for me. When I see her in her floral nightshirt, her full breasts straining against the fabric, blood rushes to my cock like water released from a dam.

She crooks a finger, calling me to her. I stand my ground. She flings the covers off and pads over to me. She's bare below the waist, and my heart flips in its cage as my dick hardens. Her shiny, bare legs are so smooth. She stands on tiptoes and kisses me, and my hands have a life of their own, reaching down to cup her butt.

Damn, my dick's gonna burst free any minute. She whimpers against my mouth. Fuck, I want to sink myself into her again.

When we come up for air, I nuzzle her nose gently. "Darling, get some sleep. I need to stay awake to guard you. Make sure nothing happens."

She pouts, and it makes me laugh. She trails a finger down my chest, and damn, her hand starts to rub the hard outline of my bulging cock.

"Sure you don't want to join me?" Her whisper is sultry, smoky in my ears.

My eyes are closed, and I can feel the drumbeat of my heart in my eardrums. "Darlin', stop, please." I hold her wrist and lift it, kissing it. I bend and pick her up in my arms. She gives out a cute little squeal. I put her on the bed then pull the sheets over her. Then I kneel near her face.

"I'll be here, don't worry," I whisper. "I'll keep getting up and checking around. But I will sleep here tonight, right next to you."

She folds her small hand in my big, gnarled, ugly hand and kisses it. Then she puts my hand next to her head as if she's going to hold it while she sleeps.

A black weight is lodged in my throat. She looks so sweet, so innocent.

"Sleep tight, sweetheart," I rumble from deep in my chest, my voice hoarse.

*****

I'm awake, but try telling my body that. My brain can filter sounds and light, and my eyes snap open. It takes me a few seconds to realize Dora is leaning over, watching me. I smile at her and look around. I must've fallen asleep near dawn.

But I did have the whole night to walk around the apartment building, alone with my thoughts. And my thoughts weren't good ones. Yes, it's that old ghost again, scratching at my shoulders, whispering in my ears that no matter how hard I try, if I drag Dora into this life, she'll get hurt. More than she is already. Because if I get my head blown off one day, I can't let her pick up the pieces.

I want a life with her.

And being a soldier's wife is the hardest job in the world. Being in love and letting him go at the same time. Not knowing…just not knowing, and not having control over anything.

And I'm not a soldier anymore, I'm a mercenary for hire. I'm black ops through and through. She might never again hear from me if I die in some foreign land on a deniable mission.

Is that what I want for her?

I sit up in bed while Dora goes to the bathroom. When she comes out, she heads for the dresser to get ready. That black weight is against my throat again. I can barely speak but know I have to.

"Darlin'."

She turns at my voice. Breath is heaving in my chest. I hold her eyes, those melting browns reaching deep into my soul.

"I'm gonna be here for you till this blows over. You're gonna be safe, and I'll die before anything happens to you. I wanted you to know that."

She frowns and steps toward me. She stops when I step away. The frown deepens on her face.

I clear my throat. "But this is no life for you, sweetheart. If you make a life with me, and god knows I want you to, but if you did, there's always going to be risk and danger. I don't want you to live with that."

She comes forward, and when she leans into me, I can't resist hugging her. Tight. Then I hold her shoulders, and she stares at me.

"I care for you too much, Dora. More than anyone, ever." I can feel an alien burn behind my eyes, a pressure building. "But caring for you so much is also the reason I can't be with you."

A black fist closes over my throat. My eyes are blurred, and this pain is all over me, worse than a hundred bullets perforating every cell in my body.

I wipe the tears from my eyes. "I'm sorry, Dora. As much as I want you, I can't be with you." My palms cup her beautiful face. "I'm so sorry."

CHAPTER 44
DORA

I can't comprehend what Richter's saying to me. His words are lost in my head, whirling away in a tornado, leaving only destruction behind.

He lets go of my shoulders and steps away. His eyes are red, and he makes no effort to hide his emotion. His massive chest rises and falls as he looks toward the closed blinds over the windows. He stares at them as if he can see through them, far away.

"I can't ever explain everything to you. But you've become the most important thing in my life. And the longer this goes on, the harder it gets."

I shake my head, my insides all twisted, tangled up in knots. "Richter, what are you talking about? I don't understand—"

"That's just it, sweetheart." His eyes fall back on me. "It's hard for you to understand. I mean, look at these desperate people. Criminals like Viktor and power-hungry crazy men like McGlashan." He points a finger at his chest. "In one form or the other, I have to fight them. Sometimes, I need to figure out the right and wrong for myself. Do what's right for this country and what I can live with."

I spread my hands, frowning. "But Richter, that's got nothing to do with us, right? That's your job. We—you and I—are different." I get closer to him, and my heart shudders as he steps back, putting his hands up.

"Darlin', I'll be here for you till this shit blows over." He stares at me, and I see a little of the old Richter before it vanishes again behind a red-rimmed veil of sorrow. "But when it's over, you need your life back. This ain't no way to live your life."

He might as well be squeezing his throat with his hands, suffocating me. Words are hard to form, and thorns are penetrating my heart, making it bleed.

"I'm in control of my life, Richter. I can make my own decisions. And I want to be with you." I wrap my hands around his waist and rest my head on his chest. His body is ramrod stiff, and I feel him shaking. I still can't believe what he's saying.

My eyes close when his arm comes around my shoulder, bringing with it that familiar, comfortable feeling of being in a protective shell.

"No one's gonna hurt you," he whispers. "I'll make sure of that. But I can't be what you want me to be. And I don't want to see you get hurt."

"I won't. Trust me."

He separates us gently. My eyes are burning with unshed tears, and when he gently kisses my forehead, a drop rolls down my cheek. My heart is empty, shattered, broken pieces scattered against my ribs.

"You will get hurt, sweetheart. And I can't bear the thought of that. I'm sorry." He chokes on his last words. "I'll be outside. You're safe here, don't worry."

Then he walks out the door, leaving me standing there.

Did Richter just break up with me?

It's happened before, but never has it hurt like this. Never has it felt this raw, like a festering wound eating me from the inside, slowly hollowing me out.

Why did he do that? Suddenly I'm angry. Bitterness and frustration take over my shock.

I'm standing by my writing desk in the bedroom, staring at my Mac. I pick it up and hurl it onto the bed. I kick the chair.

Then I crumple on the chair, head buried in my hands on the table. My eyes burn, and my heart feels like it's been seared in a furnace.

I don't know if I'm angry with him or feel sorry for him.

I'm angry if he's hiding something from me. I already checked online, and Richter Blane isn't married. He doesn't have any other family apart from Cal and Sam.

Besides, I don't think he's the sort of person who could carry out that sort of a lie. No, Richter is the kind of guy who wears his heart on his sleeve. He laid his soul bare to me. He's been hurt before. He's damaged. I know that. I feel it like I feel the air in my lungs.

And I think it's the fear of what happened to his previous girlfriend that drives him still. That guilt never left him. He holds himself accountable, although it wasn't his fault. That speaks volumes about his character.

But it's not right.

"Damn you, Richter," I whisper through my tears. We had a connection. A real, strong, durable one forged in danger, nurtured in privacy when we opened our souls to one another. I was the sunlight to his tortured night, the oasis in his desolate desert. We fit perfectly.

How could he let that go?

Deep down, I feel as sorry for him as I do for myself. He's doing what he thinks is right, but all he's doing is hurting himself even more. He really is my wounded beast, unable to walk for the huge thorn in his paw. I removed it, but now he's stuck it back in again. He's going to hobble with that wound all his life.

And my heart will be broken, because I'll never know another man like him.

A man who taught me to face my fears. Showed me what a strong, confident woman I really am. He blew away layers of dirt to show what lay underneath decades of emotional abuse at the hands of my father and brother. *The real me.*

He gave me wings to fly then brutally cut them down.

But I'll never forget what he left me with. If it hadn't been for him, my life would be poorer. My tears come anew, hot lava scorching down my cheeks. I hate crying. These stupid, ugly tears never solve anything. They just make me feel worse.

My phone rings. I've been picking it up, but it's never been Richter. At first, I've called him, sent him texts, until his silence stopped me. A girl has her pride, right? Why the fuck should I beg him? It's his loss.

Oh, but it's not just his. It's my loss as well.

I dry my cheeks as I focus on my phone. It's Dad, and he keeps calling. I can't speak to him now, but I also know that sooner or later I have to.

The phone beeps with a text from my dad.

Please, pick up the phone. It's very important.

He might be a difficult and temperamental man, but he's still my father. And I do love him in my own way, which is the same as him, I guess. I sigh and clutch my forehead. Why does my life have to be so complicated? I wish I could have a drink, but it's too damn early for a G&T.

But I do have time for one person. I call Julia, and she picks up on the first ring.

"Hey, gorgeous. How are you?" she trills down the line.

Hearing her voice breaks the dam again. Stupid, I know. But I can't help it.

Julia listens patiently before assuring me she'll come over as soon as work's over.

I hang up to find Dad has sent me another text. I take a deep breath and call him back.

"Dora. Good to hear your voice." He sounds relaxed—unnaturally so. My dad's voice normally has a hard edge when he speaks to me. He thinks it's the right way to speak to me, to show he's boss.

I say nothing. He speaks again. "Honey, are you there?" The mellowness is putting me on guard. His voice is like honey.

"What do you want, Dad?"

"Now, now. Can I not ring my darling daughter for a chat? Especially when I've missed her so much?"

This is weird. I forget my own troubles for a while. "Are you feeling all right, Dad?"

"Of course. Look, I happened to be in the neighborhood. Can I come over?"

I hesitate. I don't want to see him when I'm in this state. But it saves me from having to go to his mansion up in Bethesda, the pristine, perfect, soulless place where I grew up as his prisoner.

"Give me half an hour," I say and hang up.

CHAPTER 45
DORA

I have a shower and clean myself up the best I can. I put on a new dress to make me feel better. It doesn't. As I look at myself in the mirror, all I can think of is Richter's large hands roaming all over my body, pulling down the zipper at the back of my dress. I want to be naked with him again.

I close my eyes.

Fuck this.

I literally run downstairs, grab the bottle of gin, pour two fingers, mix in some tonic, then down the damn thing. It's fizzy and sharp and helps to numb my brain for a while.

The doorbell rings. It must be Dad. I go to hide the bottle, then stop myself. He can watch me drink in the daytime. Do I care anymore?

Hell no.

Fortified by the drink but by no means tipsy, I walk into the hallway. I look through the peephole. Dad is standing in front of the door in a killer business suit with a handkerchief in the top left pocket. I open the door. Behind Dad, I can see Brandon parked on the opposite side of the road. He's leaning against the SUV, observing us. I quickly switch my attention back to Dad, hoping and praying Brandon won't come over to investigate. I don't want to have to explain my life to Dad. Not right now. Maybe not ever.

My father has a tall, imposing physique. His black hair—which he dyes to hide the gray—is swept back from his forehead. His black eyebrows are thick, and he has a strong jawline and sharp blue eyes. The contrast between his eyes and tanned skin can be startling. He's not a man who tolerates fools and has built his business empire on that foundation. Unfortunately for me, he makes it too obvious he's always regarded me as foolish.

Now, even considering that makes my blood boil.

He throws his arms wide open, a big smile on his face. "Darlin'! I missed you!"

He pulls me into a hug. I bear it without a grin, stiffly, and disengage from him quickly. We're still on the doorstep, and I did this for Brandon's benefit, so he can see my dad is not a threat.

"Aren't you going to ask your old man to come in?" There's a note of impatience in his voice.

When I look into his eyes, there is a hint of concern as well. He looks me up and down. "Are you okay, darlin'? You look good."

"Not bad," I say in a flat voice. I turn, and he follows me inside. I go straight to the kitchen and lean against the counter, facing him.

Dad stands still for a while, observing me. He does this very well. It's his way of intimidating people. He stares until it becomes unnerving. Usually I'm the first one to look away. But not today. I carry on staring back at him, arms crossed on my chest.

He relents eventually. His brows crinkle, and his eyes soften. "So, darlin'. Tell me where you've been."

"Like I said, Dad, to see a friend."

"Who, exactly? I know all your friends, don't I?"

"Do you?" I raise an eyebrow. "Or maybe you think you do."

The look of surprise on his face is lost quickly in a frown. That too changes rapidly, and he smiles. Inwardly I feel uneasy, but I keep my face impassive. Dad's on a charm offensive. There has to be a reason.

"Well, who is it?" he asks.

This isn't an innocent question. Dad isn't interested in my life. He just wants a name so he can dig up anything and everything he can find on them.

"A personal friend. A man, if you must know."

I see a fire glint in his eyes. "And who is he? Anyone I've met before?" His voice is lower, and we both know he's getting closer to losing his temper.

"No. You haven't met him before. And I'd like it to stay that way."

"Why's that?" He frowns.

I'm done playing. He wants the truth. Well, after all these years, he can have it.

"Because he's my friend, not yours. Because it's my life to live the way I see fit. I don't tell you how to live yours, so I don't see why you should tell me how to live mine. You're my father, so I'll always respect and love you. But if you try to keep tabs on me all the time, force me to be someone I'm not, then you're not welcome to any part of my life anymore."

There, I said it. The words sit between us, the proverbial gorilla in the room, invisible but sucking up all the space inside.

I might as well have slapped him across the face. His calm, cool, unruffled exterior vanishes. It's like I chucked a rock at an expensive mirror. The cracks appear quickly, spreading. I see the fixed smile on his face fading until it's replaced by the habitual snarl.

"You dare talk to me like that? Who clothed and fed you all these years? I worked night and day to give you everything. You never saw my sacrifice. My pain. And this is the thanks I get?" He huffs, shaking his head. "What's gotten into you, Dora? Ever since you disappeared to Maine and met this new guy, it seems like you're a changed person. What happened to my obedient little girl?"

I feel like I'm going to gag. I spread my arms. "Can't you see the irony in that?" I point my finger at him. "I'm not your obedient, nice little girl anymore. I'm an adult. But you choose to treat me like a child. You hate everything I do, including my career, only because it's not one you chose for me."

Dad's staring at me as if I'm some mad stranger off the street. I don't care. He has to hear this.

"And you say you clothed and fed me? Yes, you did, like every father does. But you were never there for me." I count the facts off my fingers. "Were you there for my hockey matches? No. For my school plays? No. Jesus, even on my prom night, you had a business meeting. Or whatever. If it wasn't for Jessica, the housekeeper, I would have been on my own. Do you know how lonely I was? You could've been close to me, but you chose to ignore me instead. All your attention was focused on James. And when I grew up, all you wanted to do was control me. Make me act, speak, *be* a certain way. Your way."

Dad's face falls. That cracked mirror doesn't hold an image anymore. The fractures are too wide, too numerous. Maybe the image was never there, and I was never going to see myself in it. It's a shame that I fooled myself for so long.

He looks down and rubs his jaw. He looks hurt, which hurts me too. I feel empty inside suddenly. This is not what I wanted. Hell, have I ever wanted this? I wanted to be close to him. To feel loved, cherished, valued—what any child wants from her father.

There's a poisonous fog behind my eyes, burning and irritating. I feel terribly lonely all of a sudden, like I've been left to stand alone on a clifftop, at the edge of a precipice. I felt this way that night at Dale City. The night my life changed. Only has it really changed for the better?

Richter's words float into my thoughts like a birdsong in early morning.

Don't put yourself down.

I can't stop the tears all of a sudden. I cover my face, and the black river of sorrow and shame pours out of me. But it doesn't last long. I don't want to be this way in front of Dad. Whether he likes it or not, I'm a different person. I have to show him this regardless of the pain inside me. I can't let that pain make me weak. I'll bear it, stand up like the mountain I climbed with Richter.

Dad doesn't come close to me as I stifle the tears, stem the tide of melancholy threatening to burst the dam. All my life, I've had to hide my real self. Not just from him.

From myself too, because I didn't have the strength to stand up to him.

So now he knows the real me—and it occurs to me that maybe he did all along. Maybe that's what is so fucked up about this. He chose to make me in his own mold and ignore me as I was.

Whatever.

I'm done with this now. I'm through. I need a new life.

When I look back at him, his eyes are like slits. He seems deep in thought. He sighs then opens his mouth to say something. I'm staring back at him, willing him to speak.

Dad closes his mouth and opts for silence. Then he smiles. "Okay, darlin'. I think you need some time to think things through. You're angry. I'm sorry. I just want what's best for you."

Hope flickers inside me. Can I have a new relationship with him after all these years? It would need work, but it would be amazing if I could.

"Really?" I sniff. I tear off a paper towel and wipe my nose.

"Yes, of course." He stands very still, observing me. "That's why I want you to come with me to an opening ceremony. It will be great." His face becomes animated, voice excited. "It's a new media city, and it belongs to me. To us, I mean," he corrects hurriedly. "Five brand-new TV stations over a twenty-acre area. There's going to be a strip mall and housing for staff as well. City Planning gave us the green light last year. Today the first station will open."

I turn around slowly and get myself a glass of water. "Is this why you came?" I say with my back turned to him. "To tell me about your new business venture?"

I face him, sipping the water.

"Well, no, not just that. Also because I haven't seen you for so long."

You didn't see me the six months before that either, I tell myself. But I don't say it out loud. It won't change anything.

Dad continues, "This place will be huge, darlin'. It's outside Arlington, and it's going to create thousands of jobs. James, Cassandra, and I are going to the opening."

I know this is crunch time.

Cassandra is his fourth blond bimbo wife, and James, my brother, is the heir to his media empire. Cassandra will be on Dad's right arm tonight, and I'll be on the left, plastic smile fixed on my face as the flashbulbs pop. It's what I've done all my life. Apparently, this is what the daughters of media moguls do: go with the flow, maintain the status quo, and yourself be damned.

"Big opening, huh?" I hope he can hear the sarcasm in my voice.

Even if he does, he ignores it blithely. "Yes. I need you to be there, Dora." His voice is harder now, matching the glint in his eyes.

"I see. And what did you think of what I just said? You know, the bits about you ignoring me then trying to control my life?"

"Dora, come on. I don't know what's gotten into you. Can we talk about this later, please?"

I shake my head at him. I'm tired all of a sudden. Some things never change.

"Just go, Dad." I move toward the hallway.

I can feel his anger radiate in waves as he stomps behind me. "Dora, stop!"

I do stop, right in front of the door. Dad's lips are thin with anger, jaws clenched. "You will be there. This is your family, the most important thing you've ever had."

I open the door. "I'll think about it and let you know."

Dad doesn't move a muscle. He stares at me, and I stare back. "It's tomorrow evening. I'll have the car pick you up at 6 p.m."

"Goodbye, Dad."

He stares at me for a long while then shakes his head. He walks out, and I shut the door softly behind him.

CHAPTER 46
DORA

I lean against the door after he leaves. I feel better for standing up to him, but it's drained me. I stumble to the staircase and sink onto it, holding my head. I feel like my insides have been nicked by a very sharp knife.

I'm a million kinds of messed up right now. All over the place. Twisted into knots so tight I haven't got a clue how to untangle them.

But I do feel *cleaner*. That's the only way I can describe it. I feel fresher. Sounds weird when so much is bent beyond shape and my heart is shattered like a hundred shards of glass I'll cut myself on if I pick them up. Best to leave them where they are for now. But yes, I feel like I've shed old skin and grown a new hide.

Hopefully, Dad will look at me differently from today.

I'm so lost in my thoughts the knock on the door almost makes me yelp. I look through the peephole before opening. It's Brandon, but I look behind him at the parked car. Richter is sitting there, staring at me. When our eyes meet, he looks away quickly. It sends a pang reverberating through me, like the plucking of the strings of an old, out-of-tune guitar.

Brandon asks, "Are you all right?"

"Yeah, fine. That was my dad, by the way."

He nods slowly. "Okay."

There's an awkward silence as I ponder my next question. Before I can speak, however, my heart jolts as I catch a flicker of movement behind Brandon. Richter's getting out of his car. He rolls his shoulders and glances around then walks slowly towards us.

Brandon steps to one side. When Richter arrives, there's a silent communication between the two of them, and Brandon leaves.

Richter rubs his elbow with one hand. He won't look at me, but I'm staring at him point blank. This couldn't be more awkward.

"Do you, uh, need anything?" he asks.

It's a stupid question, and when I raise my eyebrows at him, he closes his eyes and rocks back.

"Well," he drawls, "if you need anything, I'll be in my car. Unless I have to go back to base, but then Brandon and Team Onyx will be here. And I'll be back in an hour, at the most."

I'm not sure why he's telling me he's going to be around. Is it to make me feel worse?

"My friend's coming in a couple of hours," I tell him. "Julia. The one I called earlier."

He slants his head to the side and frowns. "The one you called when we were back in Montrose?"

His forehead clears, and a distant light jumps in his eyes. I feel it too, the memories of the mountains of Montrose, now tinged with such sadness for me. I sigh and look down at my feet.

When I look up, pain twists his features. He clenches his jaw then passes a hand down his face.

"Yes, that was Julia."

"Okay," he sighs. "Is she coming alone? Does she know she might be followed?"

"I did tell her, and she knows to be on the lookout."

He thinks for a while, keeping his eyes to the ground, tapping his lips. "I'll tell you what, sweetheart. Tell her to stop where she is now. I'll escort her down here. That way, at least I'll know if anyone's trailing her." He hands over his phone to me. "Call her, please. It's important."

*****

Julia arrives early. I see her coming down the street from my bedroom window. Richter's car is close behind. He walks Julia to the door. When I open the door, he returns silently to his car.

I close the door, and within seconds, Julia and I are hugging, rocking back and forth while I cry into her shoulder.

Julia and I share everything, and it's such a relief to see her. She's blond and pretty, and the summer dress she's wearing shows off her curves.

Julia raises her eyebrows. "Say, who was the guy who stopped me? I mean, he got out of his car and told me to drive slowly. He had this ID from some security company."

"Oh, that was Richter," I say, trying hard to keep my face impassive. But Julia is looking at me with the hint of a smile on the corners of her lips, and I avert my face, pinching my lower lip.

"Just one of the guys who helped me out from that mess, you know."

"One of those guys, huh?" Julia prods me in the ribs, and I squirm, red faced. "He shook my hand when I arrived here. Do you know what he said?"

For the first time, Julia's face becomes serious. I frown, as I didn't see Julia shake hands with Richter.

"No, what did he say?"

Julia leans closer. "He told me to look after you. Said you've been through a lot."

I take a deep breath, releasing it slowly.

Julia lowers her voice. "Honey, I can tell. He cares for you. Anything I should know about?" She wiggles her eyebrows in that way I usually find irresistibly funny, only this time round, it's not funny.

Actually, it's pretty damn sad.

Tears burn at the backs of my eyes, and I turn my back to Julia. As I walk to the kitchen, she runs after me, faces me, and then pulls me into a bear hug.

"Tell me what happened! Did he hurt you? Have these guys—"

"No, no." I wipe my cheeks angrily. "It's nothing like that. They've been nothing but good to me."

Julia squeezes my shoulder and looks at me intently. "Let's get a drink," she suggests. Right now, that sounds like a great idea.

We sit down with the bottle of gin at the kitchen table. I tell her everything. She listens with her mouth hanging open, lost for words.

I blush when I tell her about Richter.

"So, tell me." She drops her voice and wiggles her eyebrows. "Was he everything you dreamed of?"

"Stop it, Jules." I giggle, my face burning up. Then immediately, sadness cloaks my heart like a shadow. My chin lowers to my chest.

Julia squeezes my hand, leaning forward. "Why did he break it off?"

"I don't know. He acted so cold. So distant. He doesn't answer my calls. I know it's over, Jules."

"Give him some time. Men need that sometimes. You know they don't handle emotional closeness very well. They need space."

I snort. "Oh, he's got fucking space now."

And so do I. A forlorn, empty space where my beating heart used to be.

Again, the sadness is overwhelming. The gin is working in my veins now. It's making me feel moodier. My head lowers again.

Julia comes around the table and puts her arms around my shoulders. She holds me as I cry softly.

CHAPTER 47
RICHTER

Three days have passed. She's stopped calling and sending texts. The urge to call her back is so strong it's almost physical. In between hunting for the Russian mafia chapters in the seedier parts of Virginia, I've hit the gym hard. When I'm punching the heavy bag, I'm hitting my own sad self, trying to beat my thoughts into shape and doing whatever I can to keep my mind off her.

It's not working.

Especially when I'm parked outside her house, where I stay as long as I can. We're still working on the case, but I make sure I'm there in the evenings to relieve Brandon. I settle down in the backseat of the Yukon with my thermos and take out a burger. I have a blanket that keeps me warm at night. I wait till the lights in her window go out. And yeah, I know she sees me too.

I stick around most of the day as well unless we have meetings or chase down new leads, like we got today.

It's late evening, and we've got intel that four Bratva bosses are meeting with a local gang. With any luck, Viktor might be there. So Cal and I are staking out the place. He's gone for a recon with the drone, and I'm keeping watch from the car.

I've stared at the phone so many times I've lost count. I've read each and every one of the messages she sent me more than once. I don't know why I'm doing it, because it's killing me.

The last two she left will haunt me until the day I die.

Don't let your past destroy your future.

You can't walk looking backward.

My finger touches the screen as if I can feel her again by touching her words. This girl just reached inside the closed iron doors guarding my heart and plucked the damn thing right out.

That's what it feels like. I left my heart in her possession the day I broke up with her. What's left is a yawning, empty space. An empty iron cage.

How does she know me so well? Maybe I'll never figure it out. Because what she said in that text is exactly what I'm doing. I don't want our relationship to end up like the one with Charlotte did. Part of me says it's stupid, while another part says I'm better off being cautious and not hurting the only woman I've come to care for more than myself.

The admission doesn't surprise me, because both parts of me are proclaiming the one undeniable truth: I care for Dora so much I'm willing to sacrifice my happiness for her. Sacrifice myself for her. What does that mean?

I love her. No matter how many winding paths I take, how many heart-rending barriers I crash through, I come to the same conclusion.

I've never felt about anyone like this before. This is what love must feel like.

This is so messed up.

Whatever I do, whichever way I twist and turn, I end up hurting more. I broke up with her to not break her heart in the future, but I've broken her heart now. And what of mine? My hard, calloused, scarred heart? For so long, I haven't allowed any emotion near it. But Dora's touch made the blood flow in my heart again, like a waterfall frozen in the winter, waking up as it feels spring's first rays of sunshine.

One day, you'll trip up.

Haven't I fallen for her already?

My fists clench, and a heavy black weight lodges at the back of my throat. I'm shaking. Lights dim and brighten in my eyes. I'm made for killing enemies, for violence, yet I don't know how to fight this. If this is love, why the hell does it hurt so much?

I can't bear this pain inside me. My head falls back against the headrest of the car seat, and my mouth opens.

Am I letting go of the best thing that's ever happened to me?

Don't let your past destroy your future.

There's a loud rap on my window. My eyes are blurry with beads of moisture, and it seems there's more than one person out there. Slowly, Caleb's face comes into focus.

I lower the window. I'm outside a warehouse where a chapter of the Bratva is having a meeting. With any luck, Viktor might be in there. Caleb and I are here to scope the place out.

"What the fuck is wrong with you? I've been knocking on the window for ages." Caleb frowns. No wasting time with my bro. He knows me and gets straight to the point.

I swallow, but the block in my throat just gets heavier. I feel like shit, like acid bleach is smeared down my throat and stomach, and I'm slowly corroding from inside. I have to breathe out and shake my head before I can answer Caleb.

"Nothing. What did the drone show?"

Caleb holds the drone in his hand and doesn't reply. He gets into the passenger seat next to me. The night is warm, summery, but to me, the warmth feels oppressive.

We sit in silence for a while. To our right, across a disused yard, lies the derelict warehouse. There's a collection of limos and SUVs near it. Gangsters' cars.

Caleb turns to look at me, and I ignore him. But his stare does prickle my skin.

"What's got into you?" he asks. "Ever since you came back from Dora's house that day, you've been like this." He takes a deep breath. "Fuck."

He knows it. He's my brother. We've been looking after each other since first grade.

"I've never seen you like this," he says quietly. "Not even when Charlotte died."

His words are like a slap to my face. My chin falls to my chest, and I grip my forehead. Then I bare my lips in a snarl and breathe heavily. I feel like… God help me. I want to fight someone, break something.

Or maybe fall at someone's feet. Beg for her forgiveness.

I don't know. I'm so fucking tangled up inside I don't recognize myself.

"I'm sorry," Caleb says. "It's just the way I see it. You've been so different lately. Head in the clouds." He smiles suddenly. "Remember when Mom put that daisy chain necklace around your neck? You were about eight?"

The sudden change of topic throws me. Then I smile too. "You remember that?"

"Yeah. Mom said she never had a girl, so you could wear it for a day to make her happy. And you did."

Memories crowd my head. It's weird how quickly life passes you by, leaving nothing but memories.

"Yeah," I say.

"I wanna see you happy like that again, bro. I don't know exactly what's going on between you and Dora. I know you'll keep it inside you until it kills you."

He turns to face me. My emotions are a maelstrom as I stare at him. He's my brother, and he's such a strong man—both inside and outside. He's the only confidant I have, apart from Dora. And I guess I don't have her anymore.

I let out a ragged breath. "I don't know what to do about it, Cal."

Cal is quiet for a while then replies. "The trouble is you're pushing her away because of your own fears. You're scared she could get hurt. Scared she could leak classified information. But nothing's happened. She's fine, and nothing's hit the papers. I think she's quite capable of looking after herself."

"I know that," I say in frustration. "That's not the point."

"The point is what I said. You wanna do this to yourself, go ahead. I'm saying you're being unfair—both to yourself and to her. She can decide what to do with her life. You broke it off, right?"

I nod in silence.

"It's your insecurity. Reality, as you can see, is very different. Don't punish yourself for what happened with Charlotte. No one could have saved her in the end. You being here wouldn't have made a difference."

I close my eyes. Thoughts I keep buried deep inside bubble up to the surface. Getting the letter in Ramallah. Coming back home. Visiting her gravestone with flowers. Breaking down in tears.

But through it all, like fog parting, I hear Caleb's voice as well. It's as if this mist has surrounded my head all this time, and his words are puncturing the murkiness like pinpoints of yellow light.

"You need to wake up, bro. Start living the life you have instead of holding on to what's gone."

Caleb smirks. "And most of all, I can't have you as leader of this outfit while you're acting like a lovesick teenager."

"I'm not," I growl.

"You are," he says. "I was watching this movie last week. This guy is stuck in jail, and he's trying to break out. He keeps getting caught, but he doesn't give up. Eventually he succeeds." He gives me a punch on the shoulder. "It's time you broke out of your jail."

He's right, of course. I've been looking at this all wrong. Sometimes you can get too deep in yourself and not see the man in the mirror. I need to find that man I used to be. Tell him it's all right for him to be himself.

Because Dora saw that man. He revealed himself to her. So why the hell am I hiding behind, as Cal calls it, my insecurities?

A flicker of movement catches my eye. On the far right, in front of the warehouse, a man comes out, a gun hanging from a shoulder strap. He's joined by another three, and they take up position around the cars.

"Guess the meeting's started," I say. "These are the guards."

"Time to move," Cal says.

I pick up the radio to alert Brandon and Ken. They're on standby on the other side.

Cal and I pack our weapons and run out swiftly. We move like shadows, barely visible to anyone watching. The guards don't stand a chance. They drop like flies.

Brandon and Ken catch up with us. They've done a recon from behind.

"Neutralized two guys at the back," Brandon whispers. "All clear now."

The four of us fan out. The warehouse has fire escape stairs that snake up to the top. They're unlocked. We go up the stairs quickly.

I open one of the doors at the top and train my weapon down. There's a cluster of people inside in the middle. A group of men are sitting at two tables facing each other. Others stand around them. No one has weapons out, but I know they're all packing.

I look hard but can't see Viktor. We circle around until we have them covered. They can't see us up here.

"Put your weapons down!" I shout. "This is the police. You are surrounded!"

The men are startled and look up. Several go for their guns, but I yell again, and they stop. Oliver and his men rush in from the gates below. Within seconds, the gangsters are surrounded. I come down the stairs, my rifle trained on them.

We have extra help for this mission. Ten men from another private security group called Matador are here, too. They work with us occasionally.

I head over to Casey, their leader. He's got his phone out and is checking the photo of Viktor against the men lined up.

"He's not here," I tell him.

My own phone vibrates. It's a message from Dora, and immediately it grabs my attention. Not just because it's from her. It's the content.

It's about my dad. We need to talk.

Five seconds later, another text. My heart soars when I read the two simple words.

Call me.

CHAPTER 48

DORA

I thought long and hard about telling Richter about Dad's big opening ceremony. I didn't want him to see this as a desperate, pathetic attempt on my part to get back with him. I've stopped calling him for the last three days. If he doesn't want to be in touch, that's up to him. His loss, as far as I'm concerned. But a little voice in my head is also telling me I don't want to do this alone. I know McGlashan will be there. So will half of DC and all the newspapers and media vultures. I know nothing will happen. Way deep down, I have this belief that Dad won't do anything to hurt me. But...I would feel safer with some protection. No, that's not what I mean. I would feel safer with *Richter* being there.

But I'll be damned if I ask him. My heart is broken, but I'm not desperate. I'll have to pick up the broken pieces, and hard as it is, I will move on.

It's the night of the opening tomorrow. I don't want to go, but I don't have a choice. Dad has been insisting virtually every hour. I must say there has been a change in the language he uses. There are a lot more endearments, and he doesn't speak to me as if I'm a child being scolded. We're still not close, but at least I dare to hope we might have a different relationship one day.

I need to choose a dress, and Julia's come around to help. She's lending me her black heels to go with my little black dress. She's helping to fix the dark-green jade brooch around my neck when she glances at me in the mirror.

"He didn't call you back even once?"

"No."

"And when did you send him the message about Joanne?"

"Two hours ago." And ten minutes. Not that I'm keeping track of time. Not at all.

Julia finishes fixing the brooch and goes back to the curls in my hair.

"Do you think I did the right thing?"

"By sending him the text? Yeah, of course. You can't not tell him, Dora."

It's good to know that Julia agrees with me. It felt like the right thing to do. Then why hasn't he replied yet? The options run through my mind. He could've lost his phone. Could he have been hurt while on a mission? This last thought suddenly chills my bones. A cold dread settles in my heart like a block of ice. Without realizing it, I've gasped out loud.

Julia straightens. "What is it?"

I stand up to face her. "What if he's injured or worse, and that's why he hasn't replied? In his line of work, that happens, right?"

"He also knows how to look after himself, honey. He's built like a brick shithouse, right?"

I can't help worrying. All this time, I've been thinking he's ignoring me. It's awful to think there might be another reason.

I make up my mind and check the Cartier watch on my wrist. I have two hours before Dad's car arrives to pick me up. I've got my own car in the driveway, a Tesla similar to Julia's.

"I'm going to check out where he works. Someone will be around."

Julia's mouth falls open. "What? No, you can't do that."

"Why not? And what if something has happened to him?"

Julia smiles sadly. "If something did happen to him, maybe he wants to spare you the knowledge?"

I shake my head. Of course she's right. After all, that's one of the reasons Richter did this, so I won't worry about him getting wounded or even worse.

Well, it hasn't worked, has it? I'm still worried about him. Sounds silly. Maybe it's time for me to stop doing this. Wish it was as easy as it sounds.

Julia opens her mouth to say something, but before she can answer, my phone beeps again. It doesn't just beep and stop. It keeps beeping insistently.

It's a call.

The phone is resting on the custom-built dressing table. I lean forward and snatch it up. My heart soars when I see who's calling. It's Richter. I mouth silently to Julia, who makes an O with her mouth and presses her palms to her face.

"Hello." My mouth is so dry I have to swallow twice before I speak.

"Hey, sweetheart." Richter's voice is his usual growl, but it's also unexpectedly tender, warm.

It's just so great to hear him again.

"Hi, uh, hi."

Okay, that's weird. Why can't I stop sounding like a flustered teenager? I just stood up to my dad, for heaven's sake. Yet two words from Richter reduce me to a puddle on the floor.

"You called?" *Just great, Dora.* State the obvious. Nothing like it.

"Yes," he drawls. There's a hint of a smile in his voice. "And you're answering the phone. Right?"

"I, uh, yeah. Oh, shit." I flop down on the chair. My head is swimming, and my cheeks burn.

"How are you?" he asks.

I pause for a while, as I'm not sure how to answer. Part of me can't help but think, *How the hell do you think I am?* I want to say it, shout it out in fact, but know it won't resolve anything.

I guess he picks up on my silence, because he follows it up quickly with another question. It's a loaded one, and it makes my pulse surge.

"Guess we need to meet up, right?"

"I think so. Where are you?"

"I'm right outside. In my car."

I half expected that, because when I look out my window in the morning, I see his GMC Yukon parked opposite. The car comes and goes in the daytime, but there's always one of the Cyborg Security guys out there. When I turn the lights out at night, Richter's GMC is back again.

"I need to tell you this. Tomorrow night, I'm going out." It sounds like I'm asking for permission from him, which is weird. But I also know there's a reason the guys are still keeping such a close watch on me. Especially Richter.

"I see. But I'm not sure how safe that is. Where are you going, and with who?" His voice is suddenly flat, cold.

I say quickly, "It's to the opening ceremony of my dad's new media company. The one that's tied in with all of this, as a matter of fact."

"Really?"

"Yeah. This is why we need to talk."

He pauses and breathes heavily down the phone. "Open the door," he says simply, then hangs up.

The time it takes me to move from upstairs to the front door is obviously more than it takes Richter to travel twice the distance. He's standing back, wearing a white T-shirt, arms folded across his chest. His forearm muscles ripple, and the hard slabs of his pecs move beneath the tight shirt when he shifts. The grays are smoldering when he holds me in his eyes. His stance is rigid, awkward, but his eyes give his true feelings away.

He's hurting as badly as I am. I can see it in the taut line of his jaw, the firm press of his lips. I try not to linger on his lips.

I don't know how much time passes. But we've not seen each other for five days, and I can't stop drinking him in with my eyes.

Finally, he clears his throat. His voice has steel underlining it when he speaks.

"We know your dad is connected with this, sweet...I mean Dora." He coughs into his hand. He takes a deep breath and stares at the floor for a few seconds.

At that instant, I want to run to him, put my head on his never-ending chest, and feel his arms fall over me like cooling shadow. But I don't. I can't. I stand there, breath frozen in my aching chest, watching him struggle with his words.

He looks up eventually. There's a desperate, haunted look in his eyes, almost as if he wants to convey something to me in silence.

Richter, it's working.

He says, "Tell me more about this."

I do, and he leans against the wall, listening intently.

"McGlashan's gonna be there, right?" he asks after I've finished. "He got your dad the rights for the land on which he built this massive building."

"Yeah, and so will all the glitterati. Loads of senators, their wives, and the media, of course."

Richter rubs the beard on his cheeks. It's definitely longer, not the neat trim I'm used to. His white tee has stains and smudges on it. His jeans are creased and worn.

He says, " I don't think it's safe for you to go to this event." He lifts up a hand and counts off on his fingers.

"Capitol Hill Police will be on security. It won't be easy for our guys to get past them. Even when we do, if this place is big, which I'm assuming it will be, we can't keep eyes on you all the time. Plus, it's going to be crowded."

I press my lips together. I don't want to go and hang with Dad and his fake-chested wife, but I did promise.

"I have to go, Richter."

He pauses again, staring at me, and this time, it lasts longer. I hold his eyes, because it's nice just to look at him again.

When he speaks, his tone is more mellow and strangely subdued. "In that case, can I ask you something?"

"Sure, go ahead."

He takes his time before replying. "This is something I've done before. I could come as *your* security. For personal protection. But no one can know that, obviously. So maybe I could be your date?"

My eyes feel like they're going to pop out. Richter as my personal protection?

As my date?

Hell to the yeah for both. The butterflies in my stomach are spreading their wings at a nuclear rate, flapping against my belly.

Richter's staring at me with a hopeful expression on his face.

I love that look! Then there's also the thought of seeing him in a suit, a sleek, wide-shouldered sex god in a black dinner jacket. Richter in a tux? The mental image is making me salivate.

"Dora?" His voice is deep. "What do you think?"

"Uh." The problem is I don't know what this means for us.

The whole situation leaves more questions than answers, and I'm not sure if I'm happy with that. But Richter does make sense. Dad is tied in with McGlashan. Could he be right about me being in danger? Not from Dad; I know that. But the events of the last few days and what Joanne Asher said surface in my mind like a slick of black oil on water.

His voice is flat, low, with a trace of hurt in it. "Don't worry if it's a problem. I'm still going to be around the place in case something happens. What's the address?"

That melts my heart. He's worried enough about me to be there even if he can't come as my date.

Inside, I'm quivering like a leaf in the wind.

If you care so much about me, why did you act like such a jerk?

There's a weight in my neck, and it's pressing against my vocal cords like a hulking black rock. I press fingers to my forehead.

"Richter, it's just that…" My words trail off. *It's just that I can't take this on-and-off bullshit.* God, why does this have to be so complicated?

"Look," I manage to say. "Can you come back in five minutes, please? I'll call you."

"Sure thing. But don't leave it too last minute. What time are you leaving tomorrow?"

"Six o'clock. Just give me five minutes, I'll call you back." I close the door on him quickly.

I can't think straight with him standing there. I close my eyes and lean my back against the door. Oh god, I want him to be there so badly. But not if it's going to give me false ideas of us getting back together.

I'm more conflicted than I've ever been before, more torn than the ripped fragments of my heart.

But if I'm thinking with a cool head, I know I need protection. And who better than Richter? Okay, so my heart will flip-flop like a salmon jumping out of a stream. But at least he'll be there, and, well…I can't deny that I want him there, too.

CHAPTER 49

DORA

I make up my mind to say yes and then go up the stairs. Julia is waiting with an inquisitive look on her face.

"What happened?"

When I tell her, she gasps. "He offered to go with you, right?"

"Yes."

"You didn't ask him, but he offered to be your date." She puts a hand on her hip. "Do you know what that means, girl?"

"It doesn't mean anything," I say, acting nonchalant, but my heart is running like a treadmill.

"Oh, you've got to be blind to say that. Anyone can see. He wants it bad."

I slump down on a chair. "Stop it, Jules."

Jules is staring at me, thunderstruck. "What the hell? You're not interested in him anymore?"

I guess my face says it all, because her expression softens immediately. She sits down next to me and holds my hand. "Oh, honey."

There's burning behind my eyes, and I want it to go away. The black weight rises up my throat, suffusing my mind like a dark shadow. I don't want to think anymore. I've made my mind up, but I still feel like I'm stuck between a rock and a hard place.

"For your information," I say, "I said I'll call him back."

"Look at it this way," Julia says. "Him being your protection tomorrow night is a good idea, right?"

I sniff. "I know that."

"And you get a chance to clear the air with him. If he wants to, of course."

"Right." I exhale. Kill two birds with one stone. Just hope my heart doesn't get more damaged in the process.

"Thanks, Jules," I say, meaning it.

She gives my hand a squeeze and smiles. "You're welcome."

*****

I can barely sleep that night. Dreams of Richter in a suit, holding me as we dance in an empty ballroom, fill the hours as I toss and turn in bed. I eventually pass out, and the beeping alarm wakes me at eight a.m.

As I brush my teeth, I peek out through the blinds. Sure enough, Richter's there. He's on the sidewalk, doing some stretches. I don't think he sees me. I keep looking, wondering how weird this situation is. I want him next to me, not out there.

I send him a text then meet him at the door. He comes in to use the bathroom. I speak to him when he comes out.

"I need to do some shopping." Again, it's weird that I have to ask him about this, but he's going to follow me regardless, so I might as well.

"No sweat. I'll take you."

We get in the car and drive in silence. I sneak glances at him. His beard is definitely longer now, and so is his hair. It falls over his forehead. His eyes are fixed on the road, face like granite.

I'm caught by surprise when he speaks.

"Douglas, the NSA chief, is still protesting that McGlashan is innocent. We've told him about Joanne, and he wants to see her personally."

I know that Joanne is in another safe house, guarded round the clock.

"What did you say?"

"I refused, citing operational risk. I don't like the fact that someone as high up as Douglas is backing up McGlashan."

I'm just glad we're talking after all this time, even if it is about his work. Besides, it affects me as well. I need to know.

"What do you make of it?" I ask.

He sighs. "I don't know. Sometimes I think the whole chain is rotten. All the way up to POTUS."

"If the CIA hatched a plan to kill your father to stop him from spilling secrets to the KGB, then the CIA would like to keep it quiet, right?" I venture.

He glances at me. "Darn right. At any given time, the CIA has hundreds of operations going down worldwide. Not sure what good it does." He snorts. "If anything goes belly up, they need to cover their backs." He shakes his head. "That's what this is all about. McGlashan's gearing up for a major campaign, and he can't risk someone like Jozdani leaking this stuff to the media."

"That's why he's kidnapped his son, Andre," I say. "Are we any closer to finding him?"

"We?" His face breaks into a ghost-like grin, so beautiful and yet so sad. My heart aches when he looks at me.

"Yes, we," I say, trying to stop my rising pulse from drowning out my voice. "I got shot at too, remember?"

The second I say it, regret washes over me. Richter frowns, his nostrils flare, and he blinks rapidly, turning his attention back to the road.

"I'm sorry," I say, staring out the window. A black shadow of frustration unfurls over me, blotting out the sun, darkening my mind.

Richter says nothing. His face is rigid, hewn out of stone, and I don't know what he's thinking.

"Will you at least acknowledge what I said?" I blurt.

He shrugs. "Thanks."

"Thanks for what? The fact that I apologized?" I'm not spoiling for a fight. I just wish he would talk to me more.

"I've got a lot to thank you for, Dora. Maybe one day I'll write it down for you."

*****

The rest of the day passes in a blur. Julia arrives in the late afternoon to help me get ready.

I text Dad to let him know I have a date for the evening and that I don't need the car. I spend an hour applying the finishing touches to my makeup before Julia leaves. I promise to call her if anything happens. It's not long before I see the familiar large shape of the GMC Yukon park opposite my house. The butterflies in my stomach have multiplied, threatening to burst out. I'm standing by the door when he knocks.

Oh my. Richter in a suit is like James Bond on steroids. The black jacket hugs his chest and shoulders, somehow making his rugged physique even more commanding. His gray eyes are glinting, his beard well trimmed and shorter. The way he moves inside, brushing closely past me, reminds me of a sleek black panther, full of sexy menace and intrigue.

I close the door, worried my surging pulse will shoot out my skull. Is that steam coming out of my ears?

He turns around when the door is shut. His aftershave smells of spice and something wooden, masculine, intricate. The sculpted jawline and those fulsome, expressive lips are holding my eyes prisoner. Shameful, sinful thoughts of having him naked, kneeling between my legs, are coursing like mad, hot hormones in my brain. I look away, hoping like fuck I didn't just gasp out loud, and look down. His chest isn't much help either, as the shining cloth of that jacket is doing a poor job of hiding the solid slabs of his pec muscles.

"Dora," he rumbles, his voice low, a hint of danger in it that makes me shiver. No one has ever made me feel like that just by saying my name.

We say nothing, just look at each other for a while, drinking each other in as if we're dying of thirst.

Or should I say hunger.

Because that's what I see in his eyes: a raw, primal need that blazes in his eyes as they move slowly up and down my body. He lingers over the black dress, and his mouth opens slightly as his eyes move from my legs slowly back up to my face.

"You look stunning," he says with a slight shake of his head.

I clear my throat. "You look nice in that suit too."

"Thank you."

Somehow, I force my eyes away from his magnetic face. I walk into the living room, and he follows so closely that I can almost touch him.

We sit on the sofa, facing each other, five feet of electricity dancing between us.

I look down at my hands, playing with them. So much seems to have happened. So much water has flowed under the bridge. But all of a sudden, it feels like I'm reliving those magical days we had up in rural Virginia. Where I discovered an inner strength, peace in nature, and a man strong as a rock.

I'll never forget those days no matter what happens between Richter and me.

That time seems pure and unblemished, like a dream seen in the sweetest of sleeps. Trust reality to bring it crashing down. Why can't I go back to dreaming again?

"Listen to me, sweetheart," Richter says.

My eyes fly to him. He's leaning forward, his face serious but his eyes swirling, melting. His mouth is soft, and I so want to feel it on mine.

But I remind myself of the reason he's here.

"Introduce me to your dad as your date for the evening, or friend, or whatever you wish. Use my real name. But don't mention Cyborg Security or any word of what we do."

I nod. "I know that."

"Good." His eyes roam all over me before coming back to my face. He swallows, a touch of color sprouting on his neck. "Stay by my side," he continues. "If you have to leave to the restrooms, tell me where you're going. Any new faces you meet, please let me know who they are. Got that?"

I raise my eyebrows. "Anything else?"

His features soften. "Not for now. I just want to keep you safe. That's all."

"Sure." I look down at my splayed fingers. "How's Joanne?"

"She's holding up all right. She's in contact with Jozdani, but she doesn't know where he is. He won't tell her, and I don't blame him. He's searching for Andre as well."

"Hiding in plain sight, in other words. And we still have no idea where her son is." I shake my head, my heart wrenching as I recall Joanne's tearful face.

"One person will know," Richter says, his lips curling upward in a ferocious snarl. "Viktor."

CHAPTER 50

RICHTER

I couldn't speak when I saw her as she opened the door. She stood there like a shimmering vision of heartbreaking beauty, her voluptuous breasts straining at the confines of her dress. That cleavage was so enticing my dick went from soft to rock hard in seconds. The swell of her hips was so pronounced my palms just itched to reach over and cup them, pull her over to me, and sink my lips onto hers, push my hardness into her, make her mine again.

But all I did was cross the threshold and enter.

Seeing her again has blown my brain to bits. I can't stop my eyes from roving all over her body. I just hope she can't see my hard dick, making it awkward for me to walk around. How the hell am I going to survive tonight?

And now what she's just revealed is almost too much to handle.

I call Cal to let him know that we're moving out in ten minutes. I also make sure he has Brandon and Ken, along with Team Onyx, on standby for tonight if the shit hits the fan.

"Take care, bro," Cal says.

"I will. Can we do a quick comms check?"

I make sure I'm hooked up on the right channel to all the guys. "I'll have to keep the microphone off as I go in," I explain to my brother. "But once all the introductions are made, I can slip it back on."

"Roger that, Alpha one zero." That's my call sign. Cal is Alpha two zero.

"Over and out," I say.

"Richter?"

I turn to see Dora observing me in silence. I blink and walk toward her. Which isn't a good idea, since getting close to her, feeling her body heat, pushes all other thoughts away, leaving the blood to rush into my cock, demanding attention.

"It's almost time to go. Would you like a drink?"

I shake my head. I'm driving, plus I don't know what's going to happen tonight.

I wait for her to set the alarm, lock the door, then walk with her to my car. This feels like a very domestic routine, like we do this often, going out as a couple. My thoughts are dragged into how that didn't make sense to me last time. Living in an apartment like this, surrounded by fancy works of art and designer furniture.

But it didn't feel like that this time. I wasn't an alien person in her home. I felt comfortable, warm, and the place felt nice, inviting.

Maybe it's because I got to see her again. Or maybe the first time, I didn't expect it to look the way it did. I don't know.

All I know is I'm more at peace, relaxed now that she's close to me and I can see her. I don't give a damn about the apartment, but I'm definitely getting used to how she lives.

Two guys from Team Onyx are outside, and I check in with them. Then I hold the door open for Dora. My heart swells when she takes my offered hand to lift herself into the passenger seat.

God, she looks so awesome in that dress. Okay, it's hidden under a lightweight coat now, but I can't help thinking about it.

It takes us half an hour to get to the location outside Arlington. It used to be a retail park. Now we find brand-new glass and metallic buildings, hundreds of security guards, and the press, snapping photos of everyone. That last bit I don't like. I need to keep my face out of the media.

Barriers have been erected, and men in uniforms are checking each car before waving it through. I come to a stop at the security kiosk and wind my window down. I show them the invitation card that Dora gave me. We're waved through, and at Dora's suggestion, I follow signs for the VIP entrance. Three hefty men, all sporting AK-47s, are guarding the entrance to this particular place. Their faces change when Dora rolls her window down. Recognition is instant, and they salute. A valet appears as we come up to the lavish main entrance, the roof covered with huge chandeliers.

My car is loaded with state-of-the-art surveillance equipment, and I'm uneasy about letting the valet park it, but I guess I have no choice. Dora's also told me we won't be searched, so I've got my Colt M1911 strapped to my left ankle.

As we walk down the red carpet, flashbulbs ping and fizzle in the air. I've got my dark sunglasses on and walk as fast as I can, head bent low. Dora's aware, and she almost runs to keep pace with me, doing remarkably well in her heels. It's a relief to go up the stairs. A massive marble-floored landing leads into the main foyer of the building. There's a mini forest in the middle, with tropical plants and a fake waterfall. Bejeweled, beautiful women and suited men mingle, chatting and drinking from champagne flutes. Very bling.

Dora pulls on my hand. "Hello, Dad," she says.

I turn to look at a man a few inches shorter than me, almost bald save the back of his head, with a haughty, arrogant bearing. His chin points up, and he looks down his nose at me with crystal-blue eyes. His shiny dark-blue suit looks expensive and handmade. His cheeks are so smooth flies would slip on them. His eyes are cold and soulless. Michael Simpson, media tycoon.

I return his gaze with an unblinking stare of my own, and eventually he thrusts his hand forward. We shake as Dora introduces us.

"So, Mr. Richter," Simpson asks, "what is it that you do?"

"I work in the security industry." I could tell him about our million-dollar contracts with the Pentagon, but I get the impression he won't listen to me much.

"What type of security?"

"The classified type."

He measures me for a few more seconds, and I hold his eyes. Then he glances at his daughter.

"We need to take some photos. Can you come with me?"

I notice the coldness. No kisses. No asking how Dora is. I look at her, and it breaks my heart to see how drawn and pale her face is. She's not enjoying this any more than I am.

"I'll be back in a minute," she says.

"Oh, I'm coming with you," I say. "You can introduce me to your friends."

Dora raises her eyebrows, and I see some color returning to her cheeks. From the corner of my eye, I see her dad frowning before he clears his throat and motions for Dora to follow, ignoring me completely. I don't care, and I love it when Dora holds my hand tight. She looks up at me, lips slightly parted, face serious. I want to grab that luscious ass and sink my teeth into those lips so badly my dick jumps to attention. She moves with her hand held in mine, and it's not an accident when my knuckles graze the soft mound of her ass. I feel her stiffen.

Our eyes meet again, and I'm not hiding anything anymore. Her eyes are hazy with desire. I know that look so well. She takes a deep breath, and I grin then wink at her. A crimson tide unfurls upward from her neck, matching the ruby red of her earrings, and I swear to God, she's never looked prettier than this.

We walk through the crowd, and I can't take my eyes off her upper back, exposed apart from the thin straps of her dress.

There's a phalanx of photographers with their lenses aimed at a stage, and her father, along with a man whom I'm guessing is her brother, James, makes his way up to it.

She pulls on my hand, and I bend down to her.

"Back soon. Get ready for fake smiles."

"Knock 'em flat," I say and kiss her cheek before I even know what I'm doing.

Her eyes blink, then open wide as she swallows hard, blushing like an erupting volcano again.

She lets go of my hand and pushes her way to the stage, where the bouncers help to make way for her. A bottle blonde who looks about twenty years younger than her dad is on his right arm, and Dora joins him on the left. All of them flash their pearly whites, and I see what she meant by fake smiles.

I crane my neck, looking all around the crowded area. I'm taller than most, and not much evades my eyes. I'm focusing back on Dora, still on the stage, when a familiar face at the far-right corner catches my attention. I frown and look back. He hasn't seen me and is still talking to someone else I can't see, his head bent slightly.

Where have I seen that guy before?

Michael Simpson starts to give a speech. I'm still staring at the guy. He starts moving farther away from me, toward the back of the stage. I decide to follow, but the crowd is too thick, and I'm not the easiest person to get through a packed space. I can't exactly shove people out of the way either. I see the guy again. He's speaking into a phone now. I glance at Dora. She looks bored, staring into the crowd. I guess she's looking for me.

As I look at her, it clicks.

A sudden flood of images and sounds washes over me. My synapses are firing without control, connections whirring and whizzing through my brain at the speed of light.

Dora's face. That night in Dale City. The man holding a gun to her head.

That's him.

I'll never forget that face. He's wearing a suit now, but it's definitely him.

If he's here, where's Viktor?

Fuck. Double fuck.

The crowd laughs at some joke Simpson has made then breaks into applause. I'm jostled around by some people. Momentarily, I lose the guy. Then I catch him moving around the stage, going to the rear. He vanishes from view.

I swivel toward the stage, which Simpson and his wife are leaving. There must be a rear exit, because they're headed backward.

I can't see Dora anywhere on the stage or in the crowd. Panic grips my chest like a pair of cold steel prongs. My head swings around in every direction, but she's gone.

CHAPTER 51
DORA

I see the man next to Dad, and my gut shrivels in disgust. He comes forward, and Dad shakes his hand like he's a long-lost friend. The man is clean shaven, almost bald, and in his sixties. Dad introduces his wife and then looks for me. I'm standing a few paces behind. I have no option but to grit my teeth, put on a plastic smile, then go up to them.

Dad says, "Dora, this is Senator McGlashan. A very resourceful man."

I shake hands with the senator, feeling nauseous. His beady black eyes are lecherous, leery, and his handshake a bit too strong and lingering. But I act nice.

Where is Joanne's son, asshole? I feel like asking.

As we face the audience and Dad begins his speech, I look around for Richter. He's hard to miss, standing head and shoulders above the rest. He's more or less in the center, and his head is turned to the left. He's staring at something, and I see a deep frown marking his face. His lips are thin and stretched tight, like he does when he's stressed. I follow his gaze, but all I can see is a bunch of people, most of them listening to Dad's speech.

When the speech is over, two bodyguards move onto the stage, and amid applause, we are ushered to the back. It happens fast, and I don't get a second look at Richter. Through red curtains, we move into the backstage area. There's a crowd here too, and I can't see Dad. Bodies press against me, and the two bodyguards are around Dad, moving people away.

Dad looks behind him, and his eyes catch mine. He motions to one of the bodyguards, who comes over and makes some space for me to move forward.

Cassandra, the fourth Mrs. Simpson, leans over to me. "Wasn't he great? Those jokes were so funny!" She's gushing about my dad.

I roll my eyes then smirk at her. She carries on babbling like I'm not even there. It's all about herself, her recent shopping trip, and her dumb friends.

I can see the back of my brother, James. He's deep in conversation with a group of people. He's barely said hello to me. If I weren't here, would it matter to my family? I doubt it very much.

Suddenly I want to be as far from here as possible. I need Richter to take me outside and get some fresh air.

I excuse myself to Cassandra then head for the restroom. But this place is huge, like the backstage of a concert, and I don't have a clue where I am. A waitress tells me to keep walking straight until I come across the signs.

I walk past knots of people chatting and drinking. All of them are strangers to me, but I note several of them give me a second glance. I'm not a society girl, but I've been to enough charity and public events that my photos have been plastered over newspapers the next day. I also know the rumors about me being reclusive, isolated. Julia even found an online magazine that thinks I'm gay.

Whoop whoop, I said. *Maybe now they'll leave me alone.*

The thought does make me smile. Maybe I should do an interview about coming out just as a joke. That would get my dad's and brother's attention. Hell, they'd have a media storm on their hands.

I'm still smiling as I walk around the bend and see the signs for the restrooms. The crowd has thinned out now, and it's relatively empty.

As I approach the toilets, I see a man standing outside the men's. He's about my height and clean shaven, with dark, swarthy looks. I figure he's waiting for someone to come out of the ladies' room, so I ignore him.

But he's looking straight at me, and there's a lazy, shit-eating smile on his face.

For some reason, the smile chills my bones.

As his face comes into closer view, my feet suddenly feel like blocks of ice. My blood feels frozen. I can't move. I know that face.

It's Viktor.

What the fuck? How is he here?

An electric shock reminds me of McGlashan's connection with Viktor. But would Viktor be so brazen as to appear here, like this?

My breathing is so labored it feels as if shards of glass are puncturing my lungs. I'm not sure if this is all a dream, because as Viktor comes toward me, my legs are still made of stone. Panic has rooted me to the ground.

Do something, Dora!

A strangled yelp comes out of my throat. I finally turn, getting some purchase out of my legs. Immediately I cannon into a body. It's a man, and the wolfish grin on his face turns into a snarl as he grabs my hair and pulls my head back.

My scream is stifled as he clamps a hand over my face. I squirm as he holds me tight against his chest.

Viktor walks forward, the smile on his face bigger. But what gets my attention is the gun he's pointing at me.

"Well, well," he says in a thick accent. "Look what we have here. What a nice surprise." He cocks his head to one side and looks me up and down. I want to vomit. He makes my skin crawl.

He motions with the gun, and the guy holding me drags me to the opposite wall, where Viktor opens a fire escape door. The gun is stuck to my back as I'm dragged down two flights of stairs. My ankles twist, and I scream in pain, but it's muffled by the big hand on my face.

Within minutes, we're outside. A black SUV is waiting for us, engine running. I recognize the Lincoln Escalade with bullet holes on the side. The man drags me toward the door, which opens without a sound. I'm dumped inside like a sack of potatoes, my ribs catching the side of the seat. Pain mushrooms in my chest, and I shout, holding my ribs.

There's a crashing sound above our heads. A shower of glass fragments rains down from above, and a voice screams something incoherent. It sounds like a wounded beast, a deep and bellowing noise that echoes against the trees. I know that voice.

Richter.

Seconds later, a black shape crashes to the ground less than ten yards away. It's Richter. He rolls and stands up, a gun in his hand, pointing at the car.

"Kill him," Viktor yells.

Guns roar, and yellow-orange fire blazes toward Richter.

"No!" I scream, tears running down my cheeks.

CHAPTER 52
RICHTER

I panicked when I couldn't see Dora. I shoved men in expensive suits aside then upturned a tray full of Krystal champagne flutes, drenching a woman, and her scream brought me more unwanted attention. I stumbled and almost fell as I made my way across but managed to keep moving. When I pushed the last throng of people aside, two burly security guards were facing me.

I don't want this.

Despite the work I do for a living and how I've been trained, I'm not here to make trouble. But if Dora is in trouble, well, I'll show them a fight they'll remember till their last day. If there's a man standing in my way, I'll reorganize his face. Rip him a new one. Guess no one told these big buffoons that, because one of them rushes me.

I sway out of the way, bend my elbow, and slam it down on his neck. There's a cracking sound, and he collapses with a grunt.

The other guy shouts at me and swings with his fists. I fall to the ground, roll, and come up behind him.

The speed of my movements takes him by surprise. Before he can turn, I grab his head and smack it down on my rising knee. Even before he hits the ground, I'm off, running toward the rear of the stage.

People now scatter away from me, screaming. I can hear footsteps behind me and voices telling me to stop. The crowd thins, and the corridor bends around to the right. To my left, through the windows, I can see the ground. There's a courtyard, and I see a black Lincoln Escalade screech to a stop. A man appears, dragging a woman by the hair.

Dora.

No!

I'm one floor up. There's a few parked cars below the windows. If I fall on them, I won't break a leg. The whole situation is clear in milliseconds. No time to think. Only to process and act.

I take out the Colt and fire twice at the window. The pane wobbles as cracks spread on it. I kick it hard twice, and some of the glass falls out. I go ten paces back then run and jump, crashing through the broken glass, arms crossed in front of me.

I'm out, flying in the night air, then I'm falling, smashing onto the roof of a car, its bodywork buckling under my weight, the windscreen splintering into a spiderweb. As I roll to the ground and raise my weapon, all I can hear is the sound of gunfire. I have to take cover behind the car. The Escalade revs its engine and shoots out of the courtyard. I stand up and run, rage and frustration boiling inside me. I crouch and fire at the tires of the car, but it turns a corner and bounces on a ramp, then speeds up on the road. Shouts sound from behind me, but I'm running at full tilt, legs pumping hard. I get to the road and see the Escalade stop at a red light. I run again while speaking to Cal over the microphone embedded in my ear.

"Brandon's coming around the corner," Cal shouts in my right ear. "ETA two minutes."

"Damn. Tell him to release the drone!" I shout, panting, sweating as I'm running.

I can't see the Escalade any longer. The light turned green, and it sped down a side road. I run across, ignoring the honking from cars, gun drawn. Damn! I've lost the car, but I did see the license plate. It's a Virginia plate, and I give it to Cal. There's nothing more I can do as I stand and seethe impatiently, waiting for Brandon to arrive.

*****

DORA

My heart twisted when the bullets flew at Richter, but he did take cover quickly. I kept looking back to see him shooting at the car then running after it. For a big man, he's surprisingly quick, and there's something powerfully masculine, animalistic, as he pumps those muscular legs up and down. I will him to run faster, but the light changes, the Lincoln swings away, and I lose Richter.

The men mutter something in a language I don't understand. Viktor is sitting in the front. There's two men on either side of me.

"Where are you taking me?" I ask, fighting to keep my voice steady. There's no reply, so I raise my voice. "Viktor? I know about you and McGlashan." I don't care if he knows. I'm fearing the worst, and any leverage I have over him now is good.

He leans over and looks at me for a while without saying anything. Then he faces the road again and says something to the driver. The SUV picks up speed. We enter a maze of back roads, and the car lurches as it turns tight corners.

Soon I see the slick of light on water and moored boats. We're at a harbor of some kind. The car screeches to a stop, and the men jump out. I'm dragged out at gun point. Cranes rise way over my head, and stacks of shipping containers are arranged like giant leg boxes all around us. Straight ahead is a large boat with a plank extended from the lower deck. Other boats bob gently in the water.

"Move," a voice commands me.

I have no choice. My ankle is killing me, but I'm forced to go up the plank. Viktor is waiting for me on deck. Without a word, he turns and goes inside a cabin. I'm forced to enter. The room has a desk and two chairs, with bunk beds in two corners. A single yellow bulb gleams overhead. I'm shoved down on a chair, and my hands are tied behind me. Viktor is sitting opposite me behind the table.

"Richter knows where you are. He's going to find you," I say.

The grin on his face vanishes. He gets up and walks over to me slowly. Without warning, his hand lashes out, slapping me across the face. The blow is brutal, hard, and I taste blood on my lips. He backhands me, flinging my face the other way. Pain rocks my eyes, making the lights swim. Nausea curdles in my stomach, and along with metallic blood, I taste saline tears.

Viktor lowers his clean-shaven face to mine. "Now, let's have some ground rules. I talk, you answer. Got that?"

"Fuck you," I whisper.

He hits me again, the bastard, rocking my head to the left. I cringe, trying to make myself smaller in the chair, waiting for another blow. Instead, he pulls on my hair so hard it makes me cry out in agony.

"What did you say?"

I look at him, but his face is hazy. The light has a weird glow, giving him a fucked-up halo.

"I said you're an asshole."

He slaps me once again. I feel a cold touch on my cheek. It feels sharp and bites into my skin. The blade of a knife flashes in the light.

"Want me to cut you up, bitch?" he says quietly, as if he's speaking to a child. The knife presses harder.

"No," I whimper, tears spilling down my cheeks, mixing with snot and blood from my nose.

"Where's Jozdani?" Viktor barks.

"I don't know," I whimper.

He slaps me again, and a red-orange fireball of pain explodes across my face. He grabs my hair and makes me face him.

"That's the wrong answer, bitch," he drawls in his thick accent. "You can save yourself a lot of pain if you tell me now." He looks up at his men and grins. "These guys are like animals. Want me to set them loose on you?"

I bite back the fear and nausea threatening to engulf me.

"The CIA know you are here," I say. "They're going to find you." It's bullshit, but I need to play for time.

"Is that so?" There's a hint of amusement in his voice.

"Yes. McGlashan can't protect you anymore. It's all coming out in tomorrow's news. If you don't let me go and tell me where Joanne's son is, all of this will be tomorrow's headlines."

He frowns and stares at me. "How do you know about…" He stops just in time, not giving any more away.

I take courage from the look of confusion in his eyes.

"Oh yeah. I know all about it. And if you don't let me go, then my friends will release the news to the media. You and McGlashan are finished."

He pulls on my hair so hard the entire chair bends to the left. "Really, bitch? And what if I told you that your friends will die if that happens?"

"The news will still get published. Then McGlashan ends up in jail. And you have no protection." Pain is shooting down my scalp, setting my head on fire. But I'm not going to show this asshole any weakness.

"Enough of this!" He swears in Russian then reverts to English. "You want me to kill Joanne's son?"

Without waiting for an answer, he straightens. The pressure on my head ceases abruptly. I lean back, chest heaving, eyes streaming. I try to pull on my hands, but that only seems to make the knots tighter.

Viktor marches to a side door, opens it, and barks out a command in Russian.

A thin young man stumbles out, hands tied behind his back. His white T-shirt is stained with dark blood. Holding him by the neck is a taller man, his face impassive. The man gives the young guy a shove, and he sprawls on the floor, close to my feet. Viktor bends on one knee and lifts his head by the hair.

"This is Andre, Joanne's son," Viktor says. He puts the knife against Andre's neck. Then he turns to look at me, an evil gleam shining in his eyes. He looks like a giant reptile, a predator about to grab its prey.

"He doesn't know where his father is. But you do, and this boy's life is now in your hands."

Viktor presses the knife harder against his throat, and Andre whimpers. A drop of blood trickles down his neck.

"Please don't," I whisper.

CHAPTER 53
RICHTER

Cal's voice comes to life from the speakers as I savagely turn the Yukon's steering wheel. Brandon and I swapped places as soon as he arrived. The tires skid then rectify as the car sails around a corner, jumping the traffic lights. Send me a police car. There's no mortal force that can now stand between me and Viktor. Revenge has lit a fire in my veins, and the flames are consuming me.

"We got a visual from the drone feed." Cal's voice is on the car speaker. "He headed down south on I-295. There's an old harbor near Joint Base Anacostia-Bolling. It's not used anymore, but it's capable of mooring multiple ships."

"Is he at the harbor?" I shout over the roar of the engine.

"Yes. The drone's picking up three boats, all with lights on. I'm guessing this is how they make a getaway."

Brandon is sitting next to me, listening in silence. Behind us, Ken and Oliver are driving up with two teams.

"We can't let them set sail. What's my ETA?" I say.

"Ten minutes."

I swear and press on the gas. It's almost at full power anyway. The engine whines and the hood shakes as the Yukon rushes forward.

Every second I can't see her feels like an eternity. Every image that flashes through my mind is of her being dragged away by Viktor's men.

I don't know how I don't end up crashing the Yukon, but somehow, we manage to get to the old derelict harbor two miles south from the AFB Bolling.

We park a safe distance away, then we wait for the two teams behind us. When they arrive, my men and I fan out. I'm holding an AR-15 assault rifle with my night-vision goggles on. The microphone in my ear chirps.

"Two guards behind the stack of shipping containers. Three more on the deck of the ship."

I rush forward as the guards drop under fire from my team. The guards from the deck start shooting, but so do I. They collapse, and I'm the first member of my team on the deck. Guns are chattering, but my eyes are frantically searching for doors. I take the first cabin door and fling it open. There's a light on inside, with a table in one corner and two chairs in the middle. The chair is empty, but I can see a coil of rope on it. The rope looks like it was used to tie someone up.

There's a shout from the deck. I scramble outside to find Brandon pointing his gun out at the water.

An RIB is bobbing on the small waves, and indistinct shapes are moving on it. As I look down, I hear a scream.

"Richter!"

It's a voice I know well. Dora.

I act on pure impulse. I vault over the railing of the deck, plant my feet on the edge, and jump down into the RIB. The men on the boat hadn't expected that move. I crash land on three bodies, all of whom go splashing into the water. Brandon's rifle is chattering from above, and I know those men won't bother me again.

As I get to my feet, a shape rises in front of me. It's Viktor. He kicks me in the chest, and I fall back down. I can barely see his face, but there's no mistaking the gun he's pointing at me.

Before he can fire, someone kicks him from behind, and he stumbles forward. I roll to the side then kick his legs out. He falls down beside me, and I slam my fist against his cheek, making his head snap back. Then I jump to grab the gun arm. We tussle, but I'm bigger than Viktor, and there's only going to be one winner in this fight.

I manage to wrestle the gun from his control and throw it into the river. I whip out my own Colt from the ankle holster and point it at him. The gun is cocked and loaded, ready to fire. Viktor is at my mercy. But I put the weapon away. Blood is thrumming against my ears, a red river of rage drowning out every other thought.

A bullet is too good for Viktor. I reach down, grab him by the collar, and heave him up. His face meets my forehead with vicious force, and it snaps back. I knee him in the belly, and he doubles over with a scream. Both of us lose balance, but I grab his throat with both hands and squeeze. He makes a choking sound, and his legs shake. I increase pressure, watching the veins pop on his forehead.

"Remember killing my father, Viktor?"

He tries to say something. He's choking, flailing, his hands slapping mine. But I have a death hold on him, and I'm not letting go. His tongue begins to protrude as his face goes dark, engorged with blood.

"I want you to think of my father's face just as you take your last breath," I whisper between clenched teeth.

"Richter. Richter!"

It's Dora calling me. Not just calling; her hands are on my shoulders, clutching them from behind. She comes forward and puts her face between mine and Viktor's.

"Look at me," she says, her voice soft. "He's not worth it. Remember you wanted justice for your father? You get justice by handing him over to the cops. He talks about McGlashan."

The boat is moving in the waves, jostling against the side of the ship. My eyes are used to the dark now, and Dora's face is barely visible.

But I can feel the melting brown depths of her eyes reaching far inside me, cooling down the murderous red flames burning in my soul.

"Please," she whispers.

She's right. Of course she's right. My hands go slack. Viktor takes a breath, spluttering for air.

Dora's hand reaches out to touch my face. Her fingers are so warm, the tears on her cheek so real. I let go of Viktor and pull her over to me. Her face sinks into my neck, and I hold her so tight I'm afraid I'll hurt her. But she doesn't care. Her nails are digging fiercely into my skin as she grabs me back just as tight.

Two bodies drop into the boat, making it wobble. It's Ken and Brandon. Keeping ahold of Dora, I move to the side as they handcuff Viktor.

CHAPTER 54

DORA

A boat comes around to pick us up then drops us off at the harbor. Richter literally carries me off the boat, only letting my feet touch ground when we are on the harbor jetty. A man rushes up to him.

"Boat's under lockdown. We got all of them. Shall we call the cops?"

"Yes." Richter nods. "And stay here until they arrive." He touches his earpiece with the left hand, right arm still around my waist, like it belongs there.

"Cal?" Richter asks.

He has a conversation with his brother while we walk toward his car. Cal appears, shouting orders. Then he calls out Richter's name. Cal and Ollie have their hands on the shoulders of a shorter man, who walks between them. The man offers no resistance. He's bald, and his skin is darker. As he gets closer I can see he must be in his sixties.

"Jozdani," Richter breathes.

Ollie says, "We found him hiding on top of one of the shipping cabinets. He was armed, but surrendered without firing a shot."

Jozdani's cheeks are sunken, and he blinks rapidly. The two men on either side of him keep holding him. He looks thin, frail and tired. Wisps of hair stick to his bald scalp.

"Where's my son?" Jozdani asks, a wheeze in his voice.

"Let him go," Richter says.

Jozdani rubs his arms when they become free.

Cal says, "Your son has been taken to the hospital, Mr. Jozdani. You can go to see him, but only if you're escorted by one of us."

The engine of a car revs behind us. A black Suburban pulls up, and from the back seat, Joanne Asher emerges. She runs over to us. Tears have left dark streaks on her cheeks. She shouts out when she sees Jozdani.

"Amir!"

She runs to him, and they hug. Jozdani is the first to let go. His eyes move from Cal to Richter.

"Are you guys CIA?"

Cal smirks. "Not quite, Mr. Jozdani. But not far off either."

Jozdani looks confused then shakes his head. "Look, I just want to see my son. Please."

Richter nods. "Take him, Ollie. Cal, you stay here to sort things out. Brandon can come with us."

Richter shakes hands with Jozdani. Joanne hugs me, then Richter as well, who stands stiff and awkward as she does so.

"Thank you for saving my son," Joanne says, her eyes brimming with unshed tears.

Richter glances at Cal and Brendan, then to me. "It's our pleasure. Viktor knew he was fighting a losing battle. That's why he got desperate." He swallows and his voice falters as his eyes sweep down my body. "Dora wasn't hurt much, that's what's important."

Joanne thanks us again, then she leaves with Jozdani and Ollie. Richter watches them leave. Then he turns to Cal and Brendan.

"Where's McGlashan?" The familiar growl is back in his voice.

"Arrested by the FBI?"

"FBI?" Richter raises his eyebrows. "Don't tell me Sam arranged that."

Cal grins. "You bet she did. Turns out FBI had a file on him anyway. Not surprising, given his campaign funding comes from offshore companies where the Russian Mafia store their money."

Richter swears under his breath, then his brow clear. He still has his arm around me, and he blinks as we exchange a glance.

"What about Dora's dad?"

Cal pauses before replying, aware I'm staring at him now. "Mr. Simpson is not under any suspicion of wrong doing. Not at the moment, anyway. The FBI want to question him with regards to his dealings with McGlashan, but that's to be expected."

I let out the small sigh of relief that I was holding. Yeah, he's still my dad. Maybe now that this is over, we can have a new relationship.

*****

Richter waves to Cal and we leave the harbor. He is limping on his left ankle but still manages to walk. The sight of his familiar car is oddly reassuring.

He takes his arm off my waist, and then leans me against the side of the car. We stare at each other for a second, then his face lowers to mine, and I feel the cool intoxication of his lips as they touch mine. I open my mouth hungrily, and his wet tongue slides in, rolling around every angle of my mouth. Wetness floods my panties. His body is pressed against mine, and I can feel his hard cock straining to be let loose. Electric sparks are shooting down my spine, consuming my body.

I'm the first to break off. He looks at me, the grays swirling in the dim streetlight.

"I'm sorry," he says. "I was a fool. Letting you go was the worst thing I ever did." He swallows and continues. "I had some time to think, and I realized…" He stops and shakes his head.

When he looks at me, there's a glint in his eyes and a hardness to his jaw. But his face is softer, brows meeting in the middle like he's in pain. An exquisite delirium.

"It made me realize…" He stops again, shaking his head.

"Yes?" I urge him on. My heart is jackhammering against my ribs. My mouth is dry. "Realize what, Richter?"

The expression of pain deepens on his face. "I love you, Dora. I've loved you from the moment I first saw you." His voice thickens, choking, and his eyes glisten. "You're the best thing that's ever happened to me."

Something breaks and snaps inside me, letting loose a pent-up ocean of emotions. I'm not even aware tears are sliding down my cheeks. I can't see as my eyes blur. Richter kisses me again, and I taste the saline relief of my tears.

"I love you too," I cry over my tears when we come up for air.

Richter opens the passenger door to let me in. I watch, concerned, as he hobbles to the driver's seat. I can see from the grimace that he's in pain. I clutch his arm before he turns the ignition on.

"Are you sure you're okay?"

His teeth flash in the darkness. "I'm fine, sweetheart. It's just a sprain, not a bullet wound."

He begins to drive, and I notice another set of headlights behind us. He catches me looking.

"That's Brandon." He gives my thigh a squeeze. "It's over, darling. We're safe now. Nothing to worry about."

I smile at him then give a sigh and lean back in the seat as Richter drives. It is a relief that it's all over. Finally, we can get back to our lives—lives that Richter and I will share, I hope.

I expect him to drive back to my house, but he takes a different route.

"Where are we going?" I ask as he takes a ramp on the interstate for downtown.

"I need to get some of my stuff from the office."

He doesn't say any more than that, and I'm left to wonder what he needs that could be so important.

He puts the emergency brake on when we get to their offices and leans over to kiss me. "Stay here, sugar, okay? Just sit tight."

The headlights of Brenda's car hit our eyes, then he draws abreast. Brandon hops out, Kevlar vest on, a rifle in his hands.

Richter vanishes through the main doors, and I can see him pressing the button for the elevators. Brandon walks over and waves at me but simply walks around the car in a perimeter, keeping guard.

Richter appears soon, still limping on his left ankle but somehow managing to move quickly.

"What did you need that's so important it couldn't wait?" I ask when he climbs aboard.

He stares at me for so long and so intensely that I have to speak. "What?"

He gives a little shake of his head. "How do you always know what to say?"

"What?" Maybe it's the adrenaline settling down, leaving me exhausted, but I can't make sense of his words right now.

Without explaining, he guns the engine, and we move out in formation as before.

We drive back to my apartment, followed by Brandon's car. Richter, Brandon and the two guys guarding my building go inside to check it. When they come out, I step down from the Yukon.

Richter hugs me. He smells of sweat, aftershave, and the cordite of gunpowder. It's a strange, heady, arousing cocktail.

As we walk to the front door, I notice he's slower and has to stop once or twice. When I look at him, he's wincing, but he winks at me and grins.

We thank Brandon and the guys then close the door. Richter locks it then grabs me. He scoops me up in his arms. I squeal and squirm against him, laughing.

"Stop it. I'm not light, and you've got a bad leg."

"Yeah, but I got a mighty fine woman in my arms. Who cares about the leg?"

And with that, he begins to climb the stairs. He moves slowly, taking one step at a time, resting his foot. I wrap my arms around his neck and kiss him lightly on the lips. I do that to say thanks, but he swirls his tongue hard against my lips, and then that warm, sinful tongue slides inside my mouth.

I don't know how he goes all the way up the stairs, but he manages. When we get to the top, I get off him and turn the lights on.

When I turn back to Richter, he's on the ground.

On one knee.

He's looking up at me with a fiery, intense light in his eyes, burning a hole in my retinas.

I stare dumbfounded as he puts a hand inside his coat pocket. He pulls out a small blue velvet jewelry box.

My throat is so tight I can't breathe. My feet are rooted to the floor. I can't move.

I can't do anything except stare at Richter.

He clears his throat. "When I realized how hopelessly in love I am with you, I didn't want to wait any longer. I went and bought this the other day. I'd kept it at the office, knowing it would be safe there."

My mouth is open, but I don't care. My heart is like a swirling hurricane, each beat booming out against my ribs. The sound is drowning out my sense.

Somehow, I'm still standing. Still listening.

He opens the box and reveals a bright, shining diamond ring. It glints and sparkles in the light, mirroring the fire in his eyes.

"Dora Simpson, will you marry me?"

I wrench my eyes from the ring to his face. His eyes are wide open, chest inflated like he's holding his breath. There's hope in his eyes, a mad, eternal sparkle of crazy love, budding like a shower of meteorites in a black sky, sprouting like the tears that pool in my eyes and course down my cheeks.

I can barely speak. I can't see, but I won't dry my tears. With a cracked voice, I whisper, "Yes. Yes, I will."

The smile that appears on his face ignites like a million firecrackers. It turns night into day. He stands, grimacing with pain. I rush to him, and he holds me, hugs me, lifts me again, and nestles me against his chest hard, like he never wants to let me go.

We're both crying and talking at the same time, saying "sorry," "I love you," till we're just jabbering at each other, meaningless words mixing with our tears into a consummate, inseparable whole that is me and him.

Finally, we are one, mingling into one another like the warm swirls of currents in the sea. Like we were always meant to be.

CHAPTER 55
DORA

Near Fort Bragg, North Carolina

Carolina Beach

The private room at McCluskey's Bar in Carolina Beach is full to the brim with Army Special Forces guys, mostly vets, but some, I'm told, are still on active duty. Most are standing, chatting, sipping from drinks. Myself, Julia, Joanne, Sam, and two of Sam's friends are sitting at a table. Well, I have to sit, given the bump I'm carrying. I'm five and a half months pregnant with Richter's baby, and I couldn't be happier. The pregnancy wasn't planned. I was keen on starting a family, and so was Richter, and I guess it just happened.

I smooth down the loose vest over the burgeoning baby bump and eye with slight envy the alcoholic drinks my friends are holding. Julia catches my eye and winks.

"To the new Mrs. Blane." She grins and lifts her glass.

"Hey, it's not a done deal yet." I laugh.

The wedding is next week at a church in Arlington, where my parents were married. My relationship with Dad has improved to the point that we now actually talk. He's opened up to me about how much he loved my mother and how traumatized he was after she died giving birth to me. He never realized how much it affected him. I'm closer to Dad now, and he suggested the church. Richter and I went to visit it, and both of us agreed it would be an amazing venue for the wedding. But we couldn't get a date till next week, hence the wait.

It was ten days after arranging the church that I realized I was more than two weeks late. Richter was ecstatic. We had an engagement party up in DC, but for a gender-reveal party, Richter wanted to invite more of his Army buddies who live near Fort Bragg, where the Delta Team and Rangers are trained.

I have cousins who live in Fayetteville, North Carolina, so they're here as well. McCluskey's is owned by a former Delta operative called Burt McCluskey, and the seaside bar and hotel has become a regular haunt for the Special Forces when they have downtime—which is very little, from what Richter tells me.

"Is your house all sorted now?" Sam asks, taking a sip of her gin and tonic.

Richter has moved in with me, although he owns two apartments in DC. We have been living together the last four months, and it's been easy going. I've never lived with anyone, strange as that may sound. I always had a whole apartment to myself, and then a house, courtesy of my dad. So living with Richter is a new experience, one I definitely want to continue.

"New carpets, curtains, and painting almost done," I say. "One of the three bedrooms upstairs is being colored..." I raise my eyebrows, and all of them smile. Sam and Joanne have become part of my inner circle now. They all know that it's going to be a baby girl. I can't wait to paint the walls pink and get loads of fluffy dolls. In fact, it's Richter who's practically ordered the whole Barbie catalogue even before the baby's arrived.

Something tinkles against glass, loudly, and then I hear Cal's voice.

"Can we have silence, please."

The hubbub dies down. Cal is tall enough to be seen above the heads of most of the men in the room. Richter is standing to one corner, holding his beer bottle, proud smile on his face.

Cal says, "We all know my big brother is getting married next week. And I guess most of you know he's going to be a father soon."

There's loud cheering. Cal waits for it to die down then says, "But we don't know if it's going to be a boy or girl. Well, our mother, bless her departed soul, always wanted to have a granddaughter."

When I hear his words, a lump forms in my throat, and tears threaten my eyes. I'm more emotional these days, and I've heard from Richter several times what Cal's saying. I wish I'd met their mother, Angela. Richter talks about her a lot. She died when he finished his Special Ops training.

After a brief, loaded pause, Cal says, "But only Richter knows the answer."

Richter steps up, and the audience gives him a cheer.

Richter's voice is emotional when he speaks. I dab at my eyes. Julia reaches out and holds my hand. Richter rubs his chin once and smiles. "We found out last week. It's going to be a girl."

The cheering is louder, and several men reach forward to shake his hand.

Richter says, "Like Cal said, my mom always wanted a granddaughter. And now, her wish is fulfilled. I just wish Angela was here to see her." His voice chokes up, and he looks to the floor.

There're tears in everyone's eyes. I'm wiping my cheeks, and Sam gets up to give me a hug. Then she stands and raises her glass.

"To new beginnings," Sam toasts loudly. The whole room turns toward her.

Everyone repeats her toast. Glasses chink, people hug, and Richter gets his back slapped several times. I'm so emotional and so happy I can't stop crying.

Richter comes over and crouches by my feet. I put my face in the crook of his neck, and he holds me tight. His familiar smell is comforting, and I just want to lean against him the whole night.

"You okay, sweetheart?" he rumbles in his usual way. I run a hand over his well-trimmed beard, then we kiss.

"When I'm with you, I'm more than okay. I love you."

His hand is on my bump as he looks deep into my eyes. "I love you too, Mrs. Blane."

THANK YOU!

I hope you enjoyed the first book in the Delta Men series! I certainly had a blast writing it. All of the men featured in this book will have their own stories. So will Samantha, Richter and Caleb's sister.

Cal's story is next. Just click here!

The Hot Target (Men of Delta Book 2)

ABOUT THE AUTHOR

MM Rose is a man. He is an incurable romantic and has always been a lover of books of every kind, including romance. Many years ago, he used to write poetry. He still does when his writing schedule allows him time.

His real name is Mick Bose, and he also writes the Dan Roy series, which is a Jack Reacher–type action series, but as elements of romance kept creeping in, he couldn't stop himself from penning a romance series.

Join the readers only Facebook Group for MM Rose's books, The Readers of Rose:

Get in touch with MM Rose on his Facebook page:

https://www.facebook.com/MM-Rose-Author-125364452194065/

Made in the USA
Monee, IL
25 January 2020